RIDE
ON

Also by Gwen Cole

Cold Summer

RIDE ON

GWEN COLE

Sky Pony Press
New York

Sky Pony Press books may be purchased in bulk at special discounts for
sales promotion, corporate gifts, fund-raising, or educational purposes.
Special editions can also be created to specifications. For details, contact
the Special Sales Department, Sky Pony Press, 307 West 36th Street,
11th Floor, New York, NY 10018 or info@skyhorsepublishing.com.

Sky Pony® is a registered trademark of Skyhorse Publishing, Inc.®,
a Delaware corporation.

Visit our website at www.skyponypress.com.

10 9 8 7 6 5 4 3 2 1

Library of Congress Cataloging-in-Publication Data is available on file.

Cover design by Kate Gartner
Cover illustration by Darren Hopes

Print ISBN: 978-1-51072-993-3
Ebook ISBN: 978-1-51072-995-7

Printed in the United States of America

To Mom, because you gave me the love of horses.

0.

Seph

I haven't broken any laws. But I haven't followed any either. Never have. My father always said the only laws we need to follow are the ones our hearts say are right.

Some call me an outlaw, but others call me a cowboy. I don't rightly know what a cowboy is, but I like the sound of it better. Because every time I think of an outlaw, I think of the man who killed my father, and that is not who I am.

Cowboy.

Cade nudges my back with his warm nose, bored with me standing here like an idiot. I go back to thinking about states and repeating their names in my head. About the names people call me. It keeps me focused.

We cross over the invisible Texas state line, and I'm surprised about the lack of trouble I'm having. It makes me nervous, it being this easy. The feel of the breeze and the silence raises the hair along my arms.

Asphalt and wind. Bound and free. Life and death.

Two sides of the road for everything.

And this is one of them.

Like most of the roads, the highway is cleared of old metal. The vehicles now sit in the ditches, hollowed bones rusted into

1

the ground like artificial trees. My father told me trees used to have green leaves that grew from their branches.

My father—

I used to call him Dad back before he died years ago. When I think of him I just think, my father. My father did that, my father told me this . . .

Dad.

Dad used to tell me everything.

I like calling him that. Even if it is only in my head. It makes me feel like he's still with me.

The wind picks up, blowing dust from the west. I pull the bandana from my neck up over my nose and mouth. I do the same with Cade, tucking the cloth into his bridle to protect his lungs from prolonged exposure. My goggles still hang around my neck, so I pull them up and over my eyes, blinking the dust from my lashes.

In the north, the ground is frozen, but here it's dust.

We continue south. Cade keeps his head low and presses into my back to keep the dust from his eyes. There's an old sign up ahead with the list of cities that's been spray painted over with the names we use now. The next city is five miles south. And then the big city, Kev, is twenty. That city has its own stories and rumors, ones I hope aren't true.

I have no choice but to stop. We both need food.

There's a bridge up ahead, crossing over the highway. This is the first sign of cover that I've come across since the border, someplace where a gang of outlaws would love to hide behind. Cade lifts his head and I keep my eyes sharp.

I stop before the shadow of the bridge covers me. The flaps of my coat tug in the wind, sending dust spiraling around my feet. With the slightest movement, I brush my hand across my right thigh, feeling my holster up to the handle of my revolver, worn and familiar. I let the fear pump adrenaline through my veins, making my hands steady and sure.

They finally show themselves, and there are only four of them—a small crew for the rumors around here to be true. I wait for more to appear, but they never do. Maybe this isn't the same gang. Two men on the bridge, and two men under it.

"Good day, cowboy." The two men under the bridge step out of the shadows.

I smile to myself at the name.

None of them have bandanas over their mouths—some people don't care about their health when the world has already gone to hell.

"What brings you to Texas?" The younger man talking has tanned skin and wild hair, his words slow and drawn out, probably from somewhere east of here. He points a rifle to the ground that looks more cared for than himself.

I pull my goggles and bandana down around my neck. "Business of my own."

"How long you been on the road for?" He spits on the dirt between us while his eyes stare at me, uncaring.

"Nine years."

He laughs, a low chuckle that comes out slow. "Nobody can survive on the road for nine years, but you being a liar is the least of my worries."

The other men smile in response, like they picked up on an inside joke and can't wait to tell me.

I ignore them and answer, "Then we're in agreement to let me pass."

"Sorry, cowboy. You know that's not the way things work." He flicks a finger toward me. "Hand over your stuff and we'll let you pass. Best to keep that horse here, too. Haven't seen one that good in ages."

"Maybe you should take better care of your animals." I move my coat aside, revealing my gun. They all stand a little straighter. "And it'll be better for everyone if you let me by. I have the right to my things, and I won't give them away to people who kill and steal from the less fortunate."

"There," he says, smiling, "you're wrong. We don't steal from the less fortunate. We steal from everyone." I catch sight of something behind him when he tilts his head to the side. Two bodies lie under the bridge—an adult and a small child. Both motionless with pools of blood around their heads.

My heart pounds for me to do something about it. But I can't. I didn't come soon enough. And if I'm not careful, I'll be next.

His fingers twitch in the slightest, but I'm faster than those on the bridge. With a flick of my wrist and two bullets, the men on the bridge disappear with painful cries. By the time the remaining two have the chance to even start, my gun is already on them. Steady and straight. The moans of the wounded men drift down to meet us in the wind. I don't like shooting men, but sometimes I don't have a choice.

"They'll survive if you tend to them fast enough," I tell him, hoping they will.

The younger man has his rifle half-raised, and his partner's hand is paused over the pistol at his hip—it's rusted but probably shoots straight.

Texas. Texas with its rusted weapons.

"What are you going to do?" the leader asks, a little smirk on his lips. "Shoot us, too? You'll only get one of us by the time you get a shot off."

"Trust me, I want nothing more than to kill you both." I keep my voice calm and my anger in check. "People like you are the ones destroying our world. Not the skies or the floods. Just *you*."

4

My gun is heavy and familiar in my hand. The thing that has kept me alive. It keeps me focused in my time of need.

I can tell he isn't all there in his head. I can tell because he isn't afraid of me and he should be. He glances over his shoulder at the bodies behind him. Then he shrugs. "At least I know how to stay alive," he says. "Only the strong survive in a world of death."

"And the strong don't need to kill people to do it."

"It seems to me that you swallow your own words. You can't tell me you haven't killed."

The dust blows around my feet and the bandana brushes against my neck. The only thing not moving is my gun. Despite the adrenaline in my veins, I'm still able to stay calm. I used to repeat the state capitals to help me steady my hands, but after years of encounters like this, I no longer have to.

"I killed for the first time when I was eleven," I agree. "Again when I was twelve. Another when I was thirteen when a thief tried to gut me in my sleep. And last week I killed two men for a reason I don't want to think about again. But in no way am I like you. I only kill to save my life or for others who need me to do it for them."

"So does that mean you're gonna kill us?" The side of his mouth lifts, his eyes still daring.

"I don't make a habit of killing people in cold blood," I tell him. "If or when I kill you, you'll be conscious and you'll be armed. But right now, I need you to drop your guns, step off the road, and help your injured men."

"And then?"

"It's up to you if you want to keep living your life this way. But if I see you again, killing people who have done nothing wrong, I *will* end you."

His laugh is dry. "Are you usually this generous to people you keep at gunpoint?"

"No. So count yourself lucky."

After they drop their guns and move off the road, I slip my pistol back into its holster. They're silent as I start under the bridge with Cade keeping pace next to me. I watch his ears, waiting for them to turn back and warn me of the danger behind us.

They never do.

I can't look at the bodies as I pass them. If I do, I'll do something I will later regret.

When I'm almost out of earshot, I hear the drawn-out voice carried in the wind: "You're gonna wish you'd killed me."

I wish for a lot of things, but none of them come true.

1.

Seph

In a place with no sun, it's easy to remember things that would rather be forgotten.

And this is the worst of them.

The day was cold and gray, like any other. Dad always said the earth was so sick of us humans, it decided to start over. Too many natural disasters to count, and eventually sickness set in, plaguing every country who thought themselves lucky. It only left those strong enough to survive and start new. But we're still waiting for that chance, waiting for the sun to reappear.

We celebrated my ninth birthday with a box of stale cookies. One for each year. Dad let me have every last one of them, even when I offered half. When you're nine and starved, you can't deny food, no matter how hard you try.

We were on a road heading west, toward the rumors of warm weather and the promised glimpse of the sun, when it happened. People rushed out from the cover of rusted cars, brandishing weapons and running toward us, giving us nowhere to escape.

They surrounded us within seconds and pulled our only belongings off our backs, throwing us to the ground in movements too fast to fight. While they went through our things, others searched us. A man patted me down, touching me in places that made me flinch and kicking me in the ribs once he was done.

Not once did I cry.

Dad had taught me to be strong, but he never told me not to be scared. He said everyone should feel fear—it's how we survive and how we grow stronger.

"Without fear we are not people," he'd said to me. *"Don't let yourself be without it. Use it to survive, but don't let it control you."*

I did feel fear that day. More than I'd ever felt.

They pulled my dad to his feet and a man pointed a gun at his head. The man was bald with a scar making a line down the left side of his head and had a roughly shaven jawline.

He questioned Dad about unimportant things. Where we had gotten our food. Our water. I wished knowing those things weren't the price for someone's life. He wouldn't tell them—not wanting the people who gave us aid to also be killed. He was saving them. The people who would never know his name and how he died.

How he died for *them.*

Someone pulled me to my feet too fast for me to hold my balance, holding my small arms behind my back like I was made from twigs. I saw tears well in my dad's eyes when he looked at me, for what he knew was to come. The bald man shifted his anger, pointing his gun at me from two feet away, black against the sky.

"Please," Dad said, dropping to his knees. "I'll tell you. Just don't kill him . . . *please.*"

The man smiled, keeping the gun pointed at my head. "Then tell me, and pray I don't shoot him anyway."

Dad rambled out what he knew, giving them exact directions and an estimate of how long it would take for them to get there. While he did so, the bald man stared at me instead of him for any flicker of confusion or doubt, waiting for me to give Dad away and reveal his lies—which they were.

I stared back, expressionless—that dead stare so many have acquired. Maybe staring into the eyes of a scared child in the past would expose their lying parent. But he should've known that growing up with gray skies, and watching people die before I could walk, made me who I'd become.

Even at nine years old, I'd learned not to show my fear.

Use it, but not show it.

The man finally turned away from me and returned his focus to my dad, allowing me to breathe once more while the hands of a stranger held me in place. That's when it happened.

No warning and no time to react.

The gun exploded into the cold air.

Echoing death across the barren land.

The bald man stepped over his dying body, looking down at him like something to be squashed.

"Maybe watching you die will give your son the strength he needs to survive this world," he said, turning, a wicked grin across his face. "You'll thank me one day," he told me. "We aren't those whacked cannibals you only see from a distance or hear stories about." He came closer, putting his mouth to my ear, his breath as rancid as his voice.

"They aren't stories, little one. If you survive this, you'll thank me. That," he said, straightening, "I can promise you."

He turned without another word. They packed into a beaten truck with everything we owned and left me with nothing but a dying father.

With shaking legs and weakening courage, I knelt next to him as he bled out onto the road. The man had made sure I could watch him die by shooting him in the stomach—the slowest death he could give. I moved to put my hands over his wound, but he stopped me before I felt his blood, instead bringing them to his chest and covering them with his own. His skin was too cold.

"No boy should feel their father's blood," he said.

Thunder growled on the horizon, warning me of a coming storm. One that I was only beginning to feel within me.

With his life finally giving way, Dad spoke through cracked lips, his voice weak. "You did well, Seph. Just remember the things I taught you and trust only yourself. Do you hear?"

I nodded, everything inside me growing numb. "Please don't leave me here," I whispered. It was my last attempt to make things right. Something I should have known I couldn't do. Nobody was around for miles.

I had never known the world without my father, and I wasn't sure if I could survive without him. That's all I could think about while watching him become more still.

"Ride on," he said, squeezing my hand with the last of his strength. "Ride on."

The wind cut through me as he took his last breath.

"Dad?"

His eyes stayed half closed and I pulled my hands from his before they became stiff.

I didn't stay there for long. I knew he wouldn't have wanted me to, so I forced myself to move, not thinking, and repeating his lessons in my head. The outlaws would come back once they figured out he'd lied to them, and I needed to be far away from there when they did. I took his jacket and his boots, telling myself the whole time that it was the right thing to do. I could trade them for food and supplies, or whatever I could get. I untied the red cloth around his wrist and tied it around my own, promising him I would do things right. The way he had taught me. And the way the world had taught him.

Leaving him there was the hardest thing I ever had to do.

They left me with nothing. Just memories of their faces.

Vengeance isn't something to live for, but that man's face is one I'll remember forever. Maybe I'll see him again and maybe I won't.

I try not to think of it much.

It makes my heart feel wrong when I do.

It was nine years ago now. Every year growing harder than the last. That day tore something from my heart. Something I don't think can ever be replaced. Like a chunk of me is missing that I keep trying to find.

I'm not seeking revenge, but if I ever see that man again, I wouldn't feel bad about killing him.

2.

Avery

Someone just died. Or, if by some miracle, they haven't taken their last breath, they will soon. It's only a matter time. There's no air down in the mines when the tunnels collapse, trapping a human inside its belly to claim forever. The mine is greedy like that. It likes to take lives while we drain its soul away.

Life for a life. That's what Dad always said. "The mine is a living thing. If you don't treat it well, you'll find yourself in it forever."

I wonder if he still thought that after he found himself in its clutches.

The siren wails through town, screaming for us to come help unbury the living. I watch people run down the road toward the mountainside, feeling oddly relieved that I don't have to wonder if someone I love is trapped below. I know the feeling too well and will never miss it.

"Twice in one week," I say, my breath fogging the glass.

I steal a glance at Finn, whose nose is almost touching the window as he watches. His eyes are filled with worry, something I've been seeing more of every day.

"It doesn't feel right," he says, turning away. "It never used to be this bad."

I tear my gaze off the road and pull on my boots, not bothering to tie the laces. My coat hangs next to Finn's, wondering if it'll be worn today. This is the first cold day we've had this year.

"You're going?" he asks.

"Yeah." I tie my bandana around my neck in case I need it. It rained a few days ago, but it's already become dry again. "I've been inside all day—I need some air."

Finn holds my gaze, torn between wanting to go with me and wanting to stay away. But he gives in, pulling on his coat and stamping his feet into his boots. We never not go, even when he pretends he might stay home.

We head outside and Finn shuts the door behind us. He's wearing the knitted cap one of our neighbors made for him years ago. We move down our long pathway and start the short walk toward town—the mine's entrance sits just on the other side. Our boots kick at stones along the way, and the air nips at my nose and already makes my cheeks red. The cold season is coming fast again, as it did last year.

Jack gives a huff of annoyance behind us, hating being left behind.

Finn smiles and turns around, walking backward. "Maybe next time, Jack!" he calls. The horse gives a shake of his mane and snorts. "He really doesn't know his manners, does he?" Finn asks, turning around again. For the first time all day, he gives a quick smile.

"He gets it from you."

"From *me?* Yeah, right. I think we both very well know where he gets it from." He catches sight of more people running toward the mines, and the smile along his lips turns down. The siren has been turned off, but that doesn't mean anything good has come from it.

"Are you going to help load the train tomorrow?" I ask.

"I heard they might need extra hands since the accident last week. We could use the money."

Finn nods, still distracted by the shouting a little ways away. The happiness his eyes held a moment ago under the shadow of his hat is completely gone.

We walk through the streets, empty now that everyone is at the mine, and quicken our pace so we don't miss our chance of hearing anything. All the houses we pass look just like ours: small stone and wood cabins with only one or two windows each. There's no pattern to them. When the mine opened, the houses were built wherever there was room. Unlike Kev, where the buildings were already there when the skies darkened, our town was built after with the scraps from older buildings.

We're almost there when Axel falls into step beside Finn, pushing him in the shoulder to get one in return. The two of them have always been close enough to be brothers.

Finn shrugs off Axel so I don't leave him behind, knowing I will. "Have you heard anything?" he asks him.

"Nope, haven't been there yet." Axel shoots me a grin and says, "How's it Avery?"

"Just fine, Axel," I say, trying not to smile. His smiles are contagious. "Your dad still owes me payment from last week. He hasn't forgotten, has he?"

"He was hoping he could pay you tomorrow, once the Lawmen come to take the shipment," he says. "Is that all right?"

"You know it is."

Axel grins again. "You'll get it, don't you worry."

The mine finally comes into view, cut into the side of the bare mountainside, which used to be lined with trees. They were picked clean from the ground when the town was built, and now we have to travel for miles to find more. We weave through the thin crowd of faces we know so well. Men from the mine, dirty with soot and grime, stand at the front with their families who came to see if they had been trapped. There are tears in the wives' eyes—it could have been their husbands or sons tonight, and might be tomorrow.

We stop near the edge of the crowd and watch the entrance. The brittle wind carries the voices of the people around us. There's still someone down below.

Finn twines his fingers with mine, undoubtedly sharing my feelings, including relief that he doesn't have to work down there. There's an unspoken rule of the town—if you lose a family member to the mines, you aren't required to work in them. It's harder to get by doing smaller jobs, but to me and Finn, it's worth it. We may go hungry some days, but at least we stay together aboveground.

Before I was born, they used to dig for oil farther east of here. But once that dried up, new coal mines started sprouting up to keep the trains running. That's when our town was born. The only reason for its existence.

"It's Raymond Clarkson," Axel says, craning his neck to see around the man in front of him. He's taller than both of us.

I see Kari across the mine yard, doing everything she can to keep herself together. There are people around her, comforting her, but she sees none of them. She looks so young under the pale sky, younger than most of the married couples in town. If Gage were still alive, he and I would be keeping the Clarksons company in that group, though I spot Gage's older brother across the way, covered in the same mess of those who work below. Gage has been gone more than a year now and it's still hard to think of him. To think of the future we might've had if the sickness didn't claim him. He would be standing next to us and Axel right now.

The four of us turned to three, and I always wonder when that'll change again.

I lower my eyes, looking anywhere but in Kari's direction. "I don't want to be here anymore."

15

Finn says, "Me either." We both know what the outcome will be. He glances behind us and then to the sky. "It'll be dark soon anyway. We should get back."

He says good-bye to Axel with words I don't hear. I don't want to hear anything. Not the voices around us. Not the sobs coming from the families we know so well. And I don't want to hear Kari's screams once she finds out her husband is dead, taken too young to the thing our lives revolve around.

We walk back in silence, every step away from the mine becoming easier. At the house, we part ways—Finn goes inside to find something for dinner and I hop the fence to feed and water Jack. His wooden lean-to—along with some furniture in the house—is the last bit of wood that we own. Burning logs for the fire is expensive and we need to save our money for the winter, when we'll need them the most.

The cloth feed sack is almost empty, but he can live off one scoop a day. The special feed we give him is costly, but without him, I couldn't do most of the jobs I get paid for. Most days we're traveling between here and Kev, delivering mail or getting more supplies for people in town, whatever anyone needs.

Without Jack, all three of us would go hungry.

After I check his hooves and give him a good scratch behind his ears, I head back to the house. It's almost fully dark and only the dim flames from the candles light the inside.

I lock the door behind me and hang my coat next to Finn's. Even though the house is cold, it still smells like home. It's the only thing that hasn't changed since Mom died. I join my brother in the small kitchen and set the table for two, both of us working and not talking. I would like to say this house used to be full of laughter and warmth, but I don't think that was ever true. Not even when Dad was still here, which was years ago now. The mine took him when we turned seven, and then something entirely different took Mom just a couple years ago.

16

When the food is ready and making our stomachs growl, we sit down opposite of each other. Finn finally catches my eye and tries to give me a one-sided smile. We both look over to the empty seat at the head of the table, where Mom would sit and say a prayer. Thinking about her makes my heart ache, so I try not to do it for long.

Even though she isn't here any longer, we still take a moment before eating, maybe hoping her voice would someday replace the silence. When it doesn't, we eat our meager meal, listening to wind howl outside through the crack under the door. I've spent a lot of time at this table. The wood is worn down from years of baking and schoolwork. Mom used to teach numbers and letters to Axel and Gage, too, when they came around, which was more often than she expected.

When I look up from my plate, Finn is barely touching his food. "What's wrong?"

He blinks awake when he hears my voice, shifting in his seat.

"I went by to see Kellen today," he says, "about helping him load the train tomorrow." He picks at his potato with his fork, staring at it. "I didn't want to say before when you asked."

"And he doesn't need your help?" Nobody ever turns him down, even when they don't really need anything. "Who else is going to do it?"

Finn shakes his head. "That's not it. He does need my help but—" He finally looks up. "He showed me the storage containers . . . and it's not enough."

It's like I heard him wrong. "What do you mean, it's not enough? The Lawmen are coming tomorrow. It's been a month."

"I'm saying it's *not enough*," he says. "There's barely half of what we need to give them."

"But if we don't give them the coal, nobody will get paid—"

I don't know what else to say but I feel there's more. "Why isn't there enough?"

"He didn't say, but I think it has to do with the accidents lately. We both know there's been a lot more within the last few months, especially these last weeks." He bites the corner of his lip and his eyebrows come together—both signs he doesn't want to say something. "I think that's the last of the coal. They're getting desperate to find more, and that's why there've been more accidents. The mine is dead."

I haven't eaten anything since this morning, but the thought of food makes me sick. Mom's empty chair looms beside me. She would know what to say and do. Always did.

"Avery." At the tone of Finn's voice, I look up. "I think we might need to leave."

It's not something I ever thought I would hear. We trade with the Lawmen for payment in return—that's what we've always done. We don't live in the Wild because we don't have to.

I'm shaking my head before I even realize it. "We can't leave, Finn. This is our home. The very home Dad found before we were born, so we could stay here without any worry about freezing to death at night or fending off gangs. You know that as well as I do. He and Mom raised us here so we would be safe."

I can't think about leaving our home and our neighbors. The people I've known my whole life.

"Do you think I *want* to leave, Ave? I don't just as much as you, but I don't think we have a choice. The coal is gone, and without it, nobody gets paid. And if nobody gets paid, they can't buy anything. You know what that means," he says softly. "You're not only out of a job, but nobody will be able to live here anymore. Everyone will have to leave. How are we supposed to survive if it's only us?"

"You don't know what it's like in Kev." My throat tightens with the thought of actually living there. "That place is hell. Every time I go there, I can't help thinking maybe I won't come back. The people there—they're not like everyone here."

"I know, but I don't think we have much of a choice. What else can we do?"

I want a logical answer to pop into my head and tell me everything I need. Nothing comes because he's right. I don't like it, but he's right.

"What if they start a new mine?"

"You know it's not that easy. It'll take years just to find another coal sight, and all the close ones are already claimed."

Finn reaches his hand across the table and slips something into mine. I don't have to see it to know what it is. The smooth wood brushes against my palm. I know every inch of it better than anything else.

"Wherever we end up, we'll be together," he says. "I promise."

I curl my hand tight around the small wooden horse, still able to feel the warmth of him holding it. I will always remember the day Dad carved it for us. The season was well into winter—the windows frosted with snow and the storm howling at us to stay indoors. The whole town was snowed in for weeks. We were six. Our birthday had only been a few days earlier and Dad felt bad he couldn't get us anything.

But Dad pulled out this old piece of wood he'd been saving—for what, I still don't know. Sometimes I think he saved it because he liked to be reminded of the world he came from. The one we never knew. When the sky was an actual color instead of gray. When there were trees on the mountains and along the river. That small chunk of wood was the only proof he'd survived.

When the horse finally took shape from that piece of wood and he rubbed the last shavings off his leg, he gave it to us to share. First every other hour, and then every other day. Then those days turned into weeks and months.

Now whenever we hand over the small horse, it's because the other person needs it more. It reminds us that we have each other, no matter where we are or how much distance separates us.

"You've had this for a while," I say.

"I've been selfish."

I try to smile. "I never thought we would leave here," I admit, tears welling behind my lashes. "It scares me."

"It scares me, too," he says. "But who knows? Maybe something good will come of it. And the most important thing is we'll be together."

I smile at his attempt to lighten the mood.

Instead of finishing our dinner, we save the food for tomorrow and go to bed. In the cold season, we normally stay up longer, spending time in front of the fireplace before slipping into our cold beds.

But now I don't know if we'll ever have that again.

I still try to imagine what the suns looks like and how it feels. The books we have on our small shelf only tell us so much, but Mom used to describe it to us when we asked her to. Big and bright. Warm.

It's something I have a hard time believing.

Because all we've ever known is a brown earth and a gray sky.

3.

Seph

If I had a choice, I would circle around this town so wide the dogs couldn't even pick up our scent.

Nothing good comes from this place. Even Cade knows it, but his stomach is telling him otherwise, and so is mine. We need to eat.

We watch the town from a distance.

People walk to and from the old buildings, but from this far away, there's no way of knowing what kind of people they are. I'll find out when I'm there—when it's too late and I'm too close to them.

"What do you think, Cade?"

He says nothing, just a twitch of an ear.

"Yeah, me too."

I gather the reins and Cade starts forward with his ears pricked, hearing everything I can't. Going into towns is dangerous; I don't know if they'll take my money like civilized humans or pull me off my horse the first chance they get.

It's the risk I'm willing to take.

It's the risk I have to take.

The town is small. Maybe it used to be bigger before they tore down the surrounding houses to fix the ones in the center, but with the dust hiding everything, it's hard to tell. Windows still stand here and there, and the rest of the holes are boarded up. Boarded windows are always a sign of people living inside. I like the abandoned towns where the buildings are full of holes and the silence is only broken by an old swinging door. Sometimes I even get lucky and find something good that the scavengers missed.

My hand rests near my gun as we pass the first buildings. Work has stalled and heads crane in my direction. They stop everything to watch me with dull eyes. Not a good sign. There are no kids here. No laughter. So many things missing to make this place wrong.

I feel and hear everything—my bandana brushes against my neck, my short hair pulls with the breeze, hammering pauses and rings into a silence, and even a chain clangs against a gate somewhere to my left.

And then the eyes. They see right through to my bones. They're either warning me to leave or welcoming me, but I'm afraid to know the answer.

The buildings are crudely marked. Old signs have been painted over and others have marks scarred into their walls. The shop is located in the center of town, in a structure with wide pillars in the front, made from something similar to stone, except smoother. The only two windows are barred on the outside—the only reason they haven't broken.

The moment I dismount, the sound of work continues, like they don't want to be caught looking for too long. Ignoring my tightening stomach, I take off my ball cap and fold it into the saddlebag. My coat is already inside—the day started out oddly warm. Then I unstrap the opposite bag, full of my money and things to trade, and sling it over my shoulder.

I don't want to be here longer than I have to, so I leave Cade's reins slung loosely over his neck.

"I'll be right back," I tell him. He only snorts in return.

I walk up the cracked steps and head inside, where daylight seems to have a hard time reaching. I've never liked the absent feeling of the sky on my shoulders. The walls threaten to close in around me, but I continue without pause.

The man behind the counter is balding, wearing a tattered sweater with printed grizzly bears across the chest. He doesn't notice me, too focused on fixing a radio in his hand. I do a quick sweep of the room and find no one else. When I start across the hardwood floor, counting my steps and taking note of exits, the man finally looks up and flinches, almost dropping the old radio.

Nobody likes being surprised. One of his hands reach for something under the counter and pauses there. A gun. I don't have to see it to know.

I hold up my hands as I approach, stopping a foot away.

"You aren't from around here," he says, flicking his eyes from my pistol to my face.

"Just passing through. I don't want to cause any trouble." I lower my hands, keeping them away from the holster hanging from my hip in case he has a twitchy finger. "All I need are supplies. Then I'll be on my way."

He nods, still surveying me. "Can you pay? We don't do donations here. Especially to outlaws."

I want to say I'm not an outlaw. "I can pay in either trade or coin," I tell him instead. "Whichever you prefer."

"Coin." He still doesn't trust me but removes his hand from under the counter. It's already better than most places I've come to. "I have enough things as it is and none of it's worth anything around here. What is it that you need?"

"Feed for my horse, if you have any, enough for a week. And seven ration bars for myself."

He nods again. "Just got a shipment in yesterday."

"Where from?"

"Kev." He spits on the floor. It falls with a heavy splat. "We get everything from Kev, but it don't come cheap."

"How much?"

"For what you need—three hundred."

I cringe, acting like I don't have it. "I'll give you one-fifty."

He shakes his head. "No good. It's three hundred, or you walk. Like I said before, we don't do donations here." His hand disappears under the counter again.

"How about I give you two hundred," I tell him, "or you don't get paid at all."

Again, he shakes his head. "You won't make it to Kev without supplies. Two-fifty. I can't go any lower than that, especially for someone like you. I have quotas to keep."

"Fine. I'll take my chances or find someone who'll take two hundred." I turn to leave, making my steps determined and fast, giving him no time to think it over.

I'm almost to the door when he says, "Hold it right there."

Cade stares at me from the bottom of the steps, ears perked. I feel the barrel of a gun pointed at my back, and a sigh almost escapes my lips.

These people are so predictable.

"Take three steps back and let me see those hands."

"I thought we could be reasonable about this," I tell him, not moving. "My money is good as anyone else's."

His steps echo around the counter and stop behind me, probably a couple feet away.

"And that's exactly why I'm taking it. You loners don't belong here. You bring nothing but trouble."

"Now that's where you're mistaken," I say. I crouch and spin, my pistol pressed up into his crotch before he has time to lower his gun to my head. He stiffens immediately. "It seems you're the one bringing trouble. Not me."

I stare up at his wide eyes, my gun steadier than the blood pumping through him. "Now, are you going to trade with me like a civilized human, or am I going to have to shoot you?"

His licks his dry lips. "I think two hundred will be fine. Just . . . don't shoot me."

"And how do I know once I turn my back, you won't do the same to me? We can both walk away from this unharmed. It's up to you if there's blood spilled on this floor."

The man drops his gun and raises his hands, palms out. "I won't. I swear."

I stand and holster my gun, nodding back to the counter.

He disappears to the back, his hands creating a symphony of crashing boxes and broken glass. Now that the man isn't a threat to me, I can finally examine the shop. Sacks of grain and boxes of random tools and utensils line the walls. No space is unused. Fishing nets hang from the ceiling. Odd pieces of furniture crowd the corners.

In a place where people don't have much, nothing ever gets thrown out. The poorer they are, the more they hoard. This place is a cave full of unwanted treasure.

It reminds me of pirates.

Pirates have ships full of things people couldn't even dream of. Ships that float on the ocean and are carried by the wind. I've never seen such a thing, but Dad used to tell stories before I fell asleep every night. He talked about things that never seemed real, but that didn't stop me from dreaming about them. Water and light, waves that make sounds I've never heard.

The ocean . . .

The man says something behind me and I spin around, pulled from my thoughts, which seem to wander farther and farther every day.

"Excuse me?"

"Do you have the money?" he asks. Nervous again, thinking I may take it without paying him. Only outlaws do that, and I like to prove them wrong.

"Oh, of course." I reach into my bag and only take out what I need, not wanting him to see that I have more than what I claim. Once I hand him the thin pieces of paper, he puts my supplies on the counter. One small sack of feed and seven ration bars. Cade only needs a few handfuls a day to survive, something that has to do with the added protein and fiber—things I know nothing about—but there's only a few days' worth left. I stuff the bars into my bag and nod my thanks, grabbing the sack with the hand that's not constantly hovering over my gun.

"Wait."

I pause and look back. The man looks between me and the door. "Don't linger here if you can help it. There's a gang that runs this town, and if they hear of you, it won't be good."

My heart tries to stay steady. "Have you seen them lately?"

He hesitates and nods. "It may already be too late. We don't get many travelers here and word spreads fast." Then he says, "I'm sorry. I always have to expect the worst from strangers coming through town."

"I understand." I nod once and walk out, my fingers white from holding the saddlebag so tight. Cade stomps the ground. I hear nothing yet, so I may be in the clear. I feed him a handful from my palm to reassure him and then go to secure the saddlebags, putting my money under his grain.

Then I hear pounding hooves.

My hands pause over the leather clasp, everything in me hoping they'll pass by and aren't who I think they are. Cade stops being restless and his ears go flat. I still have time before it's too late.

Swearing, I hook my foot into the stirrup and mount. The horses come from behind us. Closer now. I turn Cade down the street, pretending nothing is wrong, keeping him at a steady trot. We get about ten strides until a voice rings out.

"Stop right there or I shoot you in the back," he says. "It's up to you, kid."

Cade stops, giving me a moment to clear my face and harness the adrenaline flowing through me. I can get out of this. I have before and I will again.

I squeeze Cade with my right knee and he turns around to face the men behind us. There are seven of them. A good-sized gang to be going after a lone traveler like me.

"I'm just passing through," I say, making sure my voice doesn't waver. "I've done my business and now I'm leaving."

I look them over, picking out the stronger ones and studying the leader. Most of them wear wide-billed hats and long coats. Bandanas hang around their necks and unshaven jaws. Even though I'm not downwind of them, I can smell them. Unwashed with dirty clothes.

The man in the middle smiles, showing me his gold tooth. "You gotta pay the tax first. Nobody comes through town without paying."

"I don't have any more money. And even if I did, I'm not paying any tax." My hand rests near my holster—waiting. Gangs like this one make a living preying upon travelers. The same type of gang that murdered Dad in cold blood. Still, to this day, I haven't forgotten the bald man with the scar along his scalp. I never will.

"Everyone pays tax. If no tax . . ." He shrugs and brushes his coat away to reveal a gun. "It's up to you, cowboy."

Cowboy.

My mouth twitches and then I remember where I am.

I have to get away from here, and quick. Some men in town are probably willing to help them stop my escape. Anything to get more money or food. There used to be laws.

Ones where people couldn't go around killing others or stealing.

Before I can give the man my answer, a shout rings out nearby. It stops everything. An older man steps into the street, gun in hand. But instead of turning toward me like the others, he shows me his back, positioning himself between us and the riders. My hand freezes over my pistol.

"Leave him alone, Durk," the man says. "Don't you have anything better to do than prey upon every traveler passing through town?" He points back at me without turning. "He hasn't done anything wrong. And don't give him that bullshit about some tax. We all know you're full of it."

The gang leader's eyes are crazed as he stares down at him. "If you don't get out of my way, old man, you'll receive the same fate as the kid. Or maybe your family will be punished instead."

The older man shakes his head, determined. "You've already killed my family. How can you not remember the people you've killed? You're a monster. You'll sooner become a man-eater than stop murdering."

"Because the people I kill don't matter to me," Durk says. "The ones I kill don't *deserve* to live. Only the strong survive. Now get out of my way before I shoot you myself."

"No." He stands tall despite being looked down on. "I will not let you kill another for your own gain." The older man raises his gun and tilts his head back toward me. "Ride," he tells me. "And ride fast. I can only stall them for so long."

"This isn't your fight," I tell him. "There's no need for you to die."

"That's up to me," he says. The gang leader laughs without humor, still wary of the gun pointed at him. "It's about time I help someone who doesn't deserve this. Now, go."

I hesitate while Cade backs up, throwing his head and urging me to move. I try to hold him steady. The horses across from us snort, nowhere near as lively as Cade with their rough coats and protruding ribs. Still, they know a chase is coming.

The older man yells again, *"Go!"*

And I do. Cade swings around on his hind legs and shoots forward. Gunshots echo behind us, creating a scene I don't have to see to figure out how it unfolds.

They're chasing us and coming fast. I give Cade the rein he needs to pull away. His ears are flat but his focus is forward, following the road that leads out of town. Stray bullets explode into the nearby buildings as we bolt past, some of them breaking the only windows still standing. The wind rushing into my ears drowns out their shouts.

When we pass the last structure and come into open ground, I glance over my shoulder. Now with the buildings getting smaller and smaller, I don't see the gang anywhere.

It would be easy to say they gave up, that once they realized they couldn't catch me, they headed back into town to wait for their next victim. But it's always too good to be true. I turn back and urge Cade to keep going.

When the road starts to bend, I realize why they've stopped following me. They're going to cut me off. The only advantage they have is knowing the land, knowing I have no choice but to follow the road because of the steep ridge on the left side of us, created by the flash floods coming through this area.

As the small hill disappears on my right, blocking my view of everything around me, I finally see the dust drifting into the air from the horses' hooves. Cade is going fast, but it might not be fast enough.

They see me and urge their horses faster, one of the riders pulling ahead of the others, whipping his horse with the reins. The flat plains loom in the distance before me. If we can get to flat ground, with no ridges and no towns, we're gone. Their horses won't be able to keep up.

The wind howls and hooves pound the earth. I stretch low over Cade's neck, my fingers digging into his coat to urge him on. The two roads connect up ahead. We're flying across the land, yet not going fast enough. The riders appear larger as they close the distance between us. Their mouths open and close, yelling words to one another I cannot hear.

The rider in front continues to pull away from them, lying flat on his horse in a way that mimics me. Cade gives one last burst of speed and we're suddenly riding in front of them, leaving only mere feet between us and the horse behind us.

He's closing the gap.

I see him from the corner of my eye, and when I glance over my shoulder, it's already too late.

The man jumps from the back of his horse and collides with me, curling his arms around my chest, causing me to pull the reins. Cade jerks and stumbles, sending us both to the ground. My shoulder explodes with pain when I fall and the man loses his grip on me, yelling out with pain of his own. I don't have time to catch my breath or think.

Yells and shouts grow louder in the wind as the gang catches up, kicking their half-starved horses to move faster than they should be able to. My rifle is still strapped to Cade's saddle, along with the rest of my belongings—everything I own besides the clothes on my back and the pistol at my hip. He's trotting back to me, seeming unhurt but shaken.

For the first time since Dad died, I realize it's over. Cade's too far and they're coming too fast. There's a chance we could escape, but it's slim and I can do only one thing right now.

"Cade, go!" I shout at him. He stops short, his ears perked. It might be the last time I see him, and I don't even have time to think about it. "*Go!*"

He tosses his head and slowly backs away, not wanting to leave me. "Cade, *go.*"

Finally, after what seems too long, he turns and gallops away as fast as we'd come.

With Cade gone, I rush back to the man on the ground. He tries to get up but falls, holding his head where blood rushes from an unseen cut.

This man is the only thing keeping me alive right now.

I pull him to his feet and bend his arm behind his back, using him as a shield between me and the riders. With my free hand, I press my pistol against his throat. He doesn't dare move as his gang surrounds us.

They bring the noise and the dust with them. I stand steady and fight to keep my face clear of emotion. The leader, Durk, is the last of the riders. His eyes take one glance at me before searching the area.

"Go find the horse before it gets any farther," he yells at two of the men. "And be quick about it!" He dismounts, gun already in hand, and stares.

The others wait around me with their guns drawn. Sweat rolls down my temple despite the cool wind.

"Drop your gun, kid," Durk says. "We both know you're aren't gettin' out of this. And if you do it without a fight . . ." he shrugs, "maybe I'll kill you sooner than later."

"And if you take one step closer, you're going to have one less man on your crew. And don't think you won't be the next person I'll be aiming at once he's dead."

Durk cocks his head and smiles. "You really think I care about him enough to let you go?" He brings his pistol up and aims at the man's chest instead of at me.

My eyes narrow.

The man fights against my grip, and I press the gun harder against his throat. "Durk, what are you doing?" he asks. "I've been on your crew for years. Doesn't that mean anything to you?"

"No, not really." He pulls the trigger.

The man jerks against me and then slumps to the ground, his blood already soaking into the dry dirt. I can only stare at him, barely believing his own boss killed him.

With a half-dozen guns pointed at me, my own pistol hangs idly from my hand.

It's over.

"How can you do that?" I ask. "How can you kill someone who's unarmed? Someone who's been loyal to you?"

Durk steps forward, close enough for me to smell his foul breath. "Do I look like I care who I kill? My men work for me because I pay them. *Loyalty* has nothing to do with it. If Eddic here didn't want to die," he nudges his boot into the dead man's shoulder, "he shouldn't have gotten himself caught by you. You see? I didn't kill him. He killed himself. And do you know who else will get himself killed by acts of foolishness today?"

I normally use my fear and adrenaline to stay focused and calm. Keeps my hands steady when I need them to be. Not today. Not now when I can do nothing to save myself. It overcomes me and my hands threaten to shake. They haven't shaken since Dad died.

He wouldn't want this for me. Wouldn't want me to feel this way now that I've been beat. He would have wanted me to stay strong until the very end. And that's what I'll do. For him.

Keeping my back straight and forcing my hands steady, I look the man in the eye and say, "The only act of foolishness I've done today is believing someone like you could do something good."

"You're full of yourself," he says.

I shrug. "At least I'm not like you."

He looks past my shoulder and nods. When I follow his gaze, all I see is the butt of a rifle.

4.

Avery

The day starts out as a warm one. It makes me think that maybe winter isn't coming as soon as we thought. But even so, it's still dry outside, so we both head out with our bandanas around our necks in case we need them.

Finn takes off toward the tracks, where the empty train waits to be loaded, and I start hauling manure from Jack's lean-to to the greenhouse where I trade it for more potatoes. Then I feed Jack and brush his dark coat until it shines. When I finish, I slip a bridle over his head and jump onto his bare back. We don't need to go into Kev today, but he gets restless if I don't take him out.

The clouds hang low, dark with a coming storm, but I leave my jacket inside, trying to enjoy the warmer weather before it leaves us for good. For a long while, I give Jack free rein. He takes me out of town and along the river, wetting his hooves along the shallow shore. When the wind picks up and blows dust from the dry ground, I move my bandana up around my nose and mouth and head back.

Neither of us feel like riding in dust, but it was enough to stretch his legs.

The mine is closed today so they can load the train before

the Lawmen come. I follow the tracks on the outskirts of town, waving at the few people I see. As I'm passing by the Pole house, I see Darcy with her three-year-old son, Will, bringing in clothes from the drying line before it gets too dusty.

Jack slows to a stop when Will runs up to us, his cheeks warm and red. I pull my bandana down now. The wind isn't as cruel between buildings.

"Hi, Will!"

He smiles big. "Hi."

It's rare when he says more unless he's talking to his parents, but sometimes I'll catch him mumbling words to Jack.

Darcy waves and walks over, scooping up Will when she gets close. Now that he's up higher, he carefully strokes Jack's nose.

"Are you headed for the train?" she asks.

"Yeah, I was going to see if they're finished yet. Are you guys headed there, too?"

"We were, yeah," Darcy says, setting down Will. "Damon is over there right now."

"I could walk over with you and give Will a ride." I look down at the little boy. "Would you like to ride up here with me?"

He smiles again and looks to Darcy, seeing if he's allowed to. She picks him up and sets him in front of me. His little fists grab onto Jack's mane and he hangs on, using his legs.

"I think he's a natural," I tell her, nudging Jack into a walk.

Darcy walks beside us, watching Will. "I'm afraid so. It seems like we'll have to start saving for a horse, along with everything else."

I think about what Finn told me last night, about the coal being gone. What will happen today when the Lawmen come and find we don't have enough to make quota? What will happen to Will and his parents? Thoughts about the Lawmen's visit today kept me up most of the night. Apprehension rises in my stomach with every passing minute, so much that I feel sick.

"I'm sure you've heard about the coal," Darcy says, her smile vanishing. "Damon told me about it last week."

I nod but don't say anything. The train comes into view, everything here except the Lawmen to take it away. They've already finished loading it. It usually takes until noon, and yet they're done hours early—proof that something isn't right.

Nearly the whole town is here, ready for what's to come. Whatever that may be.

I carefully lift Will down into Darcy's arms, and she thanks me before going to find her husband. From up on Jack, I can see Finn on the other side of the square. There's a group of men near him, talking and laughing like they're trying to forget what's wrong. But Finn sits by himself despite them.

I slide off Jack and lead him through the crowd toward my brother. There's a streak of black across his cheek and he looks tired. He must've changed after loading the train, because he's wearing a long-sleeved thermal instead of the work clothes he left in this morning. I join him on the stone wall near the tracks, Jack greeting him with a nibble to his knee.

A smile brushes along Finn's lips. He rubs Jack's head and the horse pushes into Finn, wanting more.

"They'll be coming soon," he says.

"What do you think'll happen?"

"I don't know, but nothing good. Billy said he went to Carton last week because they sent word they were having the same problems." The Lawmen collect there first, closer to Kev, and then us. Finn runs a hand through his hair. It comes away slightly shaking. "The town was burned to the ground," he says in a low voice. "And they took everyone who survived."

My stomach tightens and the air is cold. Nothing like this

has ever happened before. The coal has always been here. Did anyone ever think it wouldn't be?

"Finn, what are we going to do?" I glance around, making sure nobody is listening to us. We don't need people to panic.

"There's nothing we can do," he says. "It's too late for that."

"What do you mean, it's too late?"

He pushes off the wall, standing straight.

"Because they're here," he says.

I follow his gaze down the tracks where the smoke of a train is coming our way. Everyone gathers in the middle of the square, trying to get the first glimpse of the Lawmen coming with it. Finn steps close and takes my hand. The familiarity of him calms me.

"No matter what happens," he whispers, "stay close to me."

The first of the riders appears along the train, followed by a dozen others, all wearing white bands around their biceps, dusty now from the day's ride. This group of Lawmen follow the same leader who comes with them each month—Torreck. He's the only man I've ever been truly afraid of. He is everything Kev stands for.

The riders gather next to the tracks, a few of them dismounting to examine the train cars. But Torreck just sits on his horse, looking over us like we're already dead. A black bandana hangs around his neck, moving when a gust of wind picks up. His beard is dark, matching the wide-brimmed hat he always wears. I can't look at the eyes under the hat for too long. They're the eyes of a man who shouldn't be in the position of power that he is.

Torreck dismounts when two men come back from the train. As they talk to him—in voices too low for us to hear—he takes off his gloves, slow and deliberate, stowing them away in his saddlebag.

He brushes his men away with a flick of his hand.

Then he says, "It seems to me you folks came up short on your payment." He eyes us all, like we're schoolchildren who need to be punished.

Mr. Wells steps forward from the crowd. He's the leader of our town. He has been ever since I could remember—most people don't live long enough to have gray hair.

"We've had trouble this month," he says, wringing his hat between his hands. "But I swear to you, we'll—"

"You'll what? 'Have more next month?'" he mocks. "We're not stupid, old man."

Mr. Wells takes another step closer. "Please—"

"We have an agreement," Torreck says. "You give us coal, and we pay you. The world doesn't survive on favors." Torreck's eyes lift from Mr. Wells, roaming the crowd around him. Nobody speaks up or moves.

Only the wind is brave enough to blow through us.

"But," Torreck continues, still looking at everyone around him. "I think we can work out a deal. Just this once."

The older man's shoulders lower with relief. "We'll get enough next month, I swear."

"I have no doubt," Torreck says. "But you're still short on your payment this month. We're not talking about next month, we're talking about now."

"But . . . as I told you, we—"

"I'm not talking about coal," he says. "There are other things worth just as much, and you seem to have plenty."

Everyone glances at one another.

Mr. Wells says, "Plenty of what?"

Torreck ignores him and walks up to Axel, standing near the front. I can see him pale, even against his tanned skin. "How old are you, boy?"

His voice is barely loud enough to hear. "Sixteen."

37

"Sixteen, eh?" He turns to look at Joshua, a couple rows back. "And you?"

I don't hear him answer, but I don't need to.

"Eighteen?" Torreck says, delighted to hear it. "That's lovely." He turns and walks back to his men, facing Mr. Wells once more. "I'm going to give you and your people two choices."

Mr. Wells nods.

"The first choice is for us to burn your town to the ground. Every single building, with people in them or not. I'm sure you heard about what happened in Carton, yes?" Again, he nods. "So, your second choice is to hand over some of your boys here. The Lawmen always need new recruits and laborers of the right age." Torreck's smile rips through us. "Consider it payment."

Finn glances over at me, his eyes filled with worry. He's a year older than Axel, someone they would take if Mr. Wells agrees to this. But he wouldn't agree, would he? We take care of each other here. Look out for one another.

When Mr. Wells hesitates, Torreck has a pistol pointed to his head in a flash. It's big and black like the night. "You better choose right, old man. Give me five of them, and your town gets another chance to live."

Mr. Wells nods once.

And my whole body goes cold.

Finn is rigid, watching five of Torreck's men take our friends from the crowd. They take Joshua, who fights them, hitting one man in the nose. They tie his wrists, another pressing him to the ground with a foot between his shoulder blades.

They take the Wright brothers, Han and Lee. Their mother screams from the crowd, sobs choking her voice.

One of the men comes closer, eyeing Finn from over the heads of people. I won't let them take him. I won't. I let Jack's reins fall to the ground, ready to fight them if need be.

But before he reaches us, he takes Oliver instead, pulling him from his father's grasp.

And the last boy they take is Axel.

Finn tenses next to me, watching Torreck pull him from the crowd. I wish I could feel relieved, but I can't. We've known Axel since we were five and he was four. He always liked to tell people that Finn was his twin and not mine.

This shouldn't be happening. They have no right to take them.

Finn's hand is suddenly missing from mine, leaving me cold and aware of what he's about to do. I catch his arm, stopping him.

"Finn don't." He looks back at me. "Please," I whisper.

"I have to."

He pushes his way through the crowd and I follow him, trying to get him to stop. But it's too late—Torreck sees him.

"Take me instead," Finn says, loud enough for everyone to hear. "I'm a year older."

Torreck smiles. "Looks to me like we've got a volunteer, boys." The others laugh.

Finn doesn't waver, his back straight and his jaw set. "Take me in his place," he says again.

Torreck surveys Finn. He isn't stupid; he sees the difference between them. He would've been the first one they took if he'd been in front. I don't realize how fast my heart is pounding until it kicks me forward, out of the crowd and toward Finn. They haven't gotten to him yet. I can still stop him.

"Finn, please don't this." I grab his arm but he's like a stone. "*Please.*"

He swallows hard and looks over at me. "I'm sorry, Ave."

A man grabs his arm and starts pulling him away, but I dig our wooden horse from my pocket and slip it into his. It's the only thing I can give him.

I shout his name. He's not trying to fight them because he wants to go. But that can't stop me. I'll fight for him to stay. Taking him away from me will tear me in two.

One of Torreck's men binds his wrists together, like they're worried he'll fight.

I can't stand here and do nothing. I move forward, breaking free from the people who try to hold me back. Someone shouts and my hands are cold and shaking.

Just for an instant, I'm able to push past the men and reach Finn. We press our foreheads together like we used to do when we were little.

Finn whispers, "I promised we would get through this together and we will. We'll figure something out, we always do."

There are already tears in my eyes, even when I try to hold them back. "Finn—"

I'm pulled away and thrown backward to the ground. Torreck stands between me and Finn, eyeing us both. I stand, feeling dirt imbedded into the palms of my hands.

"Did you have something to say, girl?" Then he shouts, "*Speak up!*"

I flinch and catch Finn's eye again. He's warning me not to do anything foolish—begging me. With a man with eyes as crazy as Torreck's, I shouldn't. I shouldn't and I have to.

"You don't have any right to do this."

"You're correct about that," he says, smiling. He steps closer and I match it, keeping the distance between us. "But who's here to stop me? You?" He looks over the crowd, catching someone's gaze. "What about you? No? I didn't think so."

I don't say anything because I can't. He's right—who can stop him?

"Now that I think about it," he says, "you just assaulted one of my men, and that's grounds for arrest."

Torreck jerks his head in my direction—a signal for his men. They come for me before I know what's happening.

The only thing able to wake me is Finn's voice. It rings out through the wind. "Avery, *run! Go!*"

I turn and run into the crowd, seeing Jack standing where I left him. His ears perk toward me as the men behind me push through, trying to follow. They're shouting for me to stop. Threatening to shoot if I don't.

I snatch the reins hanging to the ground and swing myself onto Jack's back in one smooth motion. He takes off before I even touch his sides. I glance back to look at Finn once more, but there are too many people to pick him out of the crowd.

Torreck's voice shouts for his men to ride after me, but I know it's too late for them to catch up. Jack is fast and knows the land. We're out of the town and headed west, into the Wild, before they can get off a shot.

We ride until we can't—until I hear nothing but pounding hooves and the wind in my ears.

When we stop, it's dark.

And I don't remember anything after that.

5.

Seph

I wake with my cheek pressed to the ground.

My head pounds and my eyes don't want to open, heavy like the old relics sunken into the earth. Maybe I've become one of them. Unable to ever move again. Then the wind brushes my face, telling me I'm alive and need to wake up.

When I finally open them, the gray sky is too bright and I don't know where I am. Then I hear voices behind me.

I move to touch my head, but my wrists are cuffed together with metal binds. I stare at them for a moment before I remember what happened and can piece together my downfall.

They came for me. I told Cade to leave and he did. The man's name was Durk. And he killed one of his own to get to me.

I was ready to die, like my father had.

Not this.

Why this?

I push myself up, feeling crashing—pounding—against the inside of my skull, but I won't let myself shake. I need to stay calm.

But I don't know if I'm strong enough.

I'm able to get to my knees, though. With my legs tucked

under me, I see the ten feet of chain connected to my cuffs. I'm staked to the ground like an animal. I don't know if I have the strength to stand. The wind is brittle against my bare arms, threatening to push me over and keep me down.

I remember I had nothing except my pistol when they caught me. Cade took everything with him when I told him to leave.

It makes me feel better, knowing he was able to escape.

I wouldn't want to give them the satisfaction of having me and everything I own. And I definitely don't want to condemn Cade to a life like those other horses.

Voices rise when they realize I'm awake. I remain kneeling on the ground, staring at the horizon., knowing I'll never make it where I want to go most.

A man steps in front of me, a pistol at his hip—my pistol.

I'm naked without it.

"Some of us had a bet going whether you would wake up," he says. "Wyatt hit you damn hard."

"Apparently not hard enough."

I lunge forward before he can react. My head is still spinning, but this may be the only chance I get. I'm on my feet, throwing the flat of my palm into his chest to knock him down and flip the pistol from its holster. All in the blink of an eye, I'm standing over him, pointing the gun at his head.

I breathe slowly. I feel the chain hanging from my wrists— they should have cuffed them behind my back.

The others shout. I hear their guns cock and a few circle around behind me.

I'm not going down without a fight.

"Stand down, boys." Without taking my gun off the man below me, I look up when Durk comes forward. "I thought I made myself clear when it comes to the lives of my men."

I glance down at the man, whose skin has gone pale as he looks at his boss.

Durk says, "Either you kill him or I kill him, it won't make a difference."

To prove his point, Durk takes out his gun and points it at his man. I don't want to be the cause of another death, even if he might deserve it. I remove my finger from the trigger and toss the pistol on the ground, already missing the weight of my weapon.

The man scrambles away.

Durk seems to be the only one willing to come close.

"What do you want with me?" I ask.

"I don't want you," he says. "Question is, what do I want to do *to* you? You defied the rules of my town, and that's not something I take lightly. I can't have an uprising on my hands. So after we're done with you, we're going to drag your body back into town and show them what happens to those who bend the rules."

His knife sings in the air when he pulls it from its sheath. It's at least a half foot long. He flips it over in his hand, his eyes never leaving mine. I don't move. I'm a rock. A stone.

"People like you think they can do anything they want," he says. "Go wherever they please. Steal whatever they desire." He circles me, taking his time. When he's behind me, he whispers in my ear, "You need to understand there're consequences for people who think they're above the law."

The tip of his knife touches my shoulder blade. Then he slashes it down and across my back. I cry out before I can catch myself. I can't breathe and my fists clench. The only thing I can do is close my eyes and hope for a quick death.

I'm trembling now. I can't stop it from happening—the pain is too much for me to bear. Behind me, I hear the knife drive into the ground. Durk walks in front of me again and motions one of his men forward.

Drops of blood run down my back, warm and soaking my shirt. My skin is on fire.

"I'm not as heartless as you think I am," Durk says. He takes out another knife and hands it to the man next to him. "That's why I'm going to give you a chance to defend yourself."

"And if I win?"

Durk laughs. "Nobody ever wins against Todd, but you're welcome to try." He backs toward his men, leaving my fate in my own hands. But I don't have my hands, and I don't have a gun. The man he called Todd is taller than me, with a shaved head and the shadow of a beard and eyes set deep into his skull.

He smiles.

Then rushes me.

I turn and dive for the knife behind me. The hilt points up toward the sky, the blade half-hidden in the earth. My fingers are inches from it when they snap to a stop—the chain too short for me to reach. It's too late to do anything but roll to the side, avoiding the blade about to slice my neck. I scramble to my feet and back away as much as the chain will allow.

Durk laughs behind me and I spare him a glance. "My bad," he shrugs.

Todd rushes me again, coming from the side. I duck low and hit him in the stomach, giving myself enough time to get on the other side of him. He swings wide before I can get out of reach. The knife skims across my shirt, slicing a tear through it.

I don't know how I'm supposed to beat him, and that's when I realize—I'm not supposed to. This is entertainment for Durk and his men, who probably love tormenting travelers like me.

Todd takes advantage of my hesitation. When I try to move away, he grabs the chain and jerks me forward. He plants his boot on the chain, keeping me in place and he comes down with the knife.

"*Stop!*"

Todd looks over at Durk, confused. I feel the blade of the knife against my skin, cold and sharp, a moment away from bleeding out.

Then he's off, leaving me on the ground, my chest heaving and my back burning.

"What is it?" Todd growls.

"The Lawmen are coming," Durk says. "Put your knife away."

Someone curses.

I drag myself off the ground, but only have enough energy to sit on my knees. The wind almost pushes me over, and it cuts through my shirt and into the gash across my back.

I'm weak enough to be killed—I feel it.

I watch Durk and his men shift their weight nervously and hide their weapons. But the body of the man Durk killed hours earlier lies on the ground. Face up. Eyes staring at the clouds above.

He is so still.

The thunder of hooves comes over the small rise. I don't know who the Lawmen are, or what they want, but they've already given me another chance to live—whether I wanted one or not. A half-dozen horsemen appear, all wearing long, black jackets. Each one with a white band around his right arm, some off-color depending on their time spent in the Wild. Maybe this is the gang I've heard so much about.

Durk's men shrink away, allowing more than enough room for the newcomers. Horses spraying dirt from their hooves, throwing their heads back when they're pulled to a stop. Only the leader dismounts—a bearded man with a rifle on his back. There is nothing soft about his eyes.

His boots hit the earth with a thump, his eyes seeing everything although he hasn't even looked.

"You mind explaining what's going on here, Durk?" He

has a hint of an accent—the kind that comes from southeast of here, the same as the guy under the bridge. "I thought I made myself clear last time."

"He killed one of my men," Durk says, nodding to the man on the ground. I want to shout the truth but don't have the strength. Even if I did, they wouldn't believe me. "I needed to restrain him before we contacted you."

He lies easily.

The man finally looks at me . . . and doesn't look away. Without breaking eye contact, he comes closer. The clouds rumble overhead, the wind slicing through my thin shirt more with every passing second. His gaze is too heavy.

I stare at the ground when he stands over me. His boots are worn in the right places but still in good condition. You can't find boots like that just anywhere. Good boots don't fall from the sky—that's what Dad always said.

Back in the days before, you could buy boots from a store. New boots. Not like today, when people try to sell me boots that have already been worn for years before their owners gave them up for something better.

Boots. Such a funny word for something so valuable.

I have no doubt someone will take my boots after they've killed me.

The man walks around me, pulling my thoughts to the present and away from boots. Slow and deliberate, like he's examining at every inch of me and seeing right through my skin.

And then he crouches down in front of me, moving the cuff away from my wrist with two fingers and exposing the piece of red cloth that peeks out.

He takes his hand away and asks, only loud enough for me to hear, "Did you kill that man?"

My eyes flit to the body on the ground and then to Durk. They all stare at me.

I turn back and shake my head. "No."

"I didn't think so," he says.

When he stands up, he snaps his fingers once and suddenly my ears ring with gunshots. I flinch, hands covering my head. Durk and his men fall to the ground, joining the man they accused me of killing. Seconds later, they're all dead.

"I told him to stop lying to me," the man says to himself. The only way I hear him is through the wind.

The men left standing are the ones with the white bands around their arms. They're different than any other gang I've come across. They sit on their horses and wait for their next orders instead of digging through the pockets of the dead or looking for weapons and other valuables to sell. They aren't even matching their foot sizes with the dead men's boots.

Everything comes down to boots.

Boots and pirates.

I don't understand.

"Are you going to kill me?" I ask.

The man turns, his wide-brimmed hat shadowing half his weathered face. He glances down at my wrists again and says, "No, I'm not going to kill you. We don't kill your kind. . . . We make an example of you." He walks away, but when he passes Durk's body, he pauses. As he stares down, one of his men comes over and unhooks the chain from my cuffs and pulls me to my feet. The gash across my back stings with every movement and my legs are numb. Honestly, I don't know how I'm standing. I feel like light tinder, waiting for the wind to set me on fire.

The leader holds up his hand, stopping us as we're about to pass, then bends over Durk's body. With two fingers, he flips Durk's jacket away, exposing his holster where he stowed my revolver. Durk's own pistol is in his hand—a last attempt to save his life.

One of his men ask, "Captain Hatch?"

The man over Durk—Hatch—takes my gun and rises from his crouch, flipping it over in his hands. "I don't see weapons like this every day," he says. "No rust, but well used." He pops out the cylinder, spins, and snaps it back in. "Clean, and the action is flawless." He looks at me and says, "A gun like this only belongs to someone who knows how to use it."

"What makes you think it's mine?"

Hatch only smiles.

I'm led away and pushed onto a horse where they tie my handcuffs to the horn of the saddle with a length of rope. The rest of Hatch's men mount, their wide-brimmed hats dark against the sky. I would do anything to have Cade beneath me and my gun around my hips. Here, I have nothing.

Then I think what *nothing* really means. Nothing is nothing.

Even pirates on lonely islands had something, didn't they? They still had their lives and so do I, as I'm not dead yet. But I'm not a pirate, or at least I don't think so. Dad described them as bearded men who looted towns and sailed away on ships, some never to be seen again. I still have never seen the ocean.

I've seen the big blue areas on a map before, but I'm sure that's not really what the ocean looks like. I hope it's grand.

I'm not sure if I'll ever see it now.

Hatch turns his horse away from Durk and the rest of his dead men and starts east, back the way they came.

I have no choice but to go with them.

6.

Avery

For the first time in my life, I'm truly lost.

We ran into the night and never stopped, knowing they were tracking us but not knowing when we lost them.

When I lost them, I lost myself.

Back when Mom was still alive, she told Finn and I stories of sailors who used the stars to take them home, and how those small specks in the night sky could guide them anywhere like a map. I look to the dark sky now and see nothing. Sometimes I can make out the glow of the moon, which I've never seen, but the sky seems to mostly show me nothing—nothing that can take me back home. But it doesn't matter, because I no longer belong there.

I belong with Finn, and he's gone.

And even if we do end up going back, what will we be going back to?

The river next to us is unknown to me, along with the small mountains to my left, and even the wind that brushes the back of my neck is unfamiliar.

I know I'm as good as dead. I have nothing but the clothes on my back—boots, jeans, and a long-sleeved shirt. My bandana and goggles still hang around my neck, but they do nothing to keep out the cold.

No food, no shelter.

No home, no Finn.

I kneel on the bank of the river, unable to hold back tears. I'm breathing too fast and can't control myself—I need to calm down and think. Jack nudges my shoulder, helping my heart slow to a constant, steady beat, reminding me I'm not alone.

"I'm sorry," I tell him. "I don't know what to do."

Only the wind answers, shaking me to my bones. From the way the sky looks, it'll be dawn soon. The river moves slow and my eyes follow it, and that's when I see something on the ridge about a half mile away. I stand, using Jack to steady me. Out here in the Wild, it's like my strength is gone, blown away along with everything else that used to be.

There's a person walking along the ridge, carrying a lamp flickering in the dark.

My body says to go to them, to ask for help or food, but my mind warns me not to. All my life, I've lived in a village where I could trust everyone, but when I went to Kev every week, it was the opposite.

I know nothing about the people in the Wild.

I push my fingers into Jack's coat, remembering how numb and cold they are. With winter coming soon, it's only going to get worse. I need to do this for myself and I need to do this for Finn.

Grabbing Jack's reins, I start toward the light. When we come up on the ridge, where the land is flat and rolling with dust, the man with the lantern is almost close enough to make out his face. The light dips with every other step he takes, making his limp more prominent, and I catch flashes of scarred and weathered skin beneath his hat.

Before I change my mind, I call out to him. "Hello?"

He stops immediately, holding the lantern in front of him. "Who's there?" He searches the night until his eyes land on me. "If you take another step closer, you won't live to see the day. I give no leniency toward thieves."

With one movement of his hand, he pushes his coat aside and takes a pistol from his hip.

"I'm not a thief," I say.

"Not a thief, eh?"

"No."

The old man comes closer. Then he freezes, staring like I suddenly appeared in front of him. "You ain't from around here, are ya?"

I shake my head.

"What's someone like you doin' out in a place like this?"

I need to lie to him, not wanting to appear worse off than I am. "I was out riding last night and I got turned around."

The man glances at Jack then back at me.

"That you did, girlie," he says, smiling. "That you did."

His pistol disappears and he grins wider, showing stained and crooked teeth. "Levi, at your service. And you are?"

"Avery."

"Well, Avery of not-from-around-here, how would ya like some breakfast?"

"I really don't think—"

"No, you're comin' home with me. Then I'll point you in whatever direction you need to be."

Levi throws his arm wide, inviting me.

It's either go with him, eat a warm meal, and find out where I am, or stay lost and hungry. The choice isn't hard, even though there is something unsettling about it. For the hundredth time, I wish Finn were here.

Levi leads me with his lantern, glancing back every few minutes to see if I'm still there. When the sky becomes lighter with day, he starts talking. First about the lack of fish in the rivers, then the rain that comes more often as winter draws nearer.

"You're lucky we crossed paths," he says. "I'm 'bout the only one around here who likes to travel at night instead of day."

"Why do you travel at night?"

He spits on the ground and keeps walking. "I could ask you the same thing."

"I already told you."

"That you did. But where did you say you were from?"

"I didn't."

Levi stops and looks back. I can see him better now that morning is coming. His wide-brimmed hat hides most of his white hair, but his face is full of lines and stubble. He reminds me of the traders in Kev—nothing but hard hearts and cold skin—those who travel through the Wild and become a part of it.

"Don't be smart with me, girlie," he says. "You tell me where you need to get back to or I'll leave you here without a thought in the world."

I open my mouth to say Stonewall, but stop myself. Finn isn't in Stonewall. He's being taken to Kev by the Lawmen, and that's where I need to go.

"Kev," I say.

He looks me up and down. "You don't look like you're from Kev. You look like a townie but not that type of townie."

"Are you calling me a liar?"

"I'm pointin' out an improbability."

Then he turns around and continues on, not caring for an answer.

When it's full morning, a small cabin comes into view about a quarter mile away from a river swollen with rain that must have fallen somewhere north of here. Now that day is here, I can tell what direction we're heading by where the sky is a lighter gray. It's hard sometimes, depending on the storms that pass by and where the clouds are thicker. But Mom taught us everything she knew, and I know we're heading north.

The closer we get to the cabin, the more I realize how thirsty I am. I can drink from the rivers Jack drinks from, but there's always a risk of me catching something he can't. There's an outdoor well near the cabin with a man-made pulley system, but I don't ask. Even if he doesn't give me the safest feeling, this man invited me to his home, and Mom always taught us not to be rude.

Levi motions over to the fence behind the cabin where an old donkey stands near a trough. "You can put your horse in there. You'll find some feed in the shed."

I stop short. "You don't have to share your feed."

He waves me off. "I know some people. Give him as much as he needs, then come inside when you've finished."

I walk Jack over to the gate, which squeaks when I open it, and the donkey lifts its head, attempting to look curious. Jack tentatively smells the animal and then turns to the trough, drinking deep, the same way I wish I could.

In the shed, I find a large bag of feed—enough to last months. This stuff doesn't come cheap. One handful can fill a horse's stomach for a whole day. A half-dozen saddles line the wall without a speck of dust on them. Saddles that have been recently used.

I take a large handful of food out to Jack, my stomach anxious, and look for anything else that may be wrong.

It's not hard to find once I'm looking.

Along with the donkey's small hoofprints in the ground, there are countless horse prints. Some fresh and some old. Levi can't be the only one living here.

Mom's warnings about the Wild echo in my thoughts, just out of reach. I wish I knew what's truth and what's just my paranoia. After Jack eats every last bit of feed from my palm, I rub his head and then go inside. Levi is bent over a pot of stew, and I'm surprised when I smell it.

"Is that meat?" I ask, my voice nearing the high end.

He doesn't turn but answers, "It surely is. A day can't go by when you don't eat your meat."

Sometimes we go weeks without eating fresh meat—or dried, for that matter. We have to rely on nutrition bars to get protein, and sometimes the occasional fish from the rivers. There used to be deer and rabbit in the Wild, if you went out far enough, but that was when you could still find edible plants, too.

They left us like they knew of something better.

Or they knew this place was going to hell.

"Sit down and I'll get you a bowl." Levi rummages through a dusty drawer in search for spoons, and I sit down at the small table. My stomach is nervous and hungry all at once. I don't like being here, but he's feeding me actual meat.

The moment he sets down a glass of water, it's gone before he can grasp what happened. But he gives me more without comment, and even though I'm more than hungry, I wait for him to take a bite before I start eating. I savor every bit of meat, not wanting to swallow because then it'll be gone. Mom always said things taste better if you're hungry, and I wonder if this is one of those times.

"What kind of meat is this?" I ask. "I've never tasted anything like it."

Levi sits back, lighting his pipe. "No? I suppose some of the vendors in Kev aren't ones to advertise where some of their meat comes from. Gives people the wrong idea."

He smiles—yellow teeth against brown, aged skin.

55

"Wrong idea about what?" I've stopped eating now—not knowing why.

"If people knew where their meat came from, they wouldn't buy it, now would they?"

He takes another smoke, his eyes never leaving mine. My brain works abnormally slow, wanting to believe something besides what he's saying. But I can't, because it's true. I should have known.

Somewhere far away, my spoon drops, splattering the floor with food that now tastes bitter on my tongue.

"You really didn't think it was animal meat, did ya?" he asks, smiling again like it's something funny.

"Is this why you brought me here?" Then I whisper, "To kill me?"

"I wouldn't kill you, girlie," he pauses and then continues. "You're too young and pretty for that."

I don't know what to do, but I can't breathe and my stomach lurches and everything in the room spins and I can't make it stop. I stand up so fast my chair hits the floor, but he already has a gun pointed at me, the long barrel propped up on the table. I didn't even see it before.

My hands shake at my sides—maybe out of fear or anger, I'm not sure. Because I am angry. He lied to get me to come here, gave me false hope of getting help when I needed it most. After everything I've been through in the last twenty-four hours, I won't put up with more.

"Shoot me then." I stare at him hard. "Because that's what it's going to take to keep me here, you *fucking* bastard."

"You can try. But they'll be here soon, so you don't have long."

I don't know who he's talking about, but I can guess. He's going to sell me to them.

With him between me and the door, that leaves the window

behind me. It might be stupid, but I don't think I can fight him to the door. I've never punched anyone in my life, and this man looks like he's been through hell and back.

Before he has the chance to come around the table, I grab my chair from the floor and throw it through the window. I jump after it seconds later, pieces of glass still falling, and somehow I'm able to land on my feet, saving my hands and arms from being cut. The wind and dust slice through my hair and my legs are already moving. I turn at the corner of the cabin and see Jack inside the pen. He's standing straight, alert, knowing something is wrong.

A few more yards and I'll be free from this place. I'll find Kev and then Finn, and everything will be the way it was again.

Something moves out of my periphery, but I don't respond fast enough. It hits the back of my legs, taking my feet out from under me, too fast to break my fall. My back hits the ground hard, taking my breath.

I blink, staring at the gray sky, counting the seconds until I breathe again. Air slowly enters my lungs, making me cough.

Levi presses the barrel of his gun to my chest, standing over me so I see nothing but him.

It triggers something, and I remember the lessons Mom taught Finn and me when we were old enough to handle a gun. We were miles away from Stonewall, shooting targets and learning how to load and clean our weapons. Before we were born—before the sky turned gray and the trees started dying—Mom never owned a gun. She said she never had use for one.

Now I understand she was teaching us how to live in the world that is now ours, and I realize how lucky I am to have had a mother like her.

In one quick motion, I swipe my arm up, my forearm hitting the underside of the barrel. Levi's eyes aren't on the gun, but mine are. As it flips in the air, I sit up, and when the butt of the gun is within reach, I catch it with my finger already on the trigger and the butt pressing into my shoulder.

Levi stands there with his eyes wide, surprised by what just happened.

"If you don't want to die, you're going to step away from me right now," I tell him.

He holds up his hands—more mockingly than serious—but steps away all the same.

"No need to be rash 'bout—"

"I have every right to be rash," I cut him off, standing and not lowering the gun. "Now, you're going to go back inside and stay there until I've left. You got that?"

"Every word," he says, smiling.

The moment he shuts the door, I run to the shed and grab only the things I need. I strap a saddle on Jack, making sure there's feed in the saddlebags, and just to spite him, I steal a hat hanging near the door—wide-brimmed and black—something I usually don't wear but nothing about this is anything typical for me. I slip the shotgun into its saddle holster, not letting it out of my sight.

Jack will barely stand still long enough for me to get on. Once my leg is over, we're gone and I don't look back.

7.

Seph

We ride into the night, right up to the point where I don't think I can stay conscious any longer.

They haven't given me anything to drink. The gash along my back aches with every movement of the horse. My shoulders are stiff from being forced to stay in the same position for hours.

But as I'm beginning to shut my eyes, Hatch calls out instructions to make camp for the night. He shouts for a couple to scout the area, and the rest unsaddle the horses and set up small tents.

They're effective for such a small group.

The man who'd been leading my horse dismounts as Hatch rides over to us. Hatch spares me a glance before giving orders. "Take him to Marshall. I don't want him dying of infection before we get there."

Hatch starts to turn before thinking of something else. "And Jones?"

"Yes, sir?"

"Make sure he gets something to eat, too."

I watch Hatch ride away while Jones unties the rope looped through my handcuffs that had been keeping me tethered to the saddle.

I don't understand that man. His eyes are unyielding and cold, and yet he cares if my stomach is full? It doesn't make any sense.

Jones drags me off the horse, and I have to clench my teeth to keep from crying out. It's like my back is being split in two. I can't walk right at first. My legs are numb and stiff. With night surrounding us, everyone wears heavy coats to ward off the cold. I can do nothing but envy them.

On the other side of camp, I see the flicker of a fire. A warmth I haven't felt for a long time. In the Wild, you don't start a fire unless you want to risk someone finding you, or you're stupid. Jones leads me to a guy probably a little older than me who is unsaddling his horse. His skin is a few shades darker than Hatch's and he's the only one who doesn't wear a hat. Jones motions me to stop and walks forward a few steps, muttering words I cannot hear.

"Tell Hatch I'll take care of it," the guy—Marshall—says, his voice is deeper than I expected.

Jones leaves me standing there in the wind. They know I don't have the strength to run away. I'm almost swaying on my feet as it is.

I think of pirates again, wondering if this is what it felt like to walk the gangplank. Alone, with nobody to save you and nowhere to run.

I got close to the ocean once, but a large gang on the East Coast controls all the land and wouldn't let anyone through. It was the same with the west. That's when I started south. Maybe they're like me—wanting to see the ships of the past that may still be out there. Somewhere. Or maybe the ocean is gone, too, and they're not hiding anything.

Marshall slips the bridle from his horse before giving me his attention. The animal moves off and nibbles at the dirt, probably hoping to find something more. It's like they can't help their instincts.

"Follow me," he says. "I can't do this in the dark."

I'm reluctant to move away from the horse, wondering how far I could ride before they catch me.

"There's no point in trying," Marshall says behind me. "They only ride for us, except when we tell them otherwise."

I turn and say, "You seem sure about that."

Marshall studies me until a smile breaks out. "Whatever you say, cowboy."

He takes my elbow and leads me through the small camp toward the fire. Most of the one-man tents are already set up. I've never seen such an organized group. No orders have to be shouted because everyone already knows their place, and nobody argues about menial things. Such an odd gang.

I don't see Hatch anywhere, and for that I'm glad.

The moment I feel the warmth of the fire, my fingers yearn to reach closer. I never risk starting a flame at night, and I never have the tinder to do so. Somehow I'm not surprised they do. Wherever their jackets and horses come from, I'm sure they have no problem getting wood either.

Marshall pushes me down on a rock so only half of me faces the fire. There's a man cooking a large pot of stew over the flames, and my stomach betrays my hunger. I watch him cook while Marshall reopens the wound by pulling my shirt away where the blood has dried to it and started to scab. I can only clench my teeth and pray it doesn't last long.

In the end, he has to cut away my shirt—not like it was worth saving after what it went through anyway.

The fire is the only warmth I have now. The thin cloth I called a shirt never brought much, but now that it's gone and my skin is feeling every touch of cold, I wish I was still wearing it.

"I know it might not seem like much," Marshall says behind me, "but you're lucky that you lived through today.

Durk has a killing streak we've been trying to stop for quite some time now."

After a little while, I say, "I know I am." The truth is, I'm lucky to live through every day.

He starts cleaning the wound but it doesn't hurt as much as before. Maybe my skin is so numb, I can no longer feel.

After dishing out dinner to everyone else, the cook puts a bowl in my hands. Eating with cuffs on is difficult, but I'm too hungry to care.

Nearby, a couple of men laugh. I look up to see them staring.

"He's like a little wolf that has to wait for his mother to give him food." They laugh again and the man who spoke comes closer. "How does that taste, little wolf?"

"And I'm assuming you have experience in that?" I ask.

"In what?"

"Your mother feeding you because you never learned how to feed yourself."

Before he can move to hit me, Marshall mutters, "Leave the kid alone, Jeremiah."

Marshall doesn't seem the type to give orders, but Jeremiah listens nonetheless. He retreats, still facing me.

"It seems the little wolf has a bite," he says.

Someone behind him laughs and they ignore me again, enjoying the last of their food.

Once Marshall is finished cleaning the wound, the bowl of water and once-white cloth are now red. He pushes them aside and I tense, knowing the stitches will come next. I've had to stitch myself up plenty of times and know how it'll feel.

"You can relax," Marshall says, a smile in his voice. "I'm going to use something I've made myself. I haven't had the chance to use it on anything this big before, so I'd like to see how it does."

"What is it?"

He hesitates. "It's a type of healing paste I started to make a couple years ago. My father first had the idea but couldn't finish it before he died."

"And it works?"

"It does on small wounds . . ." He's more meticulous than anyone I've met and makes sure every inch of the gash along my back is covered. After storing the salve safely away, he tips over the bowl of bloodied water and the dry earth soaks it up in a matter of seconds. Even though it rains regularly, the ground can't hold any moisture without the roots of plants or trees.

There is nothing but the wind and dirt and whoever is left to bear it.

Marshall leaves me by the fire under the watch of the man who is now cleaning the bowls he served a short while ago. When he returns with a shirt, he tells me to get up and releases my wrists so I can slip it over my head. It's a long-sleeved, white henley, the top two buttons missing. It smells like smoke and horse, but it's warmer than what I had.

At the sound of Hatch's voice, I look up to see him coming toward me, flanked by two of his men. One of them grabs me and cuffs my hands behind my back, not caring to be gentle.

Hatch stares and I stare back.

"I used to know a man," Hatch says, "who had a saying that I'll never forgot. 'Only the strong will survive this world from beginning to end.' Some say he was a crazy old man, but others thought of him as a prophet—those who thought he knew when the skies would clear and the stars would return. You know what I think?"

I say nothing.

"I think he was trying to warn the weak they needed to be culled before the world could be reborn. But I don't decide who is weak and who is strong. The world does."

Hatch turns away and his men push me forward to follow him. They flank me through the camp. On the way, I see Jeremiah and his friends, and when he yells, I can barely make out the words.

"Good luck, little wolf!"

Four words. That's all.

They march me out of camp and keep going until I see a half buried skeleton frame of a car. They push me down in front of it so my back is pressed against it, the cold seeping through my shirt.

That's when I start fighting them, knowing what they intend to do.

I try kicking and throwing my weight against them, but nothing works. Their hands hold me to the car, so tight that the gash along my back stings. But neither of them makes a move against me. They re-cuff my hands around it, and when I lunge forward in one last attempt, metal clangs on metal and the cuffs bite into my wrists.

"What is this?" I ask. "You patch me up, feed me, and then leave me out here?"

All Hatch says is, "It's up to you to live to see morning." He turns away, followed by his men.

"You can't leave me here!"

But he does, and nothing I say will bring him back. I can only see a speck of the campfire I sat next to minutes earlier. Little did I know it was the last time I'd feel warmth tonight.

I tuck my legs into my chest, my body already shaking with cold.

I'll survive if the temperature doesn't drop as it did last night. I'll survive if the wolves don't come out. I'll survive if I keep myself awake until dawn.

And if I survive, I will no longer give in so easily.

8.

Avery

It's midmorning when I realize I'm being tracked.

After I left Levi's, I didn't stop until nightfall. I was afraid he would send *them* to find me, and even though I had no clue as to which direction Kev was in, I went north anyway, hoping to find an old road with signs or some sort of trail to follow.

Now I'm still lost and am being followed by a band of riders who are slowly gaining on me. They're riding fast, no care for the horses under them, so I have no choice but to continue.

We come into a stretch of lowlands with sharp hills and blackened trees that would have stood tall years ago. I stop Jack at a small river to let him drink, wishing I didn't have to push him so hard. But at this point, it's all I can do. His ears turn back and he lifts his head, hearing them when I can't. There are too many low ridges for me to see them. My heart won't stop pounding. My second day in the Wild and I'm already in a worse position than yesterday. I don't want to think about what I'll face tomorrow.

The wind picks up and I tie my bandana around my mouth and nose. If it gets worse than this, I'm going to have to stop for Jack's sake and find shelter.

After another twenty minutes of hard riding, I come across

a dirt road that seems to have been used recently. I look both ways, wondering if either way leads to Kev. Jack won't stay still, nervous about those who follow us, and when I glance back the way we came, I know why. They're here. About a half-dozen riders come around the ridge, bandanas around their faces and guns in their hands.

Jack backs away as they come onto the road, just as grateful as I am they aren't surrounding us yet. But even though the road behind us is clear, I'm not sure we can outrun them any longer. They will run their horses into the ground before letting us go.

One of the riders breaks off from the group and approaches me, his horse lathered and breathing heavily. I pull my bandana away, but he doesn't return the favor. His eyes are dark under his hat, and there's no way to tell how old he is. Though their guns aren't pointed at me right now, they could be at any moment. If these men are anything like Levi, I have to trust my instincts.

"Come with us without any trouble," he says, "and we won't do you any harm."

Does he really expect me to believe that?

"Hello to you, too," I tell him. "It's not like we've met before. You've only been following me for half a day."

"Is that supposed to be funny?"

"Are you supposed to be dumb?"

"Excuse me?"

"Well, I assume you're dumb if you think I would go with you without a fight."

He finally pulls down his bandana, showing me a smile with a straight set of teeth surrounded by a scruff of a beard. "I knew there was a reason Levi sent us after you." The man kicks his horse forward and I tense, holding the reins so tight my fingers go numb. As he circles me, he says, "It seems this was all worth it after all, and you did give us quite a little run for it, didn't you? There's only been a few times in my life when I've have to ride this far for one person."

He's joins the rest of his gang and Jack dances under me again, wanting to run. "So, are you going to make this hard for us?"

I fight to keep my voice strong. "It sure as hell isn't going to be easy."

"The hard way then." He nods and holds up a hand, then flicks two fingers in my direction.

A rifle is pointed at me, and not two seconds pass before a gunshot echoes in my ears and my heart beats so fast it almost stops.

But I'm not the one who's been shot. The man with the rifle doubles over and falls off his horse, blood already staining the dirt beneath him. All I hear is shouting and something ringing in my ears, but when I look up, the gang is riding away faster than they arrived. Dust rises and makes a trail after them, and for a moment I wonder if I should follow. Whoever is coming up behind me must be worse.

I swallow hard, finding my mouth dry, and turn Jack around only to find the Lawmen coming toward me. My first thought is to run—that they finally caught up with me and are going to take me as they did Finn—but I remind myself these probably aren't the same men, and they may know nothing of me or what happened back home.

As they come nearer, I think of lies I can tell them. They can't find out where I'm from or what I'm doing this far from a town or they will take me. I have no doubt.

I count about ten riders in all, and four of them pass me riding hard, following the gang in the opposite direction. I hold Jack in place, still trying to calm him from everything happening at once.

"Are you all right?"

I turn to the voice—a man with a trimmed beard and dark hat. He wears a white band around his arm like the rest of them.

"I think so." I loosen my hands around the reins, letting the blood flow through them again. "They've been following me for the better half of the day."

He nods, like he already knows. "Gangs around these parts tend to get desperate. You're lucky we got here in time. Speaking of which, is there a reason you're so far out of Kev today? You should know these roads aren't safe."

I look straight into his eyes and say, "I was out visiting my grandfather today. I bring him food once a week because he prefers to live outside of town."

I almost don't think he believes me, but he nods again. "Some of the older folk can be that way. But to back up your story to be true, you wouldn't mind one of my men checking your supplies, would you? If you really are coming back from your grandfather's, you shouldn't have much with you, since Kev is less than a day's ride from here."

Luckily for me, I only grabbed what I could from Levi's before making a run for it. Jack only has a handful of food left and I ate the last of my rations this morning.

I shake my head and say, "Not at all."

He motions to one of his men, who dismounts and looks through my saddlebags.

Within those few moments—between the leader talking to the man beside him and the soldier still looking through my things—I catch a glimpse of someone else with them. Not a soldier or a trader, who sometimes travels under their protection, but a prisoner. A boy, not much older than me, sitting on the last horse being led by another soldier, hands cuffed and tethered to the saddle horn. Dark hair messy from the wind and eyes that see everything. He wears no jacket—only a white shirt—making the dark circles under his eyes more prominent.

He doesn't hold himself like a prisoner—tired and mentally beaten. He sits straight in the saddle, the lines of his jaw sharp, daring someone to look at him.

So when his eyes catch sight of mine, I can do nothing but look away.

"She's barely got anything," the soldier says, walking back to his horse.

"We'll be on our way then," the leader says. "Jeremiah and the others will catch up when they've finished." Then he turns to me and I have no time to process his odd choice of words. "You're welcome to ride with us the rest of the way to Kev. We offer protection to anyone who can keep pace."

Without waiting for a reply, he kicks his horse and they ride past, one after the other. Their prisoner is last, his eyes forward and hard until he spares me a glance—quick and almost like it never happened. Dust rises around me and I pull up my bandana, my mind already made about following them.

They're the only ones who haven't tried to kill me yet.

They ride at a steady pace. When the road opens into the flatlands again, the dust blows away from us, and I pull my bandana down to take a deep breath. I'm glad to be riding in the back, where nobody watches me and I can slip away at any time if I choose to.

I find my hand brushing over the rifle regularly, making sure it's still there. I'm ready to use it if I have to. In the Wild, there are no rules. That much I've learned.

Ahead of me, the boy stands out among those with long black jackets. His dark hair moves in rhythm to the horse under him, and his shirt tells the wind how thin it is. But he rides undefeated despite his situation.

He makes me think of Finn, and I wonder if he's being treated the same way. My heart aches not having him next to me and not knowing when I'll see him again. Was this guy caught in the middle of something he wasn't really part of, like Finn? Or does he deserve to have those handcuffs around his wrists?

From the east, I see the other Lawmen riders rejoining the group—the ones who rode after the gang a few hours earlier. The leader signals everyone to stop and he breaks away from the group to talk to those approaching. The prisoner glances over his shoulder, but not at me—something behind us. But when I look, I see nothing.

I take advantage of the moment and dismount to tighten the cinch. The saddle is old and uncomfortable—so different from mine sitting at home.

One of the soldiers rides over to me. He's older than me but young to be a part of the Lawmen.

He dismounts and immediately holds out his hand. "I'm Marshall."

I take it, surprised because barely anyone bothers to shake hands these days. Especially those from Kev. "Avery."

Marshall rubs the scruff on his face and gestures to Jack. "He's a fine animal. How long have you had him?"

"Since he was born," I say. "Why? You think I stole him?"

"I never said that."

"You were thinking it."

That's when he finally smiles. "Fair enough. But you don't want to take too long doing that," he says, gesturing to the saddle. "Hatch will want to be on the move again soon and he won't wait for anyone."

I look to their leader—the man he called Hatch—who is still talking to another Lawman soldier. "Do you think they caught up with that gang?"

Marshall laughs once, sharp. "It's Jeremiah, so I have no doubt." He leads his horse away by the reins, and I catch a glimpse of him over Jack's back talking to the prisoner. Talking to, not with, because the boy says nothing. He has an air of lawlessness that sets him apart.

As I swing my leg over the saddle, Hatch signals us to move on and the other Lawmen soldiers fall into place.

I hold Jack still a moment longer and glance back the way we came, wondering what the boy was looking for and what I must've missed.

9.

Seph

There's a girl riding with us now. She's around my age with hair a little darker than the dirt, freckles splattered across her cheeks, and eyes that I have a problem looking away from. Not just because of their blue color, but because a hundred secrets hide behind them.

She has told Hatch nothing but lies. Except the part about the gang following her—that was true.

She was being chased, but she wasn't visiting her grandfather. She isn't an "outlaw" like me, because she isn't supplied for it.

The horse is hers, but the saddle isn't—I can tell by the way she rides in it.

She isn't from Kev like she said, but for some reason she's headed there.

The gun in the saddle holster isn't hers either, but from the way she brushes her hand across it, I'm confident she knows how to use it.

And from the fear she tries to hide in her eyes, I know this is her first time in the Wild. But wherever she is from, they have good boots.

The first thing I saw this morning was a pair of boots. The

sky was a pale gray and the metal frame I was cuffed to had frost on it. My hands ached from making fists all night to keep the blood flowing through my fingers, and my toes were curled into my boots—possessions I'm always thankful for.

But the first pair of boots I saw that morning other than my own belonged to Hatch. He stood over me until I looked up. I know he had thought I wasn't going to last the night.

Marshall was the one who allowed me to stretch my shoulders for a few minutes. They walked me back to camp and Hatch disappeared without saying a word. Can't say I wasn't happy about that.

When Marshall sat me down next to the fire again, it took a good ten minutes before I could feel my hands. Someone gave me another bowl of food and Marshall checked my back. He said the healing paste worked as well as he'd hoped, but I wasn't sure if I didn't feel anything because I was cold or because it was healed. I had to take Marshall's word for it.

The morning went by like a blur. They let me take a piss and then I was on a horse again, where I continued to fight to stay awake.

The earth is drier here than it is in the north. Dust billows up from the horses' hooves, and I can't look up often without getting it in my eyes.

It was midday when the girl started riding with us, and now she rides a little ways behind, like she'll take off at the first sign of danger. I don't blame her. I don't trust these people either.

If I had a choice, I would have Cade underneath me and we'd be riding south. Nothing but the wind and squeak of the saddle in my ears. I ache for it.

I keep replaying my actions in my head, trying to figure out what I did wrong and how I could've avoided this. But if I hadn't gone into Durk's town, I'm not sure how much farther we could have gone without food. It was either go into town or risk our lives.

"You do that a lot, don't you?"

The voice wakes me from my thoughts. The group has stopped next to a river and everyone dismounts to give the horses one last break.

I look down to see Marshall standing there, waiting for an answer to his question.

"Do what?"

He unties me from the saddle horn and says, "Let your mind wander. Half the time it seems like you aren't even here."

"I'm here enough."

I swing my leg over the horse and slide off. Marshall walks me over to a boulder and sits me down. "Got to be careful about that," he tells me. "You don't want to end up like those crazy old men who think they're living in a different world."

If I am going to become one of those men, it's too late for me to do anything about it. My mind has been wandering for a good ten years.

I tell him, "There's not much else to do when you have nobody but your horse to talk to."

I smile, something I haven't done in my time with them.

In the end, Marshall nods once and says, "Don't go anywhere, all right? I don't think Jeremiah will hesitate to shoot you."

He walks off and I spot Jeremiah near the river, staring at me over the back of his horse. With nothing but plains around us, I'm sure he would take his time to line up the perfect shot.

I stay planted on the boulder, not ready to have a bullet in my back. But it doesn't stop my heel from tapping.

Down the river, I see the girl—Avery—with her horse. It's without a saddle now, the coat darker from where it sat.

Looking at the pair, I itch to glance over my shoulder—to

catch a glimpse of Cade waiting for me to come back to him. I caught sight of him the first time this morning when we were on top of a rise. I happened to look back, and the moment I saw a dark shape far behind, I knew it was him. I know every inch of him—right down to way he runs and throws his head when he wants to go faster. His gait is built into my bones.

I pull out of my thoughts and notice the girl walking toward me and glance over to see her saddle left discarded on the ground. Definitely not hers.

As she gets nearer, I see her horse favoring his left hind leg, but she doesn't notice. I make sure nobody is watching and stand, catching her attention. I face my palms out, letting her know I don't mean any harm. "May I?"

She barely nods, unsure, and I step closer to her horse.

"What are you doing?" she asks.

"He's favoring one of his hind legs. He probably picked up a pebble down by the river and it's good to catch it early before it bruises his hoof."

She stares and says, "I know that."

"Then may I?"

Before she responds, I approach her horse, moving slow to let it memorize my scent before laying a hand on its nose. It's a fine animal. Dark color and strong legs—a horse that would give Cade a run for his money, as Dad used to say. I trail his back with my hands to let him know where I'm going, all the way down to his leg. I pull it up and find the small rock in a matter of seconds, and as I walk back to my boulder, I drop it in her hands.

"Thanks," she says behind me.

I settle back down, catching Marshall's eye, but he doesn't say anything. Like they all know there's nowhere for me to run.

"What were you really doing out here?" I ask, turning to her.

She stops saddling her horse and looks up, her eyes searching for anyone nearby. "What?" she asks.

"Don't pretend you were telling the truth. I'm not blind."

She comes a little closer, making sure nobody is near enough to hear. When her eyes meet mine, I know I'll never forget them, because even though I've never seen the sky, I imagine it being that color.

"And what's it to you?"

"My own curiosity."

She tries to hide it, but her mask breaks for a moment. Long enough for me to see what she's feeling right now. I've shielded my emotions enough to know when someone else is doing it. All I have to do is watch them closely.

"Well?" I ask again.

I really want to know now. I can't come up with a good enough explanation as to why she's out here, with a saddle that isn't hers and being chased by a gang.

Avery glances around one last time and says, almost too low to hear, "I'm trying to find my brother." She swallows hard, holding more back.

"What happened to him?"

"He was taken."

"By a gang? Is that why you were running from them? And even better," I gestured with my hands toward the group of Lawmen near the water, "why would you have to lie about it?"

She shakes her head, hesitant.

"Look," I lean forward, talking just low enough for her to hear. "You can trust me. I'm not going to tell anyone."

"And how do I know that?" Her eyes shift to my cuffed hands and back, not having to use words to tell me what she's thinking.

"It's not what it looks like."

"Yeah? Then what did you do?"

When I open my mouth, Jeremiah's voice fills the silence, too close for comfort.

"He's a man killer," he says.

I look away the moment he says it, down at my shoes because I don't care to see her reaction. Even if I do tell her the truth, there's no way she would believe me now. An outlaw's word against one of these soldiers? I'm nothing. So I keep my mouth shut, leaving her to believe what she will.

Jeremiah continues, "He still had blood on his hands when we got to 'em."

"You saw it happen?" she asks.

"Didn't need to."

"So you don't know then." He begins to object but Avery cuts him off. "You know what? If I need your opinion, I'll let you know."

Jeremiah chews on something in his mouth, probably contemplating doing something stupid. But he's looking at Avery and not me. From what I've seen, I wouldn't wish his wrath on anyone.

The gang chasing Avery are all dead miles behind us, their bodies left for the wolves and vultures—the only animals still living are ones accustomed to human flesh.

I stand, drawing his attention away from her.

"Sit back down before you regret it," he says. "Because if some unfortunate event were ever to happen, I don't think one person would remember your name."

Avery speaks up behind me. "I would."

Jeremiah moves like he's about to hit me, but Marshall's hand on his arm stops him. Marshall gives him a look that sends Jeremiah walking.

The Lawmen are remounting their horses, ready to finish the ride to Kev. When I glance over my shoulder, Avery is gone, too, not wanting to be left behind. Marshall brings my horse and reties my hands to the horn once I'm settled in the saddle.

"You shouldn't provoke him," he says.

"He already hates me."

Marshall huffs a laugh and walks away. While we're waiting for a few stragglers, Avery comes up beside me and reins in her horse. "You didn't have to do that."

I think about it a moment and tell her, "Yes, I did."

Hatch yells to get the group moving, but before we continue, Avery asks, "What is your name, anyway?" I smile and she says, "Just in case Jeremiah brings it up again. It's good to be prepared."

"I fully agree."

The Lawman soldier pulls my horse forward and Avery yells, "Well?"

I call over my shoulder, "Seph."

10.

Avery

It feels like I haven't been to Kev in months, but in reality, it's been about a week. It looks the same but now I'm wanted by the very people who run this place. The group of Lawmen I'm with will know soon enough, so the moment we're inside the gates, I have to leave them.

Then, somehow, I have to find Finn.

Throughout the day, the gates into Kev are open, guarded by two Lawmen soldiers who only stop people if they look suspicious or their faces are similar to any on the wanted posters. But since the walls around the city are only the houses and shacks pressed close together, it's impossible for them to see everyone passing through.

This is the first time I've been through the gates while being with a group of Lawmen soldiers, though. People stand aside and let us pass, most of them eyeing Seph in the rear. I stay back a ways, and the moment we're through the gates, I slow down and let them continue on without me.

As though he can sense me, Seph glances over his shoulder before I'm lost within the crowd and gives me an unrecognizable look. Then they're gone. I know he's their prisoner and very well may have killed a man, but I still wonder what will become of him.

I turn Jack toward the western part of the city to see some-one who will know of news, if there is any. For the most part, I know this city well. I know the traders and shop owners, including the ones who should be avoided.

The streets are quiet today. The weather isn't perfect, but it also isn't storming yet. Dark clouds roll by above, holding their rain for another day or time. Most of the trading booths are closed, too, hinting at the coming night.

When the tavern comes into view, I pull Jack to a stop, look-ing close at the horses tethered out front. They're too nice to be anything but Lawmen horses. I dismount and lead Jack down the alleyway. It's tight between the houses and the trash people throw out their back doors, but we move unseen behind them. Some parts of town are still paved, crudely patched and resur-faced, but on the outskirts, there's dirt most days and mud when it rains. So here, Jack's hooves are silent.

The alleyway opens up behind the tavern, enough room for people to make deliveries with their horses and carts. I tie Jack's reins to the hitching post and slip through the back door. Most of the buildings in Kev are made from stone, but this one is a mix of stone and wood. At one point, it was prob-ably all wood, but since then, parts of the walls have needed to be replaced, and nothing but stone is left for building supplies. But the floors are still a rich-colored oak, now ingrained with sand and dirt but still beautiful.

Not only is this one of the oldest buildings in the city, it's the one place where the Lawmen come to drink into the night. One thing mankind hasn't forgotten about is alcohol. Even people in Stonewall asked me to bring bottles back from this place.

An older man they call Ted runs a distillery in the base-ment, but Margaret runs the tavern. And that's who I'm look-ing to see.

I walk through the dark storage room, and when I open the back door to the kitchen, a strong smell hits me that makes me stop right there in the doorway. My stomach growls, but I force my legs to move past the food before my hands begin to steal it. I see Margaret having words with one of the cooks and I start toward her, dodging some of the waitstaff on their way in and out of the kitchen. Her dark hair is thrown into a messy ponytail and her blouse has stains on it—the constant proof that she doesn't mind getting her hands dirty when it comes to running this place.

The moment Margaret's eyes are on me, I know something is wrong. She always greets me with a smile and free food, but this time her smile is dropping away and her eyes dart to the door leading out to the common room.

She drops the bowl on the counter and grabs my elbow, pulling me back toward the storeroom. Once the door's shut and we're surrounded by canned food, Margaret asks, "Why the hell did you think coming here was a smart idea?"

"I—what?"

"Avery." She stares hard. "You can't be seen in this city. If you are, you'll be arrested on sight. Don't you know that?"

"I had to come see you. I need to know if they took Finn to the barracks like they do with other new recruits. If they did, I'm sure I can get him out easily enough. I need to know. Please, Margaret."

That's when her eyes soften and she glances through the kitchen again. Lawmen soldiers come through her tavern every day, and they always talk like nobody is listening. But Margaret is always listening. "They didn't take him to the barracks with the others."

Didn't take him to the barracks. "Why not? Where did they take him?"

I feel my heart race because I already know the answer. But she says it for me anyway.

"They arrested him, sweetie." She puts her hand on my arm, as though I've already lost him. "When they tried to go after you, I guess he wounded a few men trying to stop them. You know they don't go lightly on lawbreakers."

My head feels light and Margaret sits me down on a crate. "What will they do to him?"

She shakes her head. "I'm not sure. He'll probably be sent to work somewhere. But Avery, you can't stay in the city. Someone will recognize you sooner or later and your fate won't be any better than Finn's."

"But I have to get him out of there. You know I won't leave until he's out."

Margaret sighs and pushes a strand of hair away from her face. "Okay, look. You'll stay here tonight, but in the morning, you have to leave town. You'll stay somewhere on the outskirts and out of sight. I know a place."

"I just said—"

She holds up her hand. "I'm not finished yet. Over the next few days, I'll try to find out what they plan to do with him. If they decide to send him to the quarry, it'll be easy to get to him, but they've been unpredictable these days so I can't promise anything, you understand?" I nod. "Once I hear something, I'll send Henry out to find you and we'll plan something from there. Sound good?"

"I guess . . . I don't like the idea of doing nothing and not knowing what's going on."

"I know. You'll have to ride this one out on faith, and make sure you're not seen."

"I don't know if I can," I tell her, thinking of Finn in that place, not knowing if he's all right.

But Margaret puts a hand on my shoulder and says, "You're gonna have to. For his sake."

11.

Seph

We ride deeper into the city. All eyes are on me.

Even when my heart pounds against my ribs, I show them nothing of what I feel. The only things between me and the Wild are the bonds around my wrists, but I know soon there will be more. Soon I won't even be able to see the constant sky or breathe fresh air.

That's what scares me most of all.

Being trapped.

Like an animal.

Or something less than one.

In the center of the city, about a quarter mile away, stands a building that has withstood the past. Maybe not in one piece but still functional like it once was and still is. A prison.

Before I have the chance to look down or get my bearings, I'm dragged off my horse and thrown to the ground. I hadn't noticed when our group had stopped, so close to our destination yet so far. The streets are flooded with people—multiplied from when we first entered the city.

That's why. More people have gathered to see what the Lawmen are bringing in. I see them whispering to one another—pointing. Jeremiah stands over me but he's facing the crowd—the same way the other Lawmen do.

I hear Hatch approach, pushing through his men to get to me. And when he does, I see the fury on his face.

"Get him up," he says.

Someone hauls me to my feet, keeping one hand in the crook of my elbow.

Hatch faces the crowd, seeing as many as he can before speaking.

"This is what happens when you think there is something more out there," he says. "When you think our way of life is too good for you. The old world is dead." He stops, making his words sink in, and I'm trying to figure out what this has to do with me. Hatch turns and lifts my left wrist, the other going with it because of the cuffs. He shows them the red cloth tied around it—the same thing he saw before they took me.

Is this really what everything has been about? A piece of cloth?

He says, "People like this will not survive this world so long as we are here. They are outlaws and whoever joins them will share their fate."

Hatch pushes me back toward Jeremiah and says, "Tie him to the horse." He walks back to the front while the other Lawmen remount, and Jeremiah grins as he finishes tying a length of rope to my cuffs. He remounts my horse and kicks it forward, forcing me to walk behind him with everyone's eyes on me.

Maybe Hatch hopes it to be a walk of shame, to be humiliating, but there's one thing he's missing: I have nothing to be ashamed of. I walk with my back straight and my eyes not looking away from the stares. This will not break me.

Jeremiah rides steady until the end, jerking the horse forward and trying to make me stumble. The moment Jeremiah gives me a little slack, I wrap the rope around my wrist and jerk back as quick and as hard as I can. Jeremiah falls backward off the horse, stopping the entire group of Lawmen in its tracks. Before anyone can make a move toward me, Jeremiah is already on his feet, his face red and splotchy.

I would laugh if it weren't for the fact that he's about to kill me.

His hat lies forgotten on the ground and he comes for me, one hand reaching for the pistol at his belt. I stand my ground, the eyes of a hundred people on my back.

Whatever he does will make him look like a fool.

He grabs my throat with his left hand, his right pressing the barrel of my own revolver to my temple. I hadn't realized he took it.

"Are you going to kill me the coward's way?" I ask. "Shooting a man with his own gun while he's tied. That's big of you, Jeremiah."

"Jeremiah!" Hatch's voice doesn't sway him.

But something flares in his eyes—something I've said.

I won't die today after all.

"Step away from him." Hatch comes up behind him, leaning in close so the crowd can't hear. "You know we can't do anything to him until the Sheriff has his say. Those are the rules—even though I would love nothing more than to break them right now."

"We should've killed him with Durk's men. Nobody would have known the difference," Jeremiah says, still holding the gun to my head.

"That's not the way we do things," Hatch says.

Jeremiah's hand uncurls from my throat, reluctantly taking his finger off the trigger of my pistol. Hatch signals for another Lawman soldier to lead me inside. We pass through the gates and a guard closes them behind us. I glance back to see the crowd disperse.

I'm on my own with no witnesses to say what happens here. The prison yard is nothing but dirt and a whipping post— the wood stained red. It's something I hope to never see up close. Hatch leads me through the yard, the soldier still at my side in case I decide to run. The others unsaddle the horses, a few leading them away in a different direction than the prison itself. We pass through a wide set of doors, and it's happening too soon. I look back in time to see them close, and for the first time in my life, I'm trapped in a place where I cannot see the sky.

Here, the walls are close and the lamps don't give off enough light. The echoes are loud and hide nothing. We walk down a long hallway until it opens into a larger room, where different passages break off in all directions.

Another Lawman meets Hatch here, nodding respectfully.

Hatch doesn't acknowledge him, but instead asks, "Has Torreck returned?"

"He has, sir. Yesterday morning."

"Did everything go smoothly?"

"One of the smaller towns couldn't pay in full, but Torreck took another form of payment."

Hatch actually smiles. "How many this time?"

"Six," he says. "Well—five, actually."

"Was there a casualty?"

"Not exactly, sir. One caused trouble and a few of our own were injured. Nothing serious, but Torreck decided to bring him here until he decides what to do with him."

"And I'm assuming the Sheriff has already gone for the night?"

"Yes, sir."

"It's probably for the better—he'll need a night's rest before dealing with this one." Hatch half turns and flicks his fingers, motioning for the soldier to bring me forward. "Take him up to cell block four."

"I'll take him," a voice says.

Jeremiah steps up beside me, taking hold of my arm.

Hatch looks unsure but nods anyway. "I'm going to trust he gets there unharmed."

"By the law," Jeremiah says.

Hatch agrees, "By the law."

Jeremiah leads me down a long hall until we reach a set of stairs that lead up several levels. He prods me to go first. Oil lanterns line the walls on the way up, but they do nothing to lessen the echo of our feet.

I feel him staring at my back.

"Hatch gave me orders to do something tomorrow," he says, following behind me. "I guess there was this horse following us on our way back to Kev."

Even though my heart stops, my legs keep going.

But Jeremiah holds me back, his hand on my arm. He says in my ear, "And I have reason to believe it's yours. Do you know what I'm going to do to that horse once I find it? If I find it weak, I'm going to kill it. But if it's strong enough, I'm going to run it into the ground. Would you like that? Seeing me on your animal, knowing its loyalty doesn't lie with you?"

He slams me against the stone, holding his forearm against my throat. My fists are clenched—all I have to do is hit him. But that's exactly what he wants. If I hit him, he gets to do whatever he wants to me.

Instead, I say, "If I find out you did anything to my horse, I will kill you."

It's not an empty promise—I stare at him as hard as I can.

"In that case, I'll bring you its head."

I slam my forehead into his face and his grip releases me. He shouts, holding his hand to his nose like it'll stop the bleeding. More Lawmen come down the stairs, their guns in hand.

Jeremiah shouts, "This little shit attacked me!"

Two of them grab my arms and Jeremiah rises to throw a punch. It's a hard hit across my jaw and he shakes his hand out, but even so, I barely feel it. If I could, I would hit him until the bones in my hands broke.

"Take him to four," he says, walking back the way we came. I'm pushed forward up the stairs, and behind me, Jeremiah storms away shouting orders to those who follow him. I can't help but wonder if he's going to start looking for Cade tonight.

This burning sensation in my chest keeps growing—it has been over the last couple days. Something I'm finally recognizing as anger. I haven't been around people for this long before—they're getting to me.

I think that's why pirate ships are so appealing.

I would be out on the ocean. No walls holding me in and the sky giving me whatever it pleases. I would be alone. My wrists wouldn't be chafed by metal and I wouldn't have to be locked away for something I didn't do. I wouldn't have to deal with people who do what they please and I wouldn't have to sleep with my gun already cocked.

Someone's hand smacks the back of my head and I come back to see two rows of cells on each side of the hallway. "Keep walkin'," the Lawman says.

It's dark, smelling of body odor and straw. Rusted metal bars make up each cell, and when the Lawman soldier opens the last on the left, it squeaks at the hinges. They shove me inside—the door clangs shut behind me. There's only one other person in the cell, and he's sitting in the corner with his legs drawn up to his chest.

"Put your hands through the bars," the soldier says.

I turn around, offering my wrists, and he unlocks the cuffs. He walks away and that's when I notice every other prisoner staring at me from their own cells. Some of them look at me and others at my wrist.

I pull them back through the bars, wanting the shadows to swallow me up. I'm barely holding myself together as it is—I can't get enough air and my heart won't stop racing. If I look up, I'll see the ceiling caving in on me like a never-ending nightmare.

"I know you," a voice says from the cell across from mine. As I hear the words drawn out slow, I'm certain of who it belongs to. I met him a few days ago at an overpass of a bridge. The day before everything fell apart.

He's one of the few who is more gone than I am.

I back into the corner opposite my cell mate and slide down the wall to sit.

"It's funny seeing you here," he continues, and I finally look at him. His elbows are propped up on the crossbars of his door, but his posture is so relaxed it would give anyone the impression he's been here all his life. "But I guess karma catches up to a person after you kill a certain number of people."

"Rami, will you shut the hell up?" a man shouts from a few cells down. "We don't want to hear more of your nonsense."

The one called Rami continues to stare. "Nonsense. Such a funny little word for a funny little man."

Someone slams the bars. "I swear to God, the next time I can get my hands on you, you won't be able to utter another word."

Rami rolls his eyes and says in that general direction, "Whatever you say, funny man."

A fist slams the bars again but he stops shouting. Rami winks before backing away into his own shadows of his cell.

It's quiet for a little while until a voice speaks up next to me. "There aren't any rules out in the yard, so I would watch your back if I were you. That guy killed someone this morning and nobody stopped him."

When he turns toward me, I see he's probably the same age I am. His hair is an unremarkable shade of brown and there's dried blood on the left side of his face from an unseen wound.

"So the Lawmen did nothing to stop him?" I ask, low enough so no one else can hear.

The boy smiles faintly. "If they care about us at all, they have a funny way of showing it." He points to his face.

He looks away but I don't, not understanding what kind of place I'm in. I don't know what he's done to deserve this, too. Is he like me, and in this place for the wrong reason? Or is he really someone who belongs here?

Despite the sounds of dozens of men around me and stone over my head, my eyelids become too heavy for me to hold open. The lack of sleep over the last couple days catches up, and I find myself in a place without walls.

12.

Avery

Today will be one of those days when it never quite becomes day. The clouds are thick and dark, taunting me with rain I can't run from. Not like home, where the roof was solid and no storm could break in.

On the bad days when nobody went outside—not even the miners—Finn and I would sit at the table and play old board games Mom taught us growing up. Neither one of us was better than the other. I would win and then Finn would win—almost to the point where it got boring to play, but at least neither of us could say we were better.

If the storm got worse, we would lie on my bed and stare up at the roof—just to listen to the rain and wind.

At nights when we made dinner together, we barely said a word to each other. Finn would be at the counter cutting the vegetables we earned from the town greenhouse, and I would be at the stove, trying to put together a half-decent stew. And then some nights after a hard day, we would talk about everything and anything.

Finn's long fingers would guide the knife down the vegetables and he would retell a story about one of our neighbors.

His laugh would fill the kitchen. Sometimes he got me laughing so hard tears would come from my eyes.

I can't describe the ache in my chest when I think of him and his smile. I've always loved his smile.

My hand searches my pocket for our wooden horse, but they don't find it because Finn has it, wherever he is.

I close my eyes, take a long breath, and turn back toward Jack, who stands near the river. Margaret gave me a better saddle, but I left it back at camp, if I can even call it that. I was there about a half hour before I couldn't stay still for another minute. We came as far as the river and now I don't know what to do.

My thoughts won't stop drifting to Finn and where he might be and if they are treating him badly, if and when I'll see him again, and how that will ever happen. Then I think about the Lawmen's prisoner—Seph. I don't have the slightest clue why.

Movement catches my eyes downriver.

A horse stands there, looking at me and Jack, with a saddle and bridle and supplies—riderless. I glance around and see no one. The horse is buckskin colored with black legs, now mostly covered in dirt. His nostrils flare and he takes a step forward. Jack moves from my side and approaches the horse, his movements cautious but his ears perked forward in search of a friend.

When they're close enough to touch, both horses take in the other's scent. The newcomer flinches at the smallest movements and keeps an eye on me the whole time.

I start forward slow, giving him a chance to see me. He's a healthy horse, his build just as good, or maybe even better, than Jack's. I'm careful not to spook him. He steps away at first, almost like he wants to bolt in the opposite direction, but his nostrils flare again, catching a scent that makes him want to stay.

I let him come to me. When I feel confident he's familiar enough, I lift my hand and touch his neck. He flinches but doesn't back away. It reminds me of the horses Mom used to bring in from the Wild—abandoned, unwanted things that needed a new start. It's how she made a living—selling horses to whoever could afford them.

"Where is your rider?" I whisper to him.

Both horses swivel their heads, ears pointing in the same direction. They hear something I don't, and the last thing I need is someone seeing me and reporting it to the Lawmen.

"Time to leave," I tell them.

I tug Jack's halter once and he follows me down the river and toward the rocky hills to the south. For a little while, I hear nothing. Then there's the sound of the buckskin horse following us. At the base of one of the hills, I find a small footpath that is nonexistent if you aren't looking for it.

This morning, Margaret sent Henry to show me this place. They said it'll be safe for me to camp here until she finds out news about Finn. It was hard leaving the city, willingly putting distance between us, but me being arrested will do him no good. At the top of the hill there's a divot, large enough to hold a decent campsite and deep enough to hide a fire at night. The footpath switchbacks up the hill, hidden enough behind rocks to be invisible from travelers on the road. But there's a place at the top that I can climb to where I can see the gates of Kev.

In sight while out of sight, that's what Henry said.

This is the first time I've felt safe in the Wild, and even this close to the city, I feel hidden enough to sleep tonight.

The path leading into the campsite sits between two rock faces, wide enough to fit two horses side by side. There's remnants of an old fire, and then my saddle and the supplies I left behind earlier.

I look back and watch the new horse come through the crevice into the camp. His head is low, taking in the scents on the ground, but his eyes are on me.

From the way his ribs are slightly showing, I wonder how many days he's been on his own. A few days at least. I dig around in my saddlebags until I find the feed I got from Margaret. Jack is already at my side, eating a few mouthfuls from the sack. I take it away when he's had enough, but he nudges me for more.

"You'll have more tomorrow," I tell him.

I have to ration it, not sure how long we'll be here.

I take an extra handful and step closer to the other horse. I hold my hand out, palm flat. It takes him a whole minute to come to me, but I would've waited longer. Mom was always patient with horses because that's how she gained their trust.

His soft nose brushes my hand and the feed is gone in seconds. I give him more, and every time I go back for feed, he's closer. I wipe the crumbs from my jeans and contemplate trying to take off his saddle. It needs to come off or else he'll have sores—he may have them already.

I reach for the cinch but he sidesteps, keeping a healthy distance between us. He does it again and again, and I finally throw up my hands and say, "Fine then, I guess you can get saddle sores if you want them so bad."

He stares at me.

I try approaching him again, but he backs away.

"Look, I know you don't know me, but I'm trying to help." I shake my head, almost laughing. "I sound like a crazy person," I mumble to myself. "Talking to horses and thinking they're actually going to talk back."

To my surprise, he steps closer. I keep talking to see if it'll work.

"I'm sorry I didn't introduce myself," I say. "I'm Avery. And you are?" I wait. "Well, in that case, I'll just call you Moose."

The horse flicks his tail and comes a little closer. "I've never seen a moose in real life, but I've seen a picture of one," I tell him. "I'm not saying you resemble one, because you don't, but it's one of those animals I wish I could see in person."

He presses his nose into my hand. "Do you mind if I call you Moose?"

A shake of his mane brings a smile to my lips. I talk to him while loosening the cinch and slide off the saddle. His coat is matted down with dried sweat and dirt. After checking him over, I see no sores or wounds of any kind, which is surprising. I pull the bridle over his ears and the bit slips out of his mouth.

Moose wanders over to Jack, and I realized we may have picked up a permanent member for our little group.

I crouch over the saddlebags, wondering if it's wrong to go through other people's things. I flip the leather flap, promising I won't take anything but too curious not to look. The first bag is filled with ration bars and horse feed—my first clue to knowing this horse isn't from around here. There's a lever-action rifle strapped to the saddle, which could come in handy since I only have a few more bullets left for Levi's gun. Mom had one before she traded it for a shotgun that is still hidden away in our closet, or else I never wouldn't have known what it is.

The other saddlebag is filled with personal items. I stare at the open pack, not feeling right going through things like this. There's a baseball cap at the top, like it was the last thing to be put inside. Dad had one—a faded red one with a white *P* on it. But this one is dark blue with a *KC* printed on it, frayed at the edges and well used.

It's actually reassuring—knowing this horse doesn't belong to the Lawmen with their white armbands and wide-brimmed hats. Moose belonged to someone normal—at least as much as I can tell, but definitely someone traveling a long way. Without moving anything, I can see a pair goggles and an old book with a cracked spine.

I think of home. Is someone going through the things we left behind right now? Do they even care we're gone? I close the saddlebag and get to work preparing a fire for the night, just in case I need one. Earlier, I found an old stack of wood nearby. It won't last long—it just assures me I won't freeze on the cold nights if I need a fire.

Being out here in the Wild is like sitting alone for a lifetime—with only my thoughts for company. And I'm beginning to feel like my thoughts aren't enough to fill the empty space where everything else should go.

Especially not out here, where there is nothing.

13.

Seph

Despite my exhaustion, I don't sleep well during the night. The walls are too close and the air much too still. While everything in me wants to escape this place, I somehow convince myself to wait. I know my body cannot leave this cell, but my mind can.

During the hours when sleep doesn't come, I imagine myself on Cade, riding away from here—anywhere. The way we grew up together. The nights we slept side by side to keep warm. The rivers we swam in to keep clean. I don't know what I'll do if something happens to him.

Voices rise from down the hall and I sit up, feeling every hour of lost sleep. My cellmate is awake, too, looking as dead as I must.

A pair of men, followed by a Lawman soldier, make their way from cell to cell, sliding plates of food to the prisoners. The dishes make uneven scraping sounds against the stone, each one digging deeper into me. My finger taps the floor—a twitch I haven't experienced since a run-in two years ago. Something I don't even like to think about. My heart beats at an irregular rhythm, and I close my eyes to get a hold of myself.

By the time the plates of food are pushed underneath our barred door, I've calmed down. I stand and take my plate, retreating to my corner again, only to wonder if I can stomach hard bread and a mush that doesn't resemble food. I swallow as much as I can before I think too hard on it.

"The quicker you eat it, the less you taste it," he says.

The boy in my cell hasn't said anything to me since last night—something I have absolutely no problem with.

"I think it's more my stomach than the taste."

He sets his plate down with a half smile. "Well, it tastes like horse shit to me."

"Not many people would know that."

"It was a dare," he says.

"Someone really must have hated you."

He smiles again as the cell doors open down the hall. The Lawmen usher the prisoners out. I get to my feet, wondering what they're doing. From across the hall, Rami smiles at me as his door opens and he follows the others. Our cell is the last they come to.

I step outside and follow the hall down a series of passageways, each doorway branching off blocked by more barred doors, like we're cattle following the only path we can.

"What's your name?" the boy asks behind me.

I glance down each hallway I pass, attempting to get my bearings. I finally answer, "Seph."

"Finn."

I glance over my shoulder, catching his eye in the dim light. "How long have you been here?"

"Only since yesterday."

After we go down multiple stories, I see light through the next opening and then I'm outside. I can breathe. The dark, cloudy sky is the most comforting thing I've seen within the last day. I never want to go back inside again.

Other than that, there's nothing else to really take in. The prison yard is surrounded by a tall fence, and beyond that is the city. At this point, I don't care as long as I'm under the sky. As long as there's air to breathe.

Finn steps up next to me and I see him for the first time in real light. His brown hair is cut shorter than mine and his eyes remind of someone I can't place. Blue. "Come on," he says. "I heard there's a place to shower."

I follow him across the yard, and soon I'm aware of the men I pass—every one of them looking at me like the crowd in the city when we arrived. The yard is good sized. Filled with prisoners from more than one cell block. There's a large, barred gate farther down, separating us from the prison entrance. I can see the whipping post from here. Behind us, Lawmen soldiers watch from the prison's roofs and balconies, and others patrol outside the fence. They never get too close.

Finn leads me to the other side of the yard where there are multiple outside showers—one-man stalls underneath large water barrels with hand levers. There are already lines forming, and men push others out of the way and some punches are thrown. Finn and I take our place in the back of one of the lines.

Something foul reaches my nose, growing stronger when the wind picks up. Then I spot a man pissing in a trench nearby. There are others there, too, but it's something I don't want to look at for long.

I turn back around to see the man ahead of us staring at me. His eyes flick down and then he moves off to join another line. Then it happens again and again—they whisper to each other and looks are exchanged. We move to the head of the line and I nod my head for Finn to go first. He shoots me a grateful smile and shuts the stall door behind him.

"Well lookie here," a voice says behind me. It's Rami—every one of his words drawn out in that southern way. "It seems you and I meet again, this time with only our hands to defend ourselves. Do you feel lost without your gun, cowboy?"

"I wasn't aware it was a compass," I say without turning.

He laughs. "You're a funny guy."

"I don't know any jokes."

"I do. You wanna hear one?" I don't say anything, but he continues anyway. "Knock knock."

I turn to face him. "Who's there?"

Rami smiles, his eyes a little crazed. "Me." He laughs again and then something catches his eye from across the yard. "Just who I wanted to see," he says, almost to himself.

He touches two fingers to his forehead, kind of like a salute, and walks off in that direction, leaving me to wonder.

Finn comes out of the shower, his face now blood free and hair wet. I take my turn and lock the stall door, not wishing for Rami or anyone else to find me here. I strip off my clothes and hang them on a peg near the door. The stone floor seeps cold into my bare feet, and when I pull the lever, the water is the same. A sharp breath escapes me but I don't move, loving the way it feels on my back and sore muscles.

My shoulders still ache from being in cuffs the last couple days, but oddly enough, I no longer feel anything from the gash across my back. I reach behind and touch my fingers to it. It's a scar now, still fresh, but healed over in two days.

There's no soap, so it doesn't take long. Just enough to wash the dirt away. Without anything to dry off with, I slip my pants on, figuring they'll dry on their own. I put my arms through the shirt and pull it over my head, and it clings to the wet places on my back.

When I push the door open, people are running past the showers, toward a crowd gathered a little ways off. There's yelling and pushing, but they're all trying to look at something I can't see. As I get closer, I slip past people to get to the front.

Some start to say something about it, but then they notice who I am or others whisper in their ears to tell them. I pretend to notice none of it.

I find Finn at the front, staring at a body on the ground.

The man's neck is broken. His arm is twisted under him and his eyes stare at the sky. It triggers something in me, enough to make me look up and scan the crowd. The only person not talking or looking at the body is Rami. He's across from me, wearing a smile I've already seen from him more than once.

"It's the man who was yelling at Rami last night, right after you got here," Finn says beside me.

"So he killed him for it?"

Finn says, "He's not right in the head."

Someone shouts and the crowd disperses faster than it came together. The Lawmen unlock the gate separating us from the main prison yard. There are more soldiers now than before, and they all move aside as a man on a horse comes through the gates.

More prisoners walk away as he dismounts, yelling for answers about what happened. But I'm looking for Rami and not seeing him anywhere.

Finn stiffens beside me.

I ask, "What is it?"

He shakes his head and looks around. "We should get out of here."

Everyone else leaves, and Finn starts backtracking. When his eyes flick back to the Lawman soldier coming through the gates, I follow his gaze. The man wears a dark hat and long coat just like the rest of them, white armband around his arm and a dark beard covering his jaw. But he has the presence of someone even Hatch can't compare to. He's the reason everyone left the scene so quickly and most likely the reason this town is run by fear of these men.

He walks over to the body and yells at someone to take it away, then his eyes land on me. I don't have the will to look away, even though something tells me I should.

"Do you have a problem with your legs, boy?"

I glance around, only to find myself alone. The other prisoners watch from a safe distance. I shake my head. "No."

"No, *sir*," he says, stepping closer.

"I'm not aware you're my superior." Everything inside me yells for me to shut up. But I can't. I don't want to.

"But you are my prisoner," he says. "So you *will* call me sir."

I take my time to study my surroundings, and then I meet his eye. "I'm nobody's prisoner."

Jeremiah's voice yells out from the gate, "I'd be careful of that little wolf, Torreck. He's got bite."

His name fits him.

Torreck smiles at that, but a rage pulses through his veins. He sees the red cloth around my wrist and asks, "A little young for that, aren't you?"

I don't know what he means by it—I still don't know what the cloth means to these people, but I know my answer to his question. "It was my father's."

Torreck looks at me hard now—still angry at what I said to him—ignoring the Lawmen who come to flank him and the others carrying the dead body away. "Maybe your father should've told you what happens to those who wear that."

Only the wind separates us, the yard so quiet like nobody else is here.

"Sir?" a soldier asks, daring to break the silence.

"Bind him to the post," Torreck says, turning his back.

Before I have the chance to breathe, soldiers grab my arms and pull me forward. I fight against them, but it does no good. It's not quiet anymore. The prisoners yell and Lawmen laugh and cheer. The noise draws a crowd to the prison's fence—

102

people peer in, their fingers gripping the bars. The moment we pass through the first set of gates, they lock them behind us. I glance over my shoulder and see Finn through the bars. I should have taken his advice and left when he told me to.

Why did I have to open my mouth? I could've melted away with everyone else and he never would've known I existed.

Someone grabs my shirt from the back and lifts it over my head, leaving me bare chested. They pull me forward and I don't know how my legs are moving. They cuff my hands on the other side of the post and connect them to one of many hooks on the other side—one that stretches my arms high and makes the metal cuffs dig into my wrists.

The soldiers leave me.

I try everything to control my breathing. I name the states in my head, one after another. It doesn't work. Nothing works.

Something touches my back and I flinch, but it's just Torreck coming up behind me. He chuckles in my ear and runs a finger down my back again. "By the end of this, you *will* call me sir. I won't stop until you do."

He backs away, snapping the whip to get a reaction out of me. I'm not going to give him the satisfaction—I can't. The crowd and prisoners now watch silently from behind the bars. I wait for it to come, and when it does, it's not like anything I've ever felt.

I stifle a scream and clench my jaw shut, pain coursing through every inch of me. Another one comes—I can't feel my hands and the metal digs deeper. If I didn't know better, I swear my back had been lit on fire. The leather slashes my skin with every stroke, and sweat already drips into my eyes.

Again and again. To the point where I can't take a breath.

"Have you had enough?" Torreck yells, waiting for me to say that word.

I only manage to say, "No," before my jaw trembles and I

have to force it shut. The people in the crowd shift and whisper, probably thinking they didn't hear right.

"So be it," Torreck says.

I hear him pull the whip back again, but that's when someone calls his name. I close my eyes and pray that will be the last of it.

"May I ask what you're doing?" the voice asks.

"My job."

"Torreck, can I have a word?"

He mutters a curse and walks away. The crowd sees something, or someone—I don't—because they whisper and point to an area I can't see. A thin trail of blood runs down my arm from one of my wrists. Before I hear them, a pair of Lawmen come up beside me and lift my hands off the hook. As they unlock the cuffs, I lean against the post, unable to feel my legs.

I can't feel anything. My skin is ice except for the fire on my back, and everything else is numb.

The soldiers lead me away, holding my upper arms and supporting most of my weight. They take me toward Torreck and the other man he's talking to—the one who stopped this from going any further. He's older with graying hair. His clothes are clean and unwrinkled, so different from what I've ever seen.

He's the Sheriff—the one I keep hearing about—I know he is. The one who's really in charge.

The soldiers drop me to my knees before him and I don't have the strength to try and stand.

"This is the one Hatch brought in?" the Sheriff asks, looking down.

Torreck nods. "This is him."

The Sheriff sighs. "Well, he's useless to me like this. Take him to the cellar—I'll send someone to fix him up." Then he looks to Torreck and says, "Come up to my office. We need to talk."

The Sheriff walks off, but before Torreck turns, he takes another look at me. I see something in his eyes that I've seen too many times to count—he wants to kill me. They take me inside. This time I don't have a chance to look at the sky for the last time.

The cellar is what they call the level underground, where a hall of old cells have been forgotten. People walk somewhere overhead, unaware I'm underneath them, even if I were to yell out.

It's dark here except for a window somewhere down the hall, but it's clean. Dust covers everything except for the room I'm in and it doesn't smell. It's the only one with a bed and bucket if I find myself needing to piss.

But the only thing I can do right now is lie on my stomach and let my eyes tear up every time I move. I can't even worry about the walls seeming to close in around me with every minute. The pain is too much of a distraction. The Lawmen pushed me in this room and left, laughing to themselves as I struggled to the bed on my own.

What feels like an hour later, the door at the top of the stairs opens and lets in light. The stairs creak with someone's weight as they come down.

Footsteps come closer until Marshall stands on the other side of the bars. He wears a plain shirt and carries a lantern in one hand and a bag in the other.

Down here, without the white band or jacket, I could almost forget he's a soldier.

"If I knew what happened, I would've come sooner," he says, "but they only just told me."

He puts the bag down to unlock the door and leaves it open as he joins me inside. After setting the light on the small table, he bends over my back. His fingers touch something tender and I suck in a breath.

"Well, at least this time I don't have to reopen the wound to clean it, right?"

It's meant to be a joke, but I can't laugh.

"Thanks for coming," I tell him, my voice hoarse.

Marshall nods, looking down. "Of course." He sits on the edge of the bed. "Besides, if anyone else were to see you, you wouldn't be on your feet by tomorrow."

I close my eyes and relax my back. "That's the best thing I've heard all day. You've made something amazing . . . you know that, right?"

"Guess we'll find out."

Marshall starts applying his healing paste to my back. It's so quiet down here—somewhere down the hall, water drips every minute or so, and mice scurry in the next cell.

After a while, I ask, "Why did you join them?"

His fingers pause for the shortest of moments before he answers. "Because I didn't have any other option. I was raised by my mother and she died when I turned sixteen. I couldn't find work and I found myself without a home or food to eat. The only thing I could do was become a soldier."

I can't say anything against that. People have to do whatever they can to survive, even if that means giving up your freedom. I couldn't stand for it, though.

Marshall moves down my back, working in silence until I think of something I need an answer for. "Can I ask you another question?"

"If I can answer it."

I hesitate because it's going to sound stupid to him. "What does the cloth around my wrist mean to these people?"

Marshall stops, this time completely. "You mean you don't know?"

I shake my head once and put my chin on my arm.

"It's not just here, but this is where it started. That piece of cloth represents . . . well, it represents everything this place doesn't. Freedom and the old laws where it wasn't okay going around killing people. When the Sheriff started this place, he was in complete power. Nobody could stand up to him out of fear of losing their lives. So when a few of his soldiers rebelled, they left and started a new settlement to the south. Now it's not safe here for anyone who wears a red band. He's scared of everyone else leaving, too, or maybe revolting."

"So they think I'm one of them," I say.

"Does this mean you aren't?" He continues on my back, fingers gentle.

"No, it was my father's. But I don't know if it's coincidence, or if he really was a part of that. He never told me if he was."

Marshall stands and puts the paste back in his bag. "Well, I guess the decision is up to you then."

"What decision?"

"About what side you're on." He pulls a shirt out of his bag—the same one they pulled off me. He puts it on the table near the lantern. "I'm going to have someone bring you food and I want you to eat it whether you're hungry or not, and then I want you to sleep as long as you can. And try not to move much, at least until tomorrow."

Marshall locks the door behind him, but before he walks away, I ask, "What side are you on?"

He pauses and looks back. "I don't know."

14.

Seph

I'm sitting on the bed when they come for me.

Three of them, all wearing white bands around their biceps and guns in their holsters.

I've been down here two days, and they've finally come for me.

Two days of sleeping and a full stomach has put me in a position I haven't been in since before Hatch found me. I've regained my strength, my mind is sharp again, and the scars on my back feel like they've been there for years.

I don't move to get up. My elbows rest on my knees and I rub a finger over the cloth around my wrist. I've thought a lot about it during the time I've spent down here—it was the only thing I could do to keep my mind off the walls pressing in around me and the lack of air.

Without Cade here to talk to, my mind wanders more freely.

The three Lawmen stop before my cell, then they move aside to let a fourth through. I look up to see Torreck. His hat makes even darker shadows than before, eyes sharp under the brim.

"Give me a minute with him," he says. The soldiers walk

away and he waits until they're out of earshot. "We don't get many of your kind here. If it were up to me, you'd be dead already."

"I guess I should be glad it's not up to you."

He half smiles and steps closer to the bars, looking down on me. "I don't know what the Sheriff will decide to do to you, but if we ever cross paths again, it'll end on my terms."

I stand and meet him at the bars. "If we ever meet again, make sure you have a gun."

If the bars weren't between us, I'm sure he would be strangling me right now. He doesn't hide his emotions well.

A soldier comes up behind him. "Sir, we shouldn't keep him waiting," the Lawman says.

Torreck turns without another word to me and walks away. "Take him up."

They pull me from the cell and walk upstairs with me between them. Each one with one hand on his gun. Because there's nowhere for me to run, they don't bother with handcuffs. We walk up two flights of stairs until they lead me down a different wing—one a little offset from the cell blocks. We come to a hallway with windows lining the left side. While others would look down at the city and people below, the only thing my eyes find is the sky.

I stare up at it until it's gone, and we move through a set of doors. The Sheriff sits behind a large desk, the window behind him covered with an old set of drapes. A sliver of light shines through, making a dull line across his desk.

They push me down in the chair before him and leave, the door slamming shut behind them. But they're still out there—waiting for the word if I do something stupid.

"I see you're on your feet again," the Sheriff says, "no doubt because of Marshall. Things have certainly changed with him here."

"Can we cut to the chase?" I ask. "I'm not one to have small talk with people who keep me prisoner."

The Sheriff smiles—an unpleasant thing I wish never to see again. "That's actually what I wanted to discuss with you." He leans forward, elbows on the desk. "Hatch tells me you claim to be an outlaw—one of those wanderers who never survives for long. But you wear a red cloth, so what are you really? A spy? Here to steal more people from me?"

"I don't have a home, if that's what you mean. I know you won't believe me, but the red cloth is merely a coincidence."

The man stares at me a long time, his jaw clenching and unclenching. "I'm going to ask you something, and if you lie to me, I will have you killed. I won't think twice about it, because without answers, you are nothing to me." Then he asks, "Do you wander because you're looking for it?"

I repeat the question in my head, not understanding. I don't know if I'm looking for anything. The ocean maybe, but I know where it is. I just need to get there.

"Am I looking for what?" I finally ask.

"The sky." That's when I see something in his eyes—something I've seen in a lot of people I've met, and if I were to look into my own, I would probably find it there, too. The Wild puts it in everyone.

I nod toward the covered window. "The sky is out there. All you have to do is look up." And I'm serious when I say it.

He stands, his hands pressing down on the desk. "I mean the real sky. The one hidden by the clouds that have plagued us all these years." He leans forward. "Don't you miss it?"

"I can't miss something I've never had."

Realizing what he said, he straightens, lowering his eyes. "Sometimes I forget how long it's been. I've lost count how many years it's been and how old I've come to be." Then he says, more to himself than me, "It's not natural."

110

The Sheriff reminds me of men I meet on the road whose minds are set on one thing: finding the sky. They're always looking up and always searching for something that cannot be found. It's the only thing they live for. Countless times, I've come across people who've killed themselves—hanged from crossbeams or used their own weapon against themselves.

One man had a handwritten sign pinned to his jacket. It said, *I couldn't find it.*

Too many cling to the past and don't embrace what's around them. Maybe it's easier for me since I've never seen it.

When the Sheriff turns back to me, his expression reveals nothing of what just happened. Unlike Torreck, he's become good at hiding what other people can't seem to. "Well, I was hoping you would bring me better news, but even as it is, it doesn't change my mind about your execution—"

"Wait—*what?*"

I rise from my chair, but soldiers have already come through the door, forcing my arms behind me.

"You can't kill someone for doing nothing," I say, fighting to keep my hands free. The Sheriff doesn't look at me, like his papers are more important. "Look at me, you son of a bitch!"

He does—his eyes stone-cold. "You really didn't think I would let you live, did you? I saw the way the prisoners and the people looked at you the other day. They saw someone who had enough courage to say no."

"So you're going to kill me for it?"

Without hesitation, he says, "Yes, I'm going to kill you for it. These people don't need someone like you on a pedestal, thinking another way of life would suit them better. You aren't the first to come here and have every eye on you from the start. I'm going to get rid of you like I did the rest of them. You know how?"

The cuffs snap around my wrists, rubbing against the scars already there.

"I make them disappear," he says, stepping around his desk to come face-to-face with me. I struggle against the soldiers, hoping somehow I'll be strong enough to break free. "They'll never know your name, and in a few days' time, they'll forget you ever existed." He nods to the soldiers. "Take him downstairs until morning."

The Sheriff turns his back on me. They drag me from the room as I yell curses, even after the door is shut.

They take me deeper and deeper to a cell where I don't exist and no one can hear me yelling.

15.

Seph

They come before dawn.

They drag me from the cell and cuff my hands in front. Horses wait in the prison yard—three of them. And waiting with them is Jeremiah and Marshall.

We ride through the city under dark clouds, the streets quiet with the morning haze. Nobody is out at this hour, and this is exactly what the Sheriff wants—for me to disappear. The gates are waiting open, and the soldiers nod to Jeremiah as we pass by.

Then we ride west. The horses toss their heads as they're let loose, enjoying the small freedom as much as I am. I close my eyes to let the wind take me in—the smell of horse and dirt right there with it. Letting Cade loose on a flat stretch of ground is like flying. But with metal brushing my wrists and a strange horse beneath me, I've never felt more grounded.

We don't ride for long—just enough time to let the day start and the crows stretch their wings far above us. We've stopped near the bottom of a large rise, where there's no chance for witnesses and nobody to hear gunshots. Now that it's come, I can't keep my heart beating at a normal rhythm.

Instead of the Lawmen saving me like they did a few days ago, this time they'll be the ones to kill me.

Jeremiah pulls me off the saddle and Marshall takes the horses away to tether them.

"To tell you the truth," he says, leading me by the arm, "the Sheriff was going to ask Torreck to do this for him, but after I insisted, he agreed."

"Congratulations," I say.

He stops me with a hand on my chest. "You're a little smart-ass, you know that?"

"No, but thank you for telling me, Jeremiah. It's been the highlight of my week." I can't make myself shut up again. I usually have the self-control to keep my mouth shut, but right now when it doesn't matter, I can't. So I ask, "Do you feel better telling people things so you appear smarter than you really are?"

He swings fast to land a blow to my jaw. I hit the ground on my elbows, tasting iron on my tongue. Then I realize I have nothing to lose at this point—there's no reason for me to sit here and take it. I spin up, catching him in the stomach when he's coming for me again. I start for him before he can recover, but Marshall comes up behind me, holding me back.

Jeremiah lets out a laugh and takes off his jacket. "This is going to be more satisfying than I thought," he says. "Marshall, give him his hands."

"Jeremiah—"

"The Sheriff said he wants him dead," he says. "He never said how."

Marshall hesitates behind me, but in the end, he frees me. He posts up against a large rock near the horses with a rifle loose in his hands. A sentry in case I decide to run.

"Have you ever been in a standoff, little wolf?" Jeremiah walks over to his horse and pulls out a holster and gun—my holster and gun. Without it at my hip, I feel bare.

"No, but I've seen it done," I say.

I'm lying and I love it.

"That's better than most, I suppose." He stops a few feet away and takes out my gun, checking the cylinder for ammunition. He snaps it in place and returns it to its holster. Then he holds it out to me, grip first. "There's one bullet," he says, nodding over to Marshall. "If you decide to shoot me before it's time, he's going to take care of you himself. Understand?"

I take the gun while my heart skips beats. "I understand."

This is my chance to live. Even if he might not know it yet.

I buckle the belt around my waist, where it sits unevenly on my hips—a familiar weight I never want to miss again. I check to see if the bullet is in place and return it to its holster. Jeremiah turns to face me fifty feet away, his stance wide.

Then there's nothing but the wind between us, waiting to take one of us away.

Jeremiah smiles and says, "Now let's see if you can actually use that gun of yours."

Instead of watching his hand, I watch his face. Everyone wants to look down at the thing wanting to kill them, but the face is what gives them away first.

Never look at the hands.

His smile fades, and the instant before his hand moves, his eyes twitch, giving him away.

Jeremiah's pistol is barely raised when his body flinches, the barrel of my revolver pointed at his chest. His eyes become unfocused as blood soaks the front of his shirt, features frozen in shock.

Even though Jeremiah is the sixth person I've killed, his death doesn't do anything to lighten my heart. Each life I've ended has taken a piece of me with them.

His body now lies still.

Somewhere above a crow calls out.

I slide my revolver into the holster and turn to face Marshall. He hasn't moved from the rock he leans against, his rifle still cradled in his arms.

"You know," he says, "if Jeremiah had actually listened to what Hatch said when he found your gun, he would've known you knew how to use it."

I think back to when Hatch turned it over in his hands, somehow knowing it was mine even when he found it on Durk's body.

"Are you going to kill me now?" I ask him.

Marshall laughs once and shakes his head. "No, I'm not going to kill you."

I glance back at Jeremiah, confused. "Are you going to take me back then?"

Marshall pushes off the rock, a smile etching his face. "I'm not going to do anything."

He slides the rifle back in its saddle holster and slides the reins over the horse's head.

"After all this, you're letting me go?" It sounds too good to be real. "What about the Sheriff?"

Marshall shrugs. "I guess he'll figure out what happened when we don't come back." He untethers Jeremiah's horse and mounts his own, hanging on to the reins with one hand. "So if I were you, I'd disappear as quick as you can. He isn't a man to forget anything."

"You aren't going back?"

He shakes his head, and I notice the white armband is missing from his bicep.

"I've been thinking about this for a long time, and everything that's happened within the last few days made me realize that I've already made up my mind. I just needed someone to push me."

"Where are you going to go?"

116

Marshall glances around, over my shoulder where the land opens up. Dust blows and the horizon is gray, giving nothing away to what lies behind. When he returns his gaze, he says, "I don't know. Maybe south, to see if the rumors are true."

"Well wherever it is," I tell him, "take care of yourself."

Marshall nods. "You too. And if I ever see you again, make sure you don't need me to fix you up." He kicks his horse and rides past me, Jeremiah's horse trailing after him. Before he gets too far, he turns in his saddle and half yells, "What's your name?"

I step forward and yell, "Seph."

Marshall smiles one last time and puts his fingers to his forehead, like he would tip his hat to me even though I've never seen him wear one.

I watch him ride off, the crow overhead curiously following him. After he's out of view, it hits me that I'm free again—after days behind bars and metal around my wrists. I never want that again. I will never again take my freedom for granted.

The horse Marshall left me flicks its tail and stares. I don't want to ride another horse besides Cade—even if that means walking a few days to find him—so I untie his reins, point him toward Kev, and slap his hindquarters. I don't look at Jeremiah's body as I head south, toward the road where I last saw my only friend.

Clouds roll by and the wind kicks up. It's not long before I come to a river, a little low with the dry week. At the bank, I loosen the laces and slip my feet from my boots. I roll up my jeans to my knees and wade in, taking a moment because I'm not sure how long it's going to last.

Even when I was a child, I loved the water. Any lakes or rivers we would pass by, my father—Dad, I have to remember to call him—always made time for me to wade or swim, depending on the day. Some were freezing cold, but I didn't care. It

117

was all the same to me. Sometimes I would float there and pretend I was lying on the deck of a ship somewhere. Riding the ocean to wherever it wanted to take me . . .

Someone clears their throat behind me and my hand moves for my gun before I remember I don't have any rounds left. Jeremiah only gave me one. My feet are cold in the water and I realize I don't know how long I've been standing here, my mind far enough to not even hear anyone approach.

Taking a deep breath, I turn to see the barrel of my own gun. The lever-action I left with Cade.

And the one holding it is the girl I met on the way here.

Avery. Freckles under narrowed eyes, hair braided back. She's a hard one to forget, even for me.

She recognizes me the same moment but doesn't lower the weapon. When I see her eyes again, I realize who Finn reminded me of. It was her—he's the brother she's looking for.

"You," she states.

I nod toward her. "That's my gun, so if you don't mind, could you lower it?"

She thinks about it and backs away, allowing me to come out of the water with the barrel of the gun pointed at the ground. I don't want to make my boots wet, so I just stand there.

Avery looks at me a long time before deciding to ask, "Did they let you go?"

"Not exactly." I can't stop looking at my rifle, wondering where she found it and if Cade is all right. "The Sheriff planned to have me killed, but as you can see—" I tilt my head and point to it, "—I'm still alive."

"And are you going to tell me why I shouldn't finish the job?"

"I will if you tell me where you got that gun." She glances down, a thousand questions in her mind. I tell her, "Look, I'm not going to hurt you, you have my word. But it seems to me we may be on the same side."

"And how do you figure that?"

"Because while I was in their prison, I met your brother."

Avery steps forward, everything else forgotten. "Don't you dare give me lies to get me to trust you. I told you I was looking for my brother, but that doesn't give you the right to—"

"His name is Finn, right?" She doesn't say anything, her mouth still half open. "I'm pretty sure you didn't tell me that." Then I remember something from the first night in the cell with him. "He has this small wooden horse he carries around in his pocket. Is that good enough for you?"

Everything about her drops and she bites her lip like she's holding something in. "Is he—is he all right?"

The first night I saw him, I wouldn't say he was all right, but I decide not to tell her that bit. "Yeah, he was the last time I saw him."

Avery nods and looks away. "Come on," she says. "We shouldn't stay here. It's not safe."

"And where we're going *is*?"

She starts walking and yells back, "It's better than here."

After I've laced up my boots again, I have to run to catch up with her. We continue up the rise following a narrow path. When we come to the top, where the path goes between two rock faces, I follow her into a hidden campsite.

Movement catches my eye and then I see nothing but Cade trotting toward me—his gait high and his neck arched. Just seeing him makes my heart lighter. He presses his head to my chest and I bury my face into his mane. I know he's not human, but he's the only friend I've ever had. And after everything, it's hard to believe he's here.

With Cade nibbling my shoulder, I turn to see Avery staring.

"Thank you," I say. I don't need to explain why, because we both know horses can't live on their own in the Wild, and most people would've sold him by now.

Avery nods and walks over to my saddle to replace my rifle. She looks down at the saddlebags and back at me. "I didn't take anything," she says, and then explains nodding to the rifle, "I wanted to use something long range for when I went out." I nod and she comes closer, stopping on the other side of Cade, putting her hand on his nose. "It took a long time before he let me come close enough to unsaddle him."

"And because he did, it means he trusts you."

"What's his name?" she asks.

"Cade."

For some reason, she smiles at that. "It suits him. How long have you had him?"

"Since he was small—barely taller than me. It was a brighter day than normal, so bright that people were looking up at the sky when I came into town even though there was nothing to see. There was a sign on a barn saying there was a horse for sale, and when I finally tracked down the man selling him, it's like he couldn't believe someone finally showed up." Without even meaning to, I smile wide, unable not to for such a good memory. "When he went to show me Cade, he bit the man right in the ass. I got him so cheap because nobody wanted him. They called him 'the little devil horse.'"

Avery laughs and Cade nibbles at her hair. "I can't thank you enough," I tell her. "You and your brother are some of the few people to show me kindness."

"You're lucky you found that many. Especially in Kev."

"So where you're from the people are kinder?"

Something changes and her smile fades. "Maybe at one time," she says.

I hesitate before saying, "I think we were all kind once, but it's hard to be when the rest of the world is not."

Cade lifts his head toward the east and Avery follows his gaze and takes off. I follow her up a steep path and crawl to the edge to see Kev laid out before us. Its gates are open, letting out dozens of Lawmen riders. Each squad goes in a different direction on the search for something, or someone. For me.

He warned me and I didn't listen to him.

"Who warned you of what?"

I look over, not realizing I had spoken aloud. I go back to watching the riders down below, everything inside me itching to run away. "The man who let me live. He said the Sheriff would be coming for me the moment he found out I survived. I wasn't fast enough."

I turn away, back down the hill to Cade, and after a little while, Avery follows me. "They won't find you here," she says. "Stay until morning. At least until then you'll be able to leave without being seen."

Everything in me wants to go. To get away from this place as fast as Cade can take us. But she's right. If I go now, there's a high chance of me being seen. I look up at the sky, glad I'm beneath it, and give her nod. "I'll stay."

16.

Avery

We settle into a deep silence, tending to our own horses, and I move the remaining wood to the fire pit. It'll be cold and dark in a few hours. Occasionally, I sneak glances at Seph, but he doesn't seem to ever notice. Always in his own head, it seems. He goes through his things, packing away his saddlebags so he's ready to leave tomorrow. He reloads the revolver at his hip and takes out the baseball cap. He rubs his thumb down the bill before putting it on. His dark hair pokes out from the sides, curling toward his face.

When he finally glances over, I look away. I want to ask him about Finn again but I'm not sure how to start. Evening comes fast and I start a fire, cooking a few potatoes Margaret gave me on the hot rocks next to it. I sit across from where he's settled on a rock. The wind teases his hair across his forehead, his green eyes steady. It makes the moment more real when I realize I don't even know him . . . and even more so because by tomorrow, I'll probably never see him again. So many people come into our lives just to leave again.

Again, I glance at Seph. I can't let my guard down with him, especially with prisoners or boys with colored eyes, but I'm not sure if I'm strong enough to resist. I'm more than curious about him, so maybe if I tell him things, he'll return the favor.

"My brother," I start and he looks up. "Do you have any idea what they plan to do with him?"

"Sorry, no. I was only with him less than a day until they moved me somewhere else."

"But he was well?" I stare hard without even meaning to, hanging on his every word.

Seph nods. "As well as can be. Is that what you're doing out here—waiting to see him?"

"I have a friend who is good at getting information," I explain, "so I'm waiting to hear from her." Then I continue, not knowing why. "The Lawmen took Finn when they had no right, and they would've taken me too if he hadn't stopped them."

Seph doesn't think long before he asks, "Why?"

"Because that's who they are," I tell him, keeping my thoughts off his eyes and everything that comes with them. "Our town makes money by selling coal to Kev as it always has, but somewhere over time, it became a requirement. And this month was the first time we've come up short." I can still see Finn leaning against the wall, waiting for them to come and knowing nothing good would come of it. I've wished that day over so many times. "There's a man who comes every time to collect what we have, making sure it's enough and that we don't give them trouble."

Something changes in Seph's eyes, like he knows who I'm talking about. But he doesn't stop me, so I continue. "So this time, when we didn't have enough coal for them, he decided to take another form of payment."

"He took people," Seph finishes.

I nod. "Finn wasn't one of the few they chose because he was near the back, but when they took one of our friends, he stepped forward to take his place. I guess it's my fault, really. I drew attention to myself, and when the orders came to take me along with them, Finn fought them, giving me enough time to escape."

Seph nods like it all makes sense now.

"What?"

He shakes his head. "It's nothing."

"It's obviously something."

"It's just . . . the first time I saw you, I couldn't figure you out."

"And that's something you can usually do?" I ask. "Figure people out?"

"Almost always," he nods. "But with you, there were things that didn't add up. You were riding a horse that was yours, but neither the saddle nor the rifle was. You weren't from the Wild, but you were there anyway." He puts his hand out, gesturing to me. "Now it makes sense."

I lean forward, curious. "Do you have me figured out now?"

Seph nods. "You left in a hurry, only escaping with your life and your horse." The smallest of smiles shows along his lips. "And then the Wild got to you. Somewhere along the way, you found a saddle and gun, knowing you needed one to survive. The gang chasing you before the Lawmen came was just bad luck." His eyes don't waver from mine. "And you distanced yourself from the soldiers, because even though they had no idea who you were yet, it was only a matter of time. But you decided to travel with us anyway, because everything comes back to what brought you there in the first place."

"And what's that?"

"The Wild." Seph looks past me, into the dark and wherever lies behind. "When it gets to people, they change. Did you sleep the first night?"

I decide not to answer. "I thought you said you had me all figured out."

His eyes dance with amusement. "You did sleep . . . only because you had your horse, but not very well. And from what interactions I've seen, you are as close with him as I am with Cade."

I lean back, actually impressed. How he knows the saddle and gun aren't mine is beyond me. "You got one thing wrong, though," I tell him.

He looks up, surprised. "And what's that?"

"I didn't find the saddle and gun. I stole them."

Seph thinks about it. "Are you sure I didn't say steal?"

"Yes."

"Hmm."

"That's pretty impressive, though."

He nods once in my direction. We eat our potatoes with some salt from Seph's saddlebags and the night becomes black around us. Without the fire, I would see my breath. Unlike me, Seph doesn't wear a coat—only his white shirt, the sleeves pushed up to his forearms. The cold doesn't appear to bother him.

"Now that you know my story, it's only fair you tell me yours."

"Who said anything about being fair?" I can't tell if he's serious or not, but he stares at me so long I have to look away. "Nothing in the Wild is fair, but I do pay my debts." To my surprise, Seph gets up and moves to sit next to me. He smells like horse and smoke—intoxicating because those are the smells I grew up with.

"You don't owe me anything," I tell him.

"That's not true—we both know it."

I look at Cade and Jack, their bodies close to ward off the cold. I'm not sure what I would have done with Cade if Seph never showed up, but I wouldn't have sold him.

"What do you want to know?"

"Why did the Lawmen arrest you?"

His elbows settle on his knees, his face half-turned to me. "I ran into a gang north of here and had a bit of trouble with them. Actually, a lot of trouble—more than I usually do. They were about to kill me when the Lawmen showed up. But when they caught sight of my wrist, instead of letting me go, I guess they decided I was worth taking with them."

"Jeremiah said you killed a man."

"I didn't that day," he says, making me even more curious about him than before. "The gang killed one of their own, and when the Lawmen showed up, they blamed the death on me. Then the Sheriff decided he wanted to kill me because I'm wearing this," he holds up his wrist, showing me the red cloth. "I'm not sure what it meant to my father, but around here, it's obviously not something to wear."

Seph is lucky to be alive. Countless times, I've rode into Kev only to find they killed another person who wears the red. I wonder how far the Sheriff will go to find him.

I pull my eyes off the fire. "So what are you going to do now?"

Seph acts like he doesn't hear me—still staring at the dirt in front of him.

"Seph."

He blinks and looks at me. "Sorry, what?"

"What will you do now?"

"We'll probably keep going like we were."

"To where?"

"Southeast."

"Anything in particular?" He shakes his head and tosses a pebble into the fire. "I heard that settlement is to the south," I tell him, nodding to his wrist. "Maybe you can see if the rumors are true."

Seph offers a half smile and shakes his head. "They've already caused me enough trouble." He ends the conversation by returning to his side of the fire, leaving me a bit cold on my right side. When I look into the fire again, I realize how heavy my eyes are. I make sure the stones are in place between me and the flames and unroll my thin bedroll, using my saddle as a pillow. The coat Margaret gave me is long enough to serve as a blanket.

Seph hasn't moved from his place, and I'm not sure if he's going to.

The horses shift somewhere in the dark and I close my eyes to the sound of a fire and ask myself if I should trust Seph enough to sleep near him.

17.

Seph

I hear them coming at the same time the horses do.

I'm off the ground and my gun is out by the time Avery opens her eyes. Once she does, she's as awake as I am.

"What is it?" she asks, voice rough from sleep.

"Riders." I listen closer. "No, just one."

"It might be Margaret," she says, coming to a stand. "She's the only one who knows I'm here."

I glance over. "You want to bet your life on that?"

It doesn't take long for her to grab the shotgun leaning against her saddle, and for some reason, I do a double take—her dark braid coming over her shoulder with the gun propped up in her steady hands. It's the second time I'm reminded she knows how to handle a gun.

I almost don't want to look away, but I have to, and I shake my head doing it.

We're ready when the rider comes through the gap in the rocks. I raise my revolver, but Avery holds out her hand to me. "It's okay, it's Margaret."

I holster my pistol and come up beside her, where the rider dismounts. The woman is older than us but not enough to have gray in her hair. She wears a wide hat and has a pistol strapped to her thigh—she knows what's out here.

"Avery . . ." She takes a quick glance at me. "I didn't think you'd have company."

"This is Seph. He's—" Avery hesitates, long enough for only me to catch it, "—a friend from Stonewall."

I breathe easier when she doesn't give me away. The smallest of words can reach the wrong ears, and I'm supposed to be a long ways from here by now.

Margaret nods to me. "It's nice to meet another friend of Avery's. I think I've only had the pleasure of meeting Axel." Thankfully she doesn't linger on me, so I don't have to come up with a response. I don't even know who Axel is, let alone know if it's a person and not an animal. Cade comes up behind me as she turns back to Avery, her smiling disappearing. "Avery—"

"It's nothing good, is it?" she asks, barely breathing.

"I'm afraid not. They've decided to move a large number of prisoners to the rock quarries down in Blackthorn. Finn is one of them."

Something deflates in Avery, but she manages to stay standing.

I take a step toward her without knowing why.

"When are they leaving?" Avery asks.

Margaret hesitates. "They already have." Avery backs away and sits on her rock, her skin pale. "But that's why I wanted to come myself. I think there's still a chance you can get him back."

Avery looks up. "What do you mean?"

"The Lawmen aren't going straight to Blackthorn. They have stops to make first, picking up more prisoners from different towns." Margaret kneels and draws in the dirt with her finger, making a circle. "Here's Kev, and these are the stops they have to make." She draws a line going east, then south, then southwest where it ends at Blackthorn. "If you travel directly south of here, you'll come across the set of railroad tracks. It'll take the train five days and you only need four to get there."

Margaret looks up at Avery. "I know I'm not giving you much hope at this point, but if there's a chance you can get him from them, this is where it'll happen. You can intercept them before they make it to Blackthorn."

"Four days," Avery murmurs to herself.

Margaret says, "I'm sorry I can't give you more than information."

"And I can't thank you enough for that," she says, still sounding numb.

"Do you have enough supplies to last?"

Avery nods.

"I need to be getting back, but if you find yourself in need of anything, don't hesitate to come to me, you hear?"

After Avery stands and gives her a quick embrace, whispering something in her ear, Margaret rides away from the campsite. I watch as the dust settles after her, and when I turn back, Avery is saddling Jack. Her face is stone, set in a determined type of way.

Cade watches me, waiting to see if I'll do the same. To be honest, I'm not sure what I'll do. The ocean is closer to the southeast, not south.

"Do you even know what you're going to do?" I ask.

"Right now, I don't need to," she says, tightening the cinch, her voice tightening with it. "I just need to get there in time. I'll figure it out on the way."

I give a low whistle to Cade, and he trots over to where his saddle lies. Either way, I'm leaving—I need to put distance between us and Kev, and it might as well be now.

We pack in silence, each of us gathering our things from around the campfire and holstering our guns. Cade won't stay still; he knows we're about to be off again after being still for so long. He's as eager as I am.

I mount and follow Avery out of camp, neither of us looking or speaking to each other. Never before have I minded the silence. My whole life I've been comfortable with it, even when around people . . . maybe especially around people. But right now, all I want to know is what's on her mind and what she plans to do.

At the bottom of the mountain, where Avery will go south and I'll go southeast, she reins Jack to a stop and waits for me to come up beside her. She scarcely looks at me—just glances at me quick enough for me to get a glimpse of what is going through her head.

Her thoughts are on nothing but her brother.

Staring at the reins, she says, "Wherever you're headed, I hope you don't run into any more trouble along the way."

"The same with you," I tell her, really meaning it.

Avery looks like she wants to say something, but in the end, she only nods and signals Jack forward. I watch them ride away.

Cade throws his head, wanting to follow them, but I turn him southeast. After days of dreaming about this moment, and having it finally here, I don't feel the way I thought I would. Instead, I feel like maybe I shouldn't leave her, which is strange, because since Dad died, I haven't desired company, never felt the pull of another person.

I should be happy to be free again, and I am—picking up where I left off before Durk decided to chase me into the Wild. But right now, it feels like a lifetime ago. A time I'm not sure I can go back to.

Cade stops after a quarter mile and turns his head to look

at me. Sometimes I think he knows me better than I know myself.

To the south, Avery rides steady, a trail of dust following her—her mind made up the way I wish mine was.

I don't know why, but I can't let this one go.

I turn my ball cap around and nudge Cade with my heels. "Let's go get 'em."

He starts off fast, his back hooves digging deep into the ground. When I give him his head, I realize how much I've missed him. I bend low over his neck, spreading my fingers into his mane and coat underneath, urging him to go as fast as he can. The ride only lasts long enough for me to crave more.

We come up beside them and Avery reins to a stop. "What are you doing?"

"Going south," I say, "You?"

She gives me and Cade a long look before nodding. "South."

"Then we'd best be off."

Avery flashes me a weird smile and rides off, leaving me to decide to follow her once again.

I don't think I've ever made an easier decision.

18.

Avery

We ride the entire day without saying a word, side by side and covering more miles than I could hope for. The farther south we go, the drier it gets. Dust spits up behind us and we pass towns long abandoned. We end up wearing our bandanas and goggles, but only slow down when it gets too bad for the horses to run in.

We stop at rivers to water the animals and eat while in our saddles when our stomachs growl. But mostly we just ride. Jack's hooves pound the earth beneath me, and every moment I silently thank him for his strength to take me where I can't go myself.

We pass old roads edged with the hoods of rusty cars—bones of the past, being buried with the wind. Most of the roads have already been covered, and the ones that are left won't be for much longer. Everything is giving in to a new world I'm only now starting to discover.

Leaving everything I've ever known is like waking up. I see the world as it is and not how I thought it was.

On one flat stretch of ground, we slow down with the horses' heads bent away from the dust. It blows sideways across us, stinging our exposed cheeks and arms.

When Seph shouts, I stop and look over at him. But he's looking up, and when I follow his gaze, a giant sign looms over us. The words are faded and cracked, but I can make out the shape of a person on it, holding something I don't recognize.

We steer the horses around the sign, passing more relics of civilization.

Minutes later when the dust clears, we stop in our tracks. Ruins of a city lie below us, stretching for miles and bigger than anything I've ever seen. Only the stone and concrete buildings are left, parts of them still crumbling away with every passing day. They're jagged and rough now, every much a part of this world as the one before.

Big cities like this one can never be erased, just made into something else.

Beside me, Seph pulls down his goggles and bandana in one motion, holding the reins in his free hand. Pieces of dusty hair poke out of the hole of his backwards cap, and his white shirt is no longer so white. Cade won't stay still—arching his neck and stomping the ground—while Seph doesn't move. His eyes are on the city, hard and calculating. I'm struck with how much he belongs out here.

My braid is a dusty mess and my legs and back already ache from the day's ride. In one day, I've come out of my world and into his.

"I've never seen such a big city before," I say, also freeing my nose and mouth, glad to breathe air again without inhaling dust.

Seph doesn't say anything. I don't realize I'm staring at him until he says, "We should go around."

The words don't make sense at first. And when they do—"We can't." My heart finally kicks in and tells him he's wrong. "We're already short on time, and going around the city will take the rest of the day." I shake my head, trying to calm myself. "I won't do it."

I have no idea what I plan to do at the end of these four days, but right now all I need to do is get there, and some city isn't going to stop me.

"It'll be a risk—"

"Then you don't have to follow me," I say. I kick Jack forward and we start down the old road. Cade comes up fast and they cut in front of us, blocking our path.

"You don't understand," Seph says, facing us, his back to the city. "People in there won't let you make it through alive." The way Seph's eyes change when he says this makes me think of Levi's cabin. The food he gave me and how he looked at me. "You have to trust me on this one."

"I don't have a choice. We don't have time."

He studies me for a long moment, then pulls out the lever-action from his saddle holster and cocks a round into the chamber. He turns Cade around to face the city, the butt of the rifle against his hip and the barrel pointed to the sky.

"If we're going to do this, you have to do it my way," he says.

"And what's your way?"

"Fast." He almost smiles. Almost. "We don't want them to know we're here until it's too late. There're a lot of miles from here to the other side, so you have to do exactly what I say or you're going to find yourself lost or surrounded by people you don't want to see. Can you do that?"

"I think so."

Seph nods. "Then follow me."

For the first mile, we ride at a steady gallop. Within the ruins—some of them pressing in close—it feels like we're flying down the roads with only the dust following us. After a little while, I realize Cade is navigating us with Seph watching everything

135

else. The reins are loose in his hand, the gun tight in the other. His goggles and bandana bounce up and down around his throat.

I'm glad to have him here, even if I don't want to admit it. If Mom ever found out I'm riding along with an outlaw from the Wild, she'd grow red in the face and get that *look* in her eyes. But Seph isn't like the few people I've met from the Wild.

As we ride through, I try to find signs of people living here, I don't see any. The buildings are motionless, the roofs bare. When old buildings are occupied, the windows are usually boarded up to ward off the elements, so if there are people here, they don't care about that.

With a glance back, I notice someone quickly ducking out of sight and behind a wall. It's so fast, I might've imagined it.

We turn the next corner, and the road up ahead is blocked by a long metal frame—something I have no name for. Seph pulls Cade to a stop and swings around, not even pausing to think. Jack comes up on his hind legs for a moment and takes off after them, his ears flicking behind us.

The next road leading south is blocked, too, by odd pieces of furniture and broken doors, and we are forced to keep going east, causing an uneasy feeling in my stomach.

After three more roadblocks, I yell out to Seph.

He pulls to a stop, his eyes still looking everywhere at once. "What is it? Did you see something?"

"No, but I don't think these roadblocks are accidental."

He looks both ways down the road, nodding. "I was thinking the same but hoping I was wrong. We should go back, find a way through one of them. We don't want to find out what's at the end of this road."

Somewhere ahead of us, there's a shout. Seph clicks his

tongue to gain Cade's attention and says, "Come on, Cade, find us a way out of here."

I turn Jack to follow them, forcing myself not to look behind. That shout was too close for comfort.

We don't even go a block before we see riders following our trail. They ride toward us quickly and Seph drops the reins, bringing the rifle to his shoulder as Cade comes to a halting stop. He pulls the trigger and one of the riders grabs their shoulder and falls from their horse. I know my own gun is still next to me, and yet my hands shake too much to grab for it.

"Avery, this way!" His voice brings me back.

We turn south, down the road with the broken furniture where it might be low enough for the horses to clear. The riders chase us, but don't take shots, obviously wanting us alive. Jack knows what's coming before I do—he puts distance between us and Seph, giving them enough room to jump. And all I can do is trust him. Cade clears by inches, and I feel Jack gathering himself under me and then we're over before I can take a breath.

I glance over my shoulder but the riders don't follow. I bring up Jack so we're riding next to them. "We need to rest the horses," I tell him. "They can't keep going like this."

"They're gonna have to a little while longer," he yells over the wind. "I don't like it as much as you do, but they'll be tracking us through the city until nightfall. If we're lucky, we'll be out of here by then."

I know he's right, so I keep my mouth shut and put my hand on Jack's neck, more to reassure myself than him.

19.

Seph

We don't clear the ruins before nightfall.

We're forced to find shelter in one of the stone buildings with no roof, and I leave Cade with Avery to go back over our path.

With the wind still blowing hard, our tracks will be covered within the hour. I move slowly from building to building, staying out of sight and keeping one hand on my gun. I'll do anything to keep myself from becoming a prisoner or something worse. After being in Kev for those few days, I'm more protective over my freedom than ever before.

I think that's part of why I decided to come with her.

Some piece of me wants to help Finn because I know exactly what he's going through and it's something nobody should. There's just enough light left to see the scars around my wrists.

Two of many I already have.

The one on my forearm catches my eye—it's only about two inches long but I remember how deep it was. The guy who gave it to me was old enough to have gray hair—something that's rare these days—but he wore this ridiculous hat with a feather sticking out of it.

He tried to gut me with his knife but he missed and sliced me in the arm, a wound that healed in a couple weeks.

But his hat is the thing I remember most. Actually, everything he wore.

A red vest, covered in patches. No shirt and a purple pair of pants.

I remember thinking he had to get new boots because they had holes in them. Boots with holes are no good. . . .

I'm standing in the middle of an intersection but don't remember how I got here. My wandering mind will get me killed one of these days. I turn and make my way back, climbing up the rubble and into the building where we've made camp. The horses stand in the back corner, their heads hanging low as they rest.

"I've already fed them," Avery voices, and I find her sitting against a pillar with her legs crossed at the ankle. She looks different and I realize it's her hair. She must've brushed the dust from it before braiding it up again. Darker in this light just as Finn's was in the prison.

I sit against the wall opposite of her, my mind not ready for sleep.

"It's so dry here," she says, rubbing a hand down her arm. "The next time we come to a river, we should stay long enough to wash the dust away."

"Here it's the dust," I tell her, "but in the north, there's snow. Then somewhere between the snow and dust, there's mud."

"Is the snow white there?" she asks.

I shake my head. "Gray. In some places it's hard to tell where the snow stops and the sky begins."

"The winter here is cold but we don't get much snow. And when we do, the wind blows it away like everything else." Avery looks at me a long time, a question forming that she seems unsure she wants to ask. "Where are you from?"

"I thought you were going to ask something new."

She smiles. "But the answer will be new to me."

I know she won't like the answer, but I say, "Nowhere."

"Everyone is from somewhere."

"Well, I was born in Montana, but my mother died when I was two, so my father didn't want to stay there any longer. And he was right not to. Since then, we never stayed anywhere for long, and even less as I got older and I was on my own. Those three days in Kev were the longest I've stayed in one place in seven years."

Avery pulls her legs up to her chest. "You really weren't kidding then," she says. "There was a man that came through town a few years back, and the moment I saw him I knew he was like you . . . a wanderer or an outlaw, or whatever people call you. But I just saw him as someone who didn't have a home."

"Is that what you think of me, then?"

I know that feeling of going into a new town. Having people look at me like they already know me and I don't belong there. Or belong *anywhere*.

But Avery shakes her head. "This is your home," she tells me. "Anywhere you happen to make camp at night, and anywhere during the day as long as you're with him." She nods over to Cade. "I don't think I really understood it until I was forced to leave mine. A home isn't always a place."

"But yours was," I say. "I know what you're going through, because I went through the same thing while I was in Kev. I was forced to be there and not out here where I really wanted to be. If it's any consolation, I hope you're able to make it back home someday."

"A couple days ago, I would've loved the idea," she agrees. "But now I'm not so sure."

"You don't want to go back?"

Avery shrugs and pushes her palms against the floor. "It's

not that I don't miss it. I miss everything about it, but it feels like I can't go back . . . like even if I did, nothing would be the same. The coal is gone and the town can't survive without it."

I don't know what to say, because I don't know that feeling. It would be like me deciding to stay in the same place for the rest of my life. The total opposite. Something I can't imagine.

"If it makes you feel any different, you're doing a lot better out here than most people."

She laughs once. "It sure doesn't feel like it."

"You're alive, aren't you?"

"Only because of luck."

I shake my head. "Out here, luck doesn't exist."

It's almost too dark to see now, and Avery stretches out on her bedroll, using her jacket to cover herself. I find my saddle-bags in the dark and dig out a blanket I haven't used in a while. I walk over and hand it to her. "Here, I don't need it."

Her eyes meet mine for a split second and then she reaches for it. "Thanks."

I settle against the wall again and listen to the wind and the sounds of the horses. Even with the building around me, the sky is still above to keep me calm. Avery shifts a couple of times before falling silent.

After a while, I check on Cade and unroll my own bed, knowing he'll warn me if someone comes. I fall asleep with one hand on my gun.

I wake to feet shuffling near my head. My eyes snap open and find someone looking down at me. It's not Avery.

The stranger smiles. "Good morning, cowboy."

I scramble to my feet but someone kicks me from behind, sending me into the dirt. I reach for my gun but it's gone. One of the men gets too close and I throw a punch. The other wraps his arms around me from behind, trying to lock my arms in place. I break away from him the same moment something hard comes down on my head.

The ground rushes toward me and I can't break my fall. For a moment, I don't see anything except black, and when my vision clears, everything is spinning. My cheek presses against the ground and someone ties my hands together with a piece of leather. But I still can't move—like my brain is too slow to tell my body to act.

Someone grabs me by the shoulders and hauls me to my knees, sending my brain to pound against my skull.

It takes a minute, but everything stops moving and I can finally see my attackers. There're only two of them. The man standing behind me has dark skin and tattoos running up one arm, and the one searching through my saddlebags is not much older than me but very pale. He's wearing a jumpsuit with a name tag that says CRAIG. He pulls everything out and throws it on the ground, finding nothing valuable. He hasn't figured out I keep my money at the bottom of Cade's feedbag.

It takes me mere seconds to realize Avery isn't here and neither are the horses.

"You took us on a little chase, didn't you?" the man behind me says. I don't look up at him—instead I test the knot in the leather and find it tighter than anything I can break through. They aren't taking any chances. "Everyone's been searching all night, but we were the only ones to come out this far."

He nods to his partner—whose name is probably not Craig—who then smiles back like they've already found something valuable.

"There's nothing here," Not-Craig says, tossing the saddlebags aside. "I guess we can't be lucky twice." He stands and looks down at me. "Where's the girl?"

"How am I supposed to know the answer to that?" I ask. "You're obviously the one who woke me this morning."

The guy next to me sighs. "Just go track her down—she can't be far. We gotta get them back before someone else comes and takes 'em from us."

"Well, why don't you go?" Not-Craig asks. "You're better at it than me."

"Because I'm not the one who got punched."

"Gerard—"

"*Go.*"

Not-Craig glances at me, and I notice the cut near his eye. It gives me slight satisfaction. In the end, he rolls his eyes and disappears out the hole in the wall that serves as the doorway.

"Don't you think about moving," Gerard says, keeping one finger on the trigger of his pistol. I look for mine and see it on the ground not ten feet away.

Not-Craig's footsteps return before I can think of how to get it.

Gerard says, "I thought I told you to—"

He cuts off when he sees that Not-Craig isn't alone. His hands are up and Avery is behind him, aiming her shotgun at his back.

Gerard stares because he's realizing the numbers are no longer in his favor.

But I'm staring because I've never seen this side of Avery. I get this weird feeling in my stomach, one I've never felt before. Her eyes are fierce and her hands are steady on her weapon, ready to do whatever it takes. I can't take my eyes off her.

"Put your gun down," she orders Gerard.

He hesitates and then moves too fast for her to do anything. He's behind me with the gun pressed to my head, probably smiling because he thinks he can get out of this. But if I were him, I would look into Avery's eyes and see he's already lost. Just like this city, there's nothing that can stop her.

"I'm not sure," he says, "but I'm guessing you care about this boy here a little more than I care about Craig."

I guess his name really is Craig. If it were any other moment, I would smile.

Craig's eyes go wide but Avery is unreadable. "I guess you'll find out the hard way," she says.

"About what?"

"About how wrong you are. You think I give a shit about him?" she asks, nodding in my direction. "I met him yesterday and we happen to be going in the same direction. That's it."

"Then why did you come back?" he asks.

I watch her face. She doesn't give herself away. She bluffs like she's done this before.

"I came back so you can look at that." She looks past him, and when he turns his head—believing her bluff—she shoves Craig to the ground and takes a shot. It clips Gerard in the shoulder and he goes down next to me. Avery stands over Craig and says, "Go untie his hands, and if you try anything, I'll be aiming for your legs."

He scrambles over to me, and Avery kicks away their guns. After he frees my hands, I retrieve my revolver and join Avery. Gerard is unconscious but alive, and Craig just sits there, hoping not to get shot like his partner.

"So that's what you think of me, huh?" I ask her. "I'm sorry you feel that way."

She tries not to smile but fails. "Sorry to break the news." Then on a more serious note, "The horses are outside. We should leave before someone starts looking for them."

"And hope nobody heard the gunshot," I add.

I leave Avery to watch the unconscious Gerard and Craig—after I made sure he would wake up with a lump on his head—to go saddle the horses. Cade is restless to be away from here and Jack watches the building, waiting for Avery to return.

I check the saddlebags on the gang's horses, and I'm lucky enough to find more ammunition for my lever-action. I'd been running low for the last few weeks and it's not something easy to come by.

That's another reason I can never miss—I can't afford to lose the bullets.

We ride at a steady pace with our guns out in case we see anyone else. When we stop to water the horses at a creek on the outskirts of the city, I finally ask, "Where were you this morning?"

"I went out to find water for the horses but never found a place," she says. "I didn't want to wake you. Then when I came back, I heard voices."

She sort of half shrugs, glancing over once.

"Well . . . thanks. You were really great." I look away with my face feeling hot on this cool day.

We both shift our weight as the horses drink. No matter what I do, I can't get that image of Avery out of my head—coming through that door with her gun held high.

"I know you think you don't belong out here," I blurt, turning to her again. She looks at me, waiting for me to finish. "But you do. This place isn't for everyone, not even the people who live out here. But there're some people who were born for it."

"And what if I'm not?"

"Then you ride on," I tell her. "Because sometimes you don't have a choice."

She fidgets with the bandana hanging from her neck and looks around, then says, "I haven't told you this, but I'm glad you decided to come with me." Her blue eyes meet mine. "I couldn't have gotten this far without you."

Avery looks like she wants to say something else, but Jack comes back to her and we move away from each other without another word, even though I still feel her eyes on me. We mount up and continue south. She rides ahead of me and I let her, understanding there are moments when one wants to face the Wild alone like she wants to right now.

For once I'm not thinking about pirates or boots.

I'm thinking about her.

20.

Avery

The evening of the third day, after passing countless abandoned towns and putting in hard miles, we finally come to a river. It's the first real water we've discovered since the city we later found out used to be Houston from a sign half buried in the ground. Every riverbed since has been mostly dried up, and I can't remember the last time it rained.

This one is wide enough to still be here and deep enough to swim in. I dismount and pull my bandana down, breathing in the scent of river. It runs as flat as the land here, which makes it easier to see anyone coming from at least a half mile away until little hills dot the horizon.

Seph rides up next to me and jumps off, pulling his own bandana off his face. He isn't looking at me but at the river, and I watch as a smile breaks out and his eyes brighten in their own way.

I've never seen this smile before. It's pure joy and something a bad day couldn't even take away. And today has been a bad day. It started out fine until we came to a couple bridges crisscrossing each other, an obvious spot for a gang to hang out. We had to go around, adding another mile to our trip, and could only hope our dust trail wouldn't be seen. Then we encountered a pack of wolves. They were brave until Seph shot a few rounds in the dirt between us and them. They followed us for a while, making the horses skittish, but finally gave up.

The only thing going for us is how warm the day is. And now this.

Seph catches me staring, and for some reason, I don't look away like I usually do. Maybe because he's still smiling or maybe because I feel I've witnessed something rare. Maybe both.

"Are you all right?" he asks.

I nod, wondering if my face gives me away.

"Then why are we standing here?" Seph loosens Cade's saddle and slides it off, followed by his bridle. Cade takes off toward the water and Seph follows him with a yelling run, leaving his gear on the ground. Just before the water, he skids to a stop, only to pull off his boots.

The water must be freezing but he's already up to his neck, clothes clinging to his body.

I sigh and unsaddle Jack, who seems just as eager to get into the water. After I pull his bridle off, he runs downstream toward Cade. Unlike Seph, I walk to the river. I stand on the bank and watch him float, facing the sky.

"Are you going to come in?" Seph asks, his eyes closed.

I want to. I've been wanting to for days. But now that I'm here, with Seph in the water and the sky watching us, I hesitate.

I settle with, "Maybe."

Seph opens his eyes and stands, the water coming up to his chest. "Just the other day you said you wanted to find a river to wash away all the dust, but now you don't want to? It's not so cold once you get in." When I don't say anything, he adds, "At least get your feet wet."

I take off my boots and set them next to his. Before I walk

into the river, I glance at Jack downstream. He and Cade are playful with the water and warm day, chasing the other away when they aren't looking.

The water is cold so I only let it come up to my ankles.

"You really aren't going to come in?" Seph asks.

"I want to—"

"But?"

I glance around. "I don't know."

The real answer whispers in my head, *Because I've never been swimming with a boy before. And where will I change when my clothes are wet and there's nothing but flatlands around us and suddenly everything feels awkward.*

"Come on," he says, dragging out his o's, taunting me.

Then he swims over to me, walking when it comes up to his waist. The cloth of his shirt clings to his chest and arms, and his hair drips with water. When I catch the look in his eyes, I ask, "What are you doing?"

He smiles in return—the kind of smile I've only seen from Finn when he's about to do something he shouldn't. It's a boy's smile.

"Seph—" I take a step back and then he's running toward me. "Seph, don't!"

I run up the bank, water soaking the hems of my jeans, but he's had a head start. He catches my wrist and swings me around, throwing me over his shoulder in one quick motion. "I'm going to kill you!" I shout, and yet I smile and don't know why. He runs deeper into the water until he can't run anymore and then we're both under.

The cold wants to suck away my breath, but he's right: I let myself sink down to the bottom and it's not so cold anymore. The river threatens to drag me away and I grab onto a rock, deciding to let Seph sweat a little before I let myself up. Not many parents bothered to teach their kids how to swim back in Stonewall because it's not like we ever went swimming for fun. The water is always too cold and the rivers usually too fast or not deep enough. Mom, though, she wanted us to learn, always claiming you never know when you might need to.

I let go of the rock and let myself float to the top.

Seph spins around in the water when I resurface. Relief fills his face and he doesn't try to hide it. It surprises me in a weird way, but still, I allow myself to smile and he narrows his eyes.

"That isn't funny."

"Neither is throwing me into the river."

Seph grins anyway, like he knows it. His wet shirt clings to every inch of him, and knowing mine probably does, too, I don't look down in case my cheeks turn a different color. Too many times I catch myself staring into his eyes and wonder if I'll ever see that color again once we go our own ways. I don't know if there's anyone in Stonewall with the color green, and not many have blue.

"What is it?" he asks. His voice is serious now, probably wondering why I'm staring.

The water feels warmer than before, and I know it's not the temperature changing it.

"I thought you'd be used to people staring at your eyes by now."

Seph thinks about it and shakes his head. "I'm usually not around people long enough for them to notice anything about me."

I smile at that. "Fair enough, but they are amazing."

Something crosses his face, between confusion and questioning—the same look Finn gives when he doesn't want to admit he doesn't know something.

"What?"

Seph's gaze shifts to me and I count to five before he moves closer. Close enough to see drops of water on his eyelashes. I curl my lips in to wet them, barely able to think with him being this close.

Things run through my mind like: What if he's been lying to me this whole time and brought me out here to kill me? Is he going to drown me? Is he going to kiss me? Is he going to kiss me and then drown me? But even as these horrible thoughts pass by, my heart doesn't change pace, because I don't believe them to be true. Even though my heart may have sped up when I thought of him kissing me. Gage and I would sneak into the barn once in a while to get away from the others, and he kissed me once in one of the darker corners. It was an awkward kiss, and the way I'm feeling now can't compare to it.

"Can I tell you a secret?" Seph asks, his voice a whisper.

I nod.

"I don't know the color of my eyes."

It takes me a little while to understand what he means, and when it settles in, I can feel my eyebrows draw together. "You don't?"

He shakes his head then explains with a shrug, "I only have broken glass and rivers for a reflection, and it's not like I'm going to go looking for a mirror. It's not something that ever mattered."

My reaction is slow in coming, and this ache in my heart starts to grow. How could somebody not know the color of their eyes? Seph doesn't know how good-looking he is and probably never sees the girls turn their heads when he passes through town.

And I can't believe that thought just ran through my head.

Do I actually think he's good-looking? Somewhere far, far away in my head, something whispers *yes*.

"Do you want to know?" I ask, more to distract myself than anything.

151

Seph opens his mouth, pauses, then says, "Yes."

I look deeply into them now that he's closer, seeing the darker shade around the edges. "They're green," I tell him. "The best kind of green you can think of."

"Green?"

I nod and smile.

Seph shifts a little closer, looking down at the water until he says, "I guess that means we're two parts of the world we'll never see. The sky and earth."

"Mine aren't as great as yours," I say, shaking my head.

"No, they're probably better." It's like he realizes how close he is and what he just said, and he attempts to cover up with something else. "The first time I saw Finn, I knew I recognized him from somewhere just because of his eyes. But it wasn't him, it was you."

The wind blows through us, brushing against my arms to make me shiver and putting more space between us. Now that the moment—whatever moment it was—is gone, Seph glances around.

"We could stay here tonight, if you want to," he suggests. "There was a patch of dead trees back from where we came, so we could at least dry our clothes."

"What if we haven't come far enough yet?" Because it's been on my mind this whole day. What if we didn't come far enough yet and miss the train? Miss my chance of getting Finn back? I do my best not to think of it, because every time I do, I start to panic.

"It's up to you, but the horses need a good rest."

I can tell he won't argue if I say no, and we would keep riding into the night and make a cold camp and my clothes would still be wet. I'm confident with the miles we've covered, but I'm scared it isn't enough.

"Let's stay," I decide.

Seph gives me one last smile and says, "I'll get the wood and you can change while I'm gone."

I nod.

He wades out of the water and whistles to Cade, who comes running. Seph slides up on his back and grabs a fistful of mane, his legs tight against the horse's sides. I watch them ride off, and I'm grateful he doesn't look back to see my reddening cheeks.

It doesn't take long for them to return. I've already changed and am in the process of rolling rocks into a circle for the fire. They're big, but they'll work better for drying clothes.

I straighten as Seph slides off Cade with a bundle of wood in his arms. His hair is almost dry now, windswept by riding. He drops the wood and starts a fire as I bring our gear over and settle on one of the rocks meant for sitting. Seph is already settled on his, across the campfire. The sky is still light, and yet once the fire is going, the night seems darker than before, tricking me into thinking it wasn't late. It's always hard to tell with this gray sky.

"Too bad we don't have any more of those potatoes," I say.

"Or anything that could be cooked over a fire." Seph glances at his saddlebags and then down at himself. "I should change out of these clothes." But he doesn't make a move to do it and continues to stare into the flames. He fingers the cloth around his wrist—something he does often but probably doesn't realize.

"Avery."

"Yeah?"

His eyes don't move and he takes exactly four breaths and then he says, "What do you plan to do tomorrow?" Seph looks up.

I've known this question was going to come, and until now, I've chosen to ignore it. Because— "I don't know."

153

I can't hold his gaze. I've brought him all this way and it might be for nothing. Everything I fear may happen and Finn will really be gone forever. I have no idea what I'm doing or what I'll do tomorrow. All I want is to have Finn back, and I don't even know if it's possible.

"For what?" Seph asks.

I lift my head. It takes me a few seconds to realize I've said, "I'm sorry," out loud. But it's something he deserves to be told.

"For coming all this way and me still not knowing what to do."

Then he says something that puts my heart at ease, at least for now. "We'll figure something out."

It brings a question to mind, one I can't hold back. "Why did you come with me? I never asked you to—you were planning to go somewhere else, and you don't gain anything from it, so why?"

"Why should my decisions be based on gaining something?"

"Because everybody wants something."

"Something, but not always for gain."

I lean back and exhale.

"What?" he asks.

"You don't have to tell me if you don't want to," I say. "I was just curious."

Seph looks at me a long time. "I decided to come with you because I know I can help. And your brother isn't someone who deserves to be in the position he's in, and nobody knows that better than I do. That's why I came with you."

My head shakes slightly on its own.

"You don't believe me?"

"It's not that," I say.

"Then what is it?"

"I've never met anyone like you before . . . not even close, and I keep doubting you when I shouldn't. My mind tells me I should, because I don't know you, and yet—" I shake my head again. "That's just it . . . and yet."

"It's good not to trust people."

"Are you saying I shouldn't trust you?"

It's his turn to shake his head. "No."

Seph takes a deep breath and puts more wood on the fire, ending our conversation and leaving me with more questions. When we do talk to each other—which isn't often—it never lasts long.

Sometimes there's nothing more to say than the truth.

Then before I'm ready for it, Seph reaches back and pulls his shirt over his head. I've seen Finn without a shirt countless times, but Seph isn't my brother and nothing about this is the same. The belt around his waist isn't tight enough. Fire dances off the veins running up his forearms. I'm trying not to look at his chest but my eyes deceive me.

Seph lays his shirt over the rocks and catches my eye before I turn, hoping my face hasn't given me away. Then I ask myself, why should it? Seph will always be a stranger to me, and he'll be gone once Finn is freed. All we share is a mutual goal. I repeat the same question in my head—*what is wrong with me, what is wrong with me, what is wrong with me?*

Out of the corner of my eye, Seph goes to his saddlebags for dry clothes. When I happen to look up, I catch a glimpse of his back and my heart skips a beat. I've never seen so many scars on someone's back before. They're white and straight, except one that is longer than the others, going from his shoulder to his hips—wider than the others, too.

Seph glances back, holding up a worn pair of jeans.

"Do you mind?" he asks, for some reason smiling.

"What?" Then as dumb as I sound, I say, "Oh, right, sorry."

I turn away, digging the heel of my palm into my forehead.

The night is dark now and I hear the horses near the river, enjoying the night off—then I hear Seph somewhere to my left, pulling on clothes to cover up the scars I won't forget anytime soon.

"Are you hungry?" he asks. I turn back around and he's wearing a dark T-shirt now, his boots untied.

I shake my head. My stomach is coiled tight thinking about tomorrow and there's no way I can eat anything. The horses are already here, like they know he has food. He gives a handful to each then sits down across from me, brushing the crumbs from his palms.

"I'm not hungry either," he finally says. "Not for those bars, anyway."

"We had to eat them all winter once. They're horrible."

"After a while, it's not so bad." He kind of smirks to himself. "You have to get creative with the way you eat them."

I actually laugh, surprising myself. "I don't even want to know."

But Seph turns serious after a moment, fingering the red cloth again. "I was somewhere north of here a few years ago, and I took a chance and went around this settlement because nothing about it said friendly. It was winter and there was nothing but flatlands everywhere. Even though I rationed my food, I still ran out. I went days without finding anything and I could feel myself becoming weaker and weaker.

"Then one day, I boiled some water and put some of Cade's feed into it. It made this horrible-smelling mush, but I had to eat something."

"And you did?"

He looks up and nods. "It was enough to keep me going until I came to a small town where I could buy real food. So now, every time I think those nutrition bars are bad, I remind myself they aren't as bad as having nothing, or being forced to eat something not meant for you."

I don't know what to say—I can't imagine being hungry enough to eat horse feed. Finn and I were lucky enough to live in a town where people looked out for one another—at least enough so nobody starved.

I don't understand how Seph can live out here like he does. Every story he tells me, it's another near-death experience or fighting for his life from people who want him dead for no reason. But then there are times when I see how much he loves it out here, and it makes me realize the Wild is a part of him. A part of who he is.

"You've said you don't have anything to go back to," Seph says. "Are your parents—"

He leaves it hanging and I finish it for him. I tell him, "They're both dead. Dad died when we were really young and then Mom got sick a few years ago. The doctor said he thought it was some type of cancer."

Nodding, he says, "It makes sense now, knowing you're twins."

"Why do you say that?"

"Because people usually don't go this far to save someone. You said Finn was taken with other boys his age?"

I nod.

"How many other families do you think went after those taken?"

I know the answer to that— "None."

It's not a question. People in town never so much as went to Kev for supplies—that's why they paid me to do it for them.

"What you and Finn have is something most people never find."

"Have you?"

Seph gives a sharp laugh and smiles. "No."

"Okay, then how do you know who has it?"

"Because you're here and they're not, and I can see it every time you mention his name. It's pretty obvious. There's a bond between you that is rare."

I swallow and bring the subject back to where it was. "What about you? You said your mom died when you were two, but what about your dad?"

Seph shifts his gaze to the fire, his fingers playing with a pocketknife. "I think I was nine when he died. A man shot him in the head and made me watch."

He says it so easily that it catches me off guard. My breath comes shallow for a few seconds until I right it again, but nothing brings my heart back to normal. It's one of those things that sticks with you after you hear it. Like random moments in the past I'll never forget.

Seph lets out a breath—one between a laugh and surprise. "I've never told anyone that before. I've thought it a thousand times but never said it out loud. Probably because nobody has ever asked."

When he looks at me, I don't know what to say. *I'm sorry you were nine when you saw your father murdered?* I don't have anything to say because there is nothing to say.

We sit for a long time in silence, using up the last of the wood and falling asleep next to the hot embers.

I dream about things I can't remember.

21.

Seph

I wake before Avery.

The horizon is becoming light with every minute and I pull on my cold boots. I slide onto Cade's back and I don't need to tell him anything. We ride east toward the sun we've never seen. He starts out with a steady gallop, but soon it turns into something more.

I let him go as long as he wants, running hard with his ears always forward. He turns when he's gone far enough. When we ride back into camp, Avery is packing up her things. I jump off Cade and she glances at me once without saying a word.

I'm not going to be the one to break the silence.

I roll up my dry clothes from near the cold fire but decide to change back into the shirt Marshall gave me. It's the best piece of clothing I've owned in a long time. I change quickly and when I turn back around, I catch her eye. Right then, I remember the scars on my back, and wonder if she saw them last night, too.

They healed too fast for me to remember them, unlike the many others my body holds.

"Where did you get those?" Avery finally voices.

"Kev."

Her eyebrows crease together. "But that was only a few days ago."

"You know that Lawman soldier you met before we reached the city? He's made something that heals wounds faster—so I was lucky, otherwise I probably wouldn't be here."

"That's amazing," she says, rolling up her bedroll. "How did it happen?"

I pause then, not wanting to relive that moment. "There was a man there that wanted to make a show of me . . . it's not really important."

"It's important if they punish you for things you never did," she argues, standing. She has her bedroll curled around her arm but doesn't make a move to strap it to her saddle.

Sometimes she can be stubborn when she wants to know things—that much I've learned. I suddenly feel angry. It's my choice if I want to tell her things, not hers. And this is something I want to keep to myself.

"It doesn't matter because it's already happened." My voice comes out stronger than I expect and I recoil. I turn away but don't go anywhere. I stand there and take a breath, forcing my finger not to tap against my leg and trying not to think about being tethered to that post. I don't want it.

"Seph—"

"I don't want to talk about it."

"Why?"

"Because it already happened," I say again, turning around. "What's the point of reliving something that can't be changed?"

Something serious passes over her eyes, and she says, "So you don't have to carry the burden alone."

I want to make my legs work but they won't. My entire life I've been alone, so I've thought nothing of it. And now Avery is here, offering something I've never thought possible, and still maybe don't. Will telling her really make a difference?

No.

No, it won't. How could it?

In the end, I shake my head and turn away. I saddle Cade, and I feel her eyes on me until I hear her call Jack over.

We mount in silence and continue south.

She rides a little ahead of me and never turns around.

Sometimes I think I was never meant to be around people. I never get along with them and rarely enjoy the company. They talk too much and demand answers I would rather not give.

It's not an hour later when we come to the railroad tracks.

Avery slides off her saddle and approaches them. We look east and west, both wondering if we're too late. I dismount, pull my bandana down, and stand behind her.

When she turns around, she smiles. "We've been this close since yesterday and didn't even know it."

"And now that we're here, we'd best get ready," I say. "It could come at any time."

She nods, looking east.

"Avery."

"Yeah?" She turns again.

I open my mouth. And then say, "I'm sorry."

Avery shakes her head. "There's nothing to be sorry for."

"Yes, there is. You said you've never met someone like me, but I've never met someone like *you*. You've been kind to me and I haven't repaid the favor well. I'm just—I'm not very good at this." I gesture between us, trying to make my point. "I'm used to talking to Cade but he can't talk back. So I'm sorry if I've been difficult."

She offers a small smile. "I'm lucky to have you. And I'm sorry, too. I shouldn't push you. Finn always has to remind me not to be pushy."

"Maybe I should be pushed more often."

We wait behind an outcropping of rocks near the tracks where we can't be seen when the train comes. If it ever does—we're still not sure if we missed it. Avery sits next to me, asking questions about my plan, which will most likely work. At least, I hope it will because it's all we've got.

"I don't know how many soldiers will be on the train," I admit, "but they'll be in a different train car. If anything, there will be a couple of guards. Nothing we can't handle."

She nods, saying nothing. The wind blows through the silence between us, and I wait. I wait for her to say something or maybe admit my plan won't work. Even though I've never done something like this—never had a reason to—I believe it'll work. Believing is all I've got right now.

"If you don't want to come, I can do—"

She cuts me off, "—No, I'm coming. I have to."

"Then what is it?"

Avery fingers the end of her braid, staring at some point on the brown horizon. "I'm just . . . I'm worried this will all be for nothing, and tomorrow I'll wake up and nothing will have changed. Finn may not even be on the train . . . or we might have already missed it." Her eyes flicker to me quickly but long enough to see tears.

After finding out how strong she is, it's like I've forgotten she's human.

I lean closer and thumb a tear away from her eye. Her skin is warm and I take my hand away before I do something I'll regret. I have trouble breathing, realizing how close I am to her. "Hey." I nudge her shoulder and she looks at me again. "Everything is going to be all right. I promise."

Time passes slowly and every touch of the wind is felt. For once in my life, I don't mind sitting still.

From my periphery, Cade flicks an ear to the east and I

turn my head slightly. Avery hears it, too, visibly filled with relief that we made it on time.

"Are you ready?" I ask.

"As I'll ever be."

We mount up and wait for the train to get closer. The engine grows louder and louder. The horses dance in place. I'm gripping the reins too hard and have to remind myself to relax.

The train rushes past, filling my ears with its noise. I count five cars, not including the engine train. I look at Avery and nod, and when the last train car passes by, I tap my heels into Cade's side, telling him its time.

The horses bolt from their places.

I imagine this is what the pirates feel like when they attack other ships. They come out of hiding and sneak up without being seen. In the dead of night or during a storm. Pirate ships have smaller crews, but their advantage is the element of surprise.

Or at least I hope that's how it works.

We overtake the train and the horses match its pace at a steady gallop. The train is loud and Cade doesn't want to get too close, but I need him to. There's a ladder running up the side of the last car and I inch him closer. For me, he does it. I grab hold of one of the bars with both hands and pull myself up, the rushing wind and the rattle of the train threatening to throw me off. It doesn't feel right going this fast without Cade beneath me. I ignore the unease and climb until I reach the top, crouching low on the roof. The wind feels like it'll push me off if I try to stand.

Avery has a little trouble with Jack so she has to jump a bit farther, almost losing her grip on the ladder. I go to help her but she calls me off, shaking her head.

When she reaches the top, the wind blows the loose strands of hair away from her face, braid flying behind her. Determination is set in her eyes, making her strong enough to do what she has to. She joins me on top and nods for me to go on.

Behind us, the horses back off but keep pace to never let us out of sight. I don't know about Jack, but Cade will run himself into the ground as long as I'm here. I start forward, staying low to keep my balance. On the top of each train car, we find a trapdoor with an outside latch.

We pause over the first one. Hoping the soldiers are at the front of the train, I flip the latch and swing the door open. Inside are a dozen horses, heads turning to look at me. No people. I close the latch and yell to Avery that it's only horses. I'm not sure if she can hear me but she nods. I don't tell her how many horses, because that would mean it's the two of us against a dozen Lawmen.

We continue on and come to the space between train cars. Earlier, I told her we would have to jump. It's safer than reaching for the ladder between the cars and risking falling beneath the train and also saves us a lot of time. I glance back and she nods, remembering.

I stand taller and take a running start.

Then I jump.

For a long moment, I'm suspended in the air, wondering if the wind will blow me away. The train car roof comes up fast and I almost lose my footing on the land, just able to catch myself in time. I turn back and wave her forward. Avery makes a better jump than I do and she knows it. She smiles at me and I return it and then yell, "You got lucky!"

The next train is full of supplies and we make the jump again. This time my jump is better since I know what to expect. I pause before opening the next roof hatch, hoping Finn's in here. Avery crouches across from me, waiting. The last thing I want to do is disappoint her—even when none of this is in my control.

I open the hatch.

Faces look up, some shielding their eyes from the sudden light. I scan quickly, not seeing anyone wearing white armbands.

I look back at Avery. "It's not that far. I'll jump first in case there are guards."

She nods, trying to hide every emotion on her face—anticipation, nervousness, and hope all at the same time. I swing my legs over, grab hold of the frame, and lower myself in. I let go and the drop isn't far, like I told her. The moment my feet hit the ground, my gun is in my hand and I take a moment for my eyes to adjust to the darkness. Compared to the howl up top, it's silent inside.

The hatch above me lets in a modest amount of light, but the corners are still dark. And yet nobody comes for me and I still don't spot any guards. The prisoners line the train wall, each separately chained to it.

My heart does a weird lurch because this is something I didn't plan for. I don't have a key or anything to break the cuffs if we do find him. I mouth a curse to myself.

Avery jumps down next to me and I steady her with a hand, the other still holding onto the pistol. Just because there aren't Lawmen doesn't mean it's safe. Unlike Finn, a lot of these men probably do belong here.

"No guards?" she asks.

I shake my head. Avery starts in the far corner, trying to look into their faces. Some of the men ask who she is and a few ask for her to free them. She ignores them, seeking one face, and with each passing one, I can see the hope in her eyes dwindle. Everything rides on this.

I turn and start in the opposite corner, trying to look for eyes similar to those I've looked into every day for the past week. Some of the men are sleeping and others don't have enough energy to care why I'm here.

Then I catch sight of someone familiar.

He's leaning against the wall, eyes closed. With an eye on the others next to him, I reach out and shake his arm. His eyes flicker open, focusing on me. "Seph?" He sits up straighter, looking like I'm the last person he expected to see. Then I remember—he probably thought I was dead. "What are you doing here? I thought—I thought you were killed."

I can't help but smile—and more than anything it's for Avery, because we really found him. For days, I've seen the worry on her face and fear that she would never see him again.

I tell him, "I'm here to get you out."

"But why?"

I back up a step and call, "Avery!"

She lifts her head immediately, her face asking an unspoken question.

I nod in return.

Finn stands when she gets closer, like he's seen two ghosts in one day.

"Ave." Something happens in my throat when Avery throws her arms around her brother. It gets tight and I swallow it away. I don't see a lot of affection, and now it's here right in front of me, slapping me in the face. Before now, I've never minded being alone. But now there's Avery.

"You're really here," Finn murmurs into her hair. With his hands bound, he can't hug her back and I know it's killing him.

"I could say the same," she says.

Finn pulls back, remembering something. "You can't be here. The guard comes every hour to check on us and he's due any minute."

"You sure it's soon?" I ask, probably too eager by the look on his face. This will be exactly what we need to free him.

Finn nods. "Fairly sure. I fell asleep after the last time he came."

166

"Why?" Avery asks me.

"Because we'll need the key to get him out of here. If we don't, I'll have to backtrack to the supply car and find something to break the cuffs. But if the guard comes, that's our fastest way out."

Right on cue, we hear the slamming of a door from the train car ahead of ours. I push Avery closer to Finn.

"Stay here." I run to an empty space near the middle and crouch down like the others, only hoping they don't give me away. Some are still asleep and I don't see how that's possible.

Then I catch the eye of the last person I want to see here. Rami smiles—his weird, crazy smile—his eyes dancing with amusement. I don't have time to say anything to him because the door opens, letting in light. I holster my gun; I don't want the other soldiers hearing the shot.

The guard shuts the door behind him, and strolls through the car with a rifle in his hands. When he gets closer to where I'm sitting, he catches sight of the open hatch, and his eyes go slightly wide.

"Who's in here?" he shouts, angling his gun a little higher.

When he turns his back, I rise from my crouch and take a step closer, my boots not making a sound against the straw-covered floor.

Right then, Rami says, "Behind you."

The soldier spins and I grab the barrel of his rifle before he can get a good grip on it. I tear it from his hands but he's already on top of me, tackling me to the ground with his arms around my waist.

The fall throws the air from my lungs. For a moment, I can't breathe. I knee him in the gut and he throws a punch to my jaw. Somehow I'm able to elbow him in the nose, giving myself enough time to go for his gun. But when I spin around, the soldier has pulled out a pistol—one he had hidden on him.

Blood runs down from his nose and I'm frozen in place. Just when I'm sure he's going to pull the trigger, a leg shoots out and kicks him behind the knee. He falls to his knees, giving me enough time to lunge forward and smash the butt of the rifle into his head.

He goes down and doesn't move.

I check his pulse to make sure he's still alive.

Avery steps out from her hiding place. I give her a nod and search the soldier for the keys. He has them. I toss them to Avery and she runs back to Finn, knowing we're short on time.

"You could've killed him over and over again," Rami says to me, staring at the man. "But you didn't."

"And you could have let him kill me, but you didn't," I counter. He might've tipped the guard off about me but at least he redeemed himself.

He has nothing to say to that and I leave him, stepping over the body. Avery meets me under the hatch, Finn rubbing his wrists behind her.

"Do you have the keys?" I ask, holding out my hand.

Avery doesn't ask why or protest—she just hands them over and I return to Rami, grabbing his cuffs to unlock them.

"You can either come with us or go your own way," I tell him. "But if you do anything to harm me or my friends, I will kill you."

His eyes don't change but he nods. The other prisoners start to protest, and I do everything I can to ignore them. For all I know, they're murderers, and the moment I free them, they'll jump me. I'm already taking a risk with Rami, but some part of me can't leave him here.

I grab the soldier's pistol and return to Avery, handing the gun to Finn. He takes it and shoves it into the back of his trousers.

Suddenly our group has doubled in size.

"Let's get out of here," I tell her.

She nods and I cup my hands to give her a leg up. She disappears up the hatch and I do the same with Finn.

"You ready?" I ask Rami.

He grins. "See you up there, cowboy."

I give him a lift and then he reaches down to give me his hand. I take it, still listening to the other prisoners yelling after me. I forgot how loud the train is until I pull myself out of the hole. I crouch low on the roof to steady myself against the wind. Before I shut the hatch, I drop the keys inside, giving the others a chance to escape if they decide to take it.

My eyes first go to Cade, still keeping pace behind the train, but I can tell he's wearing down from the sweat shining on his neck. I flick a finger toward the back of the train, signaling to the others, and Finn goes first, followed by Rami and then Avery. I bring up the rear, looking back to make sure nobody has noticed anything wrong.

Everything goes smoothly until the last jump.

As Avery leaps across the last gap, I'm right behind her when a shot rings out, the bullet hitting the roof right next to her boot.

She loses her balance and I don't try to stop, seeing what's about to happen. I land on the balls of my feet and dive as far as I can. Avery falls back, trying to grab onto anything to stop herself but there's nothing. The moment her hand is about to disappear over the edge, I catch her wrist. My body keeps sliding forward from the momentum, and we're both about to go over.

Someone grabs my legs just in time, stopping me with my chest on the edge.

Avery stares up at me with wide eyes, the ground rushing by under her.

I glance back to see Rami holding my legs and Finn,

crouching low with his gun up, waiting for the shooter to appear again.

"We have to get inside!" I yell, my head half turned.

Finn hears me—taking one last look to see if someone is going to show themselves—and comes over to take Avery's other hand. We pull her up together. Rami goes to the hatch and swings it open. Not a second later, they start shooting at us. I yell for the others to get through the hatch, and the moment I follow them through, I glance over my shoulder to see Torreck jumping the trains with his gun out.

I land beside Avery, and the horses are spooked with our sudden appearance—dancing in place with their ears flat against their heads.

"They're coming for us," I say.

Just as the words leave my mouth, the train lurches as they slow down. It's only a matter of time.

I throw open the train's door—I can feel them watching me, waiting for me to tell them what to do. With as much courage as I can muster, I turn around and meet their stares. Then I tell them what they want to hear.

"Rami, grab two of the nearest horses as quick as you can," I say. "And Finn, keep that gun handy because you might need it again."

Avery steps forward. "What are you planning?"

"The train is going slow enough for them to ride out of here."

"Wait—what?" It's Finn this time. He's got a face that wants to argue but I won't let him.

Rami comes up behind me with the horses, and I take the reins of the nearest one and give them to Finn, stepping close. "This is the only way we're getting out of here. I didn't come all this way to fail. Get on the damn horse, Finn."

Rami mounts up, keeping low so they can get clear of the door, but still, Finn hesitates.

"We'll be right behind you." I tell him. "But once you get out, you can't stop. Head south and we'll catch up with you. They'll be shooting once you're clear of the train."

Finn looks to Avery and she says, "We'll meet you south."

He finally nods and mounts.

Someone lands above us and I don't pause. I slap the horses' hindquarters. They don't have time to put up a fight, or maybe they're too frightened to. The horses jump from the train and land without a problem. Then they're gone, and again it's only Avery and me.

I run to the train's door and whistle for Cade and Jack, the wind whipping hair into my eyes.

When I turn back around, Torreck jumps down behind Avery. I pull her forward and swing her behind me, bringing up my gun before he has time to pull his own.

Torreck smiles and raises his hands. "You got me."

"Take your gun out with your left hand, and do it slowly or I'll put a bullet through it."

He laughs and it itches every bone in my body. "I have to admit, you're the last person I expected to see here."

"Shut up and do it."

He does and tosses the gun between us.

"Avery," I say.

She gets it and doesn't show her back to him. I take the gun from her and toss it out the door—I know the feeling of not having something familiar in your hands, and I don't want to use anything of his.

Torreck does a double take on Avery once she's at my side again. "Well I'll be," he says. "The townie girl, back to find her brother. You two make an odd pair, that's for certain."

I glance over my shoulder—Cade and Jack are here, waiting for us and keeping pace with the slowing train. We have to go before more Lawmen come.

"Avery, let's go," I tell her.

"I know who you are now," Torreck says, tapping his temple with two fingers. "It was the eyes that finally made me realize it. Don't get many with that color."

"Seph—" Avery touches my arm, urging me to go. But I can't. Something in his voice makes me stay, my legs locked in place just a little longer. The wind from the open door behind me tries to tug me away, warning me I shouldn't listen to whatever he says. My curiosity always wins, though.

"Maybe this will help you remember," he says. Then he takes off his hat, revealing a bald head with a jagged scar. My heart knows before my mind does—beating furiously inside me, and I try to make sense of it because I truly never thought I would see him again.

I don't hear the words, just feel the shape of them on my tongue, "You killed my father."

Avery's hand tightens on my arm, like she's trying to hold me back from something or maybe urging me on, I'm not sure. But there's nothing for me to do. I made a choice a long time ago—I would never seek out my father's killer. Revenge is not a thing on my heart. Not a thing to chase after. But now when my gun is pointed at his heart, a little voice whispers to pull the trigger.

I shake my head, telling it I won't give in.

"Avery, *go*." She hesitates at first, keeping her hand on my arm, and then finally goes, her footsteps ending in air.

I back away toward the door, my finger wanting to pull the trigger but my heart telling it not to. It takes everything in me not to do it.

"This isn't the last you'll see of me," he warns, a small smile still taunting me.

"You better hope it is."

I holster my gun and take a running jump onto Cade,

leaving Torreck to watch us ride away. The horses slow until the train passes us and then bolt across the tracks for the south.

I glance back to see only the dust following us.

22.

Avery

We ride until we're sure they're not following us. The horses are tiring and yet they keep moving forward, knowing the importance of our escape.

But no matter what I do, I can't stop thinking about Torreck and the fact we let him live. The recognition in his face when he saw me brought back the fear I used to feel when he rode into town every month. It hasn't changed. There's a reason that man is still alive, and every day I had wished someone would put an end to him. Seph had the chance and didn't take it. Why? Especially after he realized Torreck was the man who killed his father. He had the shot and he just left him there. Now he'll hunt us down until we're the ones at the end of his gun.

At the sight of a river, we slow down. I let Jack drink as I eye the river, wondering how deep it is. It's wide but appears to be shallow enough to cross without getting too wet.

My heart still races from the train, and I can't keep my mouth shut any longer. I turn to Seph and ask, "Why did you let him live?"

I don't bother hiding my anger. That man has ruined each of our lives in a blink of an eye, and when Seph had the moment to finish him, he did nothing.

Not only does Seph not say anything, but he looks away. Frustration builds and I kick Jack forward, across the river. Water splashes against my boots and I hear Seph and Cade starting after us.

"Avery—"

I turn Jack around sharply, stopping them in their tracks. "What, Seph?"

Seeing his eyes, I almost let it go but can't.

"I just . . ."

"You just what? You found out he was the one who killed your father and you did nothing." Then something else makes sense. "He's the one who gave you the scars on your back," I say. "Isn't he?"

Seph doesn't deny it, proving me right. He just sits there, trying to tell me something without actually speaking.

I turn Jack back around and continue across the river. Seph hesitates but follows, and I almost don't want him to. I do but I don't at the same time. I curse life for being so confusing. Or maybe it's confusing with boys.

On the opposite shore there's a hill that we'll have to climb. I dismount on the stony bank and am leading Jack by the reins when Seph stops me with a hand around my wrist. It makes my heart lurch because I never heard him coming.

I slowly face him, knowing my anger will go away as soon as I see his face. It's like trying to be angry with Finn—it never lasts.

Seph bites the corner of his lip and then says, "I was nine when I saw him for the first time. He pressed a gun to my head to threaten my dad to tell the truth. But he shot him anyway. For no reason at all."

"Seph, I—"

He shakes his head, stopping me. "He only let me live because he thought he was doing me a favor. He wanted to make me into someone I'm not. That's why I didn't kill him, Avery." He lets my wrist go and I wish he hadn't. "It's because I don't want to become like him. I don't want to be the person he thought he was making me into."

Now that I think about it, I've never seen him kill anyone. Not the guard on the train, not even the gang following us out of Houston—he shot the rider in the shoulder that brought him off his horse. I just thought he missed.

"You are nothing like him," I say, trying not to get lost in his eyes, which is almost impossible when he's this close. "And you never will be, because of this." I press my hand over his heart, feeling it beating against my palm. "Because you didn't give into revenge."

"Not yet anyway. You don't know how close I was." I pull my hand away and he catches it in his, holding tight. His hand is calloused and strong, warmer than mine. "If you weren't there, I might've."

I shake my head. "Not even then."

We stare at each other. The sky rumbles above us and for the first time in weeks, it rains. Drops of water splash into the dust, sending more up into the air until it comes down harder, keeping the dust anchored to the earth. We're soaked in seconds, neither of us making a move to find shelter.

Seph stands there with a wet bandana around his neck, his gun still belted crookedly around his hips, his shirt more gray than white in the rain. But everything tells me he doesn't care.

Because I don't either.

My heart urges me forward so hard it hurts. But I can't move.

I make a weak attempt to distract us from the moment, not knowing what else to do. "He's going to come after us."

Seph shakes his head and steps toward me. "I don't care."

Then he's kissing me. One hand is skimming across my

176

ear while the other pulls me in. His lips are wet and taste like rain and are softer than I imagined. My whole body shivers, hot and cold at once, yearning to have him closer like it can never be enough. Somehow my hand is on his chest, feeling everything through his shirt—the curves of his muscles and his beating heart. His lips tell me he wants this as much as I do. That we've already waited too long and have to make up for lost time.

How I haven't known this before now is beyond me.

Seph slowly pulls away and I open my eyes. Rain drips from his hair and I can see every shade of green staring back.

He gives me the smallest smile. And kisses me again. This time, soft—

We break away when Finn calls my name. I turn to see him appear on top of the hill. I glance back at Seph. He's already put a few feet of distance between us like it never happened, gone too soon. My heart still pounds because of it, and I worry Finn will know the moment he looks close enough.

I grab Jack's reins and start up the hill, doing everything I can to calm down. Finn barely lets me crest the hill before he engulfs me. Everything about him is familiar and it almost feels like we're back home again.

I pull away and say, "Hey."

Finn shakes his head and really looks at me. "I still can't believe you're here. How—" His mouth is open but no words come out.

"It's a long story."

"And one you'll have to tell me." He looks over my shoulder, where Seph stands silent. "Thank you."

Seph doesn't say anything and I don't turn to see his response. My heart still pounds from what happened, still remembering his lips on mine. I feel my cheeks heat before I can stop it.

"I don't know about ya'll," the guy Seph freed says, and I look over to see him next to the horses we stole from the train, "but I would rather not be here when the Lawmen come tracking us."

I haven't really gotten a good look at him until now, too busy trying not fall off a train and then get killed, but I'm not sure how I feel about him being here. He's got those lazy eyes men get from spending too much time in the Wild, dark tanned skin, and messy black hair. Probably a few years older than us. But if Seph trusts him enough to have him here, I'll try to do the same.

"Won't the rain help with that?" I ask.

He gives me a smile, showing me his canines. "Not in the slightest."

"I don't know how much farther the horses can go," I say, turning to Seph. Cade and Jack have already had a long day and their coats were shining before it rained.

"He's right, though," Seph says. "They're gonna have to carry us a bit farther before we make camp. And this rain won't stay for long, so the bigger head start we have, the better."

Finn says something I haven't thought of before now. "But where are we going?"

Nobody has an answer to that until Seph says, "What about south?"

"What's south?" Finn asks.

He shrugs, yet I know him well enough now to bet that he's hiding something. I don't mind going south because it's not going backwards. I knew I was leaving home for good when I started this journey.

"You don't wanna go south," the stranger with us says, making us all turn.

Then I ask, "Who are you?"

His face doesn't change—stuck in that half smirk and staring eyes. "Rami."

178

"Why not south, Rami?"

Rami looks at each of us and says again, in the same tone of voice, "You don't wanna go south."

The rains stops then, and we all look up. Seph couldn't have been more right. He rubs his face in his hands and asks Rami, "Just tell us why we shouldn't go south."

"The people down there . . . they don't just kill you." Levi flashes in my thoughts. Then Rami nods to Seph. "Why don't you go toward your people?"

"My people?"

He nods down to Seph's wrist, who then fingers the cloth tied around it. "They're to the west," Rami says. "That's probably the best place to go right now if the Lawmen decide to follow us. Plus," he says, shrugging, "I've never been west."

"And how do we know you're not lying and taking us into danger?"

"You don't, but why would I wanna meet those kinds of people?" He's not smiling anymore, and even though I don't know him at all, he almost looks worried.

Finn looks to me and then I look to Seph. He stands next to Cade and says, "West it is then."

23.

Seph

I've been alone most of my life. Just Cade and me. Riding wherever we want and trusting no one. Now as I ride behind three people I didn't know a week ago, I wonder how I got to be here.

Instead of going south, I'm following Avery west.

We're so close to the ocean to the south, I can almost taste it. And yet I'm still going west.

It's probably a day's ride from here. But I'm not turning that way.

I don't know why.

We ride silent and steady, Rami in the front and Finn and Avery next to each other in the middle. I bring up the rear. Avery has barely looked at me since we left the river. I know we're thinking about the same thing, yet neither of us acknowledge it.

But how can I talk to her when we're never alone?

I keep a close eye on Rami. I won't let him lead us astray, even though I believed him when he told us we shouldn't go south. I've seen fear in someone's eyes too many times to miss it.

Right before nightfall, we find an abandoned house with a cold fireplace and an actual bed in the corner. The mattress is dirty but it beats sleeping on the ground. Rami finds some almost rotting wood—something I'm seeing less and less of every day as years pass. In the north, wood is easier to find. The dead trees would stick up out of the ground where the fires never touched.

When the skies clouded over, the trees started to die and nobody could contain the forest fires once they started. They kept going until there was nothing left to burn. Down here in Texas, you're lucky if you find any trees, like the ones next to the river we swam in. I'm even surprised this house is still standing and hasn't been torn down to burn. It looks like an old farmhouse—miles and miles away from anything. The porch is still strong enough to hold weight, even when the dusty ground comes right up to the top step.

I stand in the doorway and watch Avery laugh at something Finn says. The three of them talk so easily—used to being around people. They make a fire and Finn finds actual food in the saddlebags of the Lawmen horses.

With just the two of us, it was simple. It was quiet and I knew what to do. It wasn't that different from before—like clockwork, day in and day out.

I'm realizing I really don't know how to be around people. Maybe I never did.

I step outside where I feel my heartbeat slow. I don't like the low roof and the body heat of other people, their voices that never stop. Where there's no corner that is silent.

I run my hands through my hair and take a deep breath. Cade stands with the other horses, his head hanging lower than usual. He still perks up when I come over, nudging me in the hand. The Lawmen horses are a dark gray and white, not as strong as Cade, but they'll hold their own like Jack does.

"What do you think about having all these people around?" I ask him. "It's weird, that's for sure."

He shakes his mane and it makes me smile.

"I know," I tell him. "I know."

I fold my arms over his back and stare out into the night, watching the last of the light leave the clouds on the horizon. I've never thought about the coming days before—it never mattered to me when I knew they would all be the same. But now it's all I can think about.

Where we'll end up, and if I'll decide to stay with them. About the people to the west with red cloths around their wrists. About Torreck. About the people to the south, who we don't want to see. For once, I don't know what the future holds for me.

"Seph?" I spin around and Avery is standing behind me. "Hey."

She glances back at the house before stepping closer, and she runs a hand down Cade's neck. "Look," Avery starts, "I need you to know something, and whatever you choose, I'll respect it."

I answer her with silence, waiting.

"You don't have to stay with us," she says. "We did what we set out to do, and now that Finn is—"

"—Avery."

"What?"

I shake my head, knowing I've made my decision even when everything about this is foreign. "I'm not going anywhere. Not yet."

She looks unsure and then she asks, hesitant, "Is it because we kissed?"

"It started long before then," I say, barely breathing.

Avery steps closer, one hand on Cade like she needs to steady herself. "I don't want to make you into someone you're not."

She waits for me to speak and I move my hand over hers.

"For years, I've only talked to strangers and people who I knew I wasn't going to see the next day. I have a quick mouth to get myself out of trouble and a quick hand to survive. But this," I glance at the house, "this is something I've never done. But it's also something I'm beginning to learn. Sometimes change is a good thing."

"But what about your own plans?" she asks. "What about going south?"

"The south will always be there. Besides," I say, changing my voice to match Rami's slow drawl, "We don't wanna go south."

Avery gives me a smile and I wish I had more of a sense of humor, just to see it more.

There's movement in the doorway of the farmhouse. It's Finn, looking for Avery in the darkness. "Ave?"

Avery steps away from me, leaving my hand cold on Cade. "Over here," she says.

Finn finally sees us, and the glance at me isn't a friendly one. Something inside me wants to make a remark about it—I just saved him from a fate that would take him away from her forever and he's giving me dirty looks? I know him and Avery are close, but still.

He says to Avery, "You should eat something before it gets cold."

"I'll be right there."

He hesitates, looking between us, but finally goes back inside. The wind blows a bit stronger and Avery pushes her hair behind her ear and backs away, still looking at me. "Come on," she says, not giving me any hint that she noticed her brother's odd behavior. "We have actual food tonight."

With a deep breath, I follow her. Avery settles down on a stool next to Finn, and Rami lounges on the bed sideways with his back against the wall. I stand next to the door.

Finn glances over his shoulder and comes over to give me a bowl of something unfamiliar. He steps away without a word, only smiling when he sits back down next to his sister.

This isn't the Finn I'm familiar with—one that smiled even though his face was bloodied and one who had my back when nobody else did. I don't know what has changed between us, but it has.

I look at the food in my bowl, not sure what it is. It's white and small but smells good. I take a spoonful and I can't describe the flavor. My mouth waters and I close my eyes, savoring it.

Finn's voice carries across the room. "So how did you come to be here? You've put off not telling me long enough."

"Where do you want me to start?" Avery asks.

"From the beginning," he says. "When the Lawmen chased you out of town, I thought for sure they would catch you. It's been killing me not knowing where you've been all this time."

I lean against the door and eat my food. I listen as Avery retells her story, hearing it again but in a new way now that it's Finn she's telling it to. When she comes to the part about me, Finn doesn't even glance over his shoulder when Avery meets my gaze. She tells him about our trouble in Houston and the long days of riding.

But what she doesn't tell him is about our night at the river, or any other time we stopped. Because she doesn't want Finn to know there's anything more going on between us.

Maybe she doesn't want me here. Earlier she started by saying I didn't have to stay with them—she never asked me to. My heart pounds at the thought of being unwanted.

Avery finishes her story and even though they're still talking with each other, I can't listen. Half of my heart is here and the other is out there—where I think I belong.

"Can I talk to you for a minute?" Finn asks Avery, glancing back at me. "Outside."

Avery nods.

They pass by me to go outside and Rami pushes himself off the bed. I put my bowl on the table but don't move any farther from the door.

"I guess I should thank you for getting me out of there," he says, putting another log on the fire.

"Why are you still here?" I ask. "Don't you have someplace to go back to?"

He tilts his head—not quite a shake. "Not anymore. Plus, when life sets you on a path, you should take it."

"And that's what you're doing?"

"That's what I'm doing," he agrees. "Never liked the Lawmen, so I might as well find a common enemy."

"And who is that, exactly?"

Rami glances at my wrist. "I don't know, you tell me."

"I've only heard a few things—I'm not even sure if they're real."

"People call them Reds," says Rami, "but I don't know if that's their real name or if they even have one. I don't know anything more than they hate the Lawmen. Maybe they're just another gang trying to gain followers." He ends with a shrug.

Rami turns back to the fire and I decide to check on Cade before we turn in for the night. In my haste to escape Rami, I forget Finn and Avery are outside, and I hear the tail end of what appears to be an argument. But instead of making myself visible, I press against the house and listen.

"Then why is he still with us?" Finn asks. "We've never needed anyone before now, and we'll be better off without both of them."

"Seph knows the Wild more than anyone. We need—"

"—we *don't* need him," he says. "You know we can't trust anyone, especially outlaws like him."

Avery pauses. "Without Seph, I wouldn't be alive, and *you* wouldn't be free right now." Finn has nothing to say to that, and she continues, "Just give him a chance, okay? At least until we know where we're going."

There's a long moment when I'm not sure he's going to say anything, then his voice comes even quieter than before. "I'm sorry, you're right. It's just . . . everything has changed and nothing feels safe anymore."

"Nothing *is* safe, but as long as we're together, we'll get through it. Okay?"

I hear them returning and I slip back inside, taking my place next to the door. Rami doesn't comment on my quick return, and the twins come back a minute later. Finn and Avery take the bed, and Rami rolls out a bedroll in front of the fire.

When nobody is looking, I slip out the door, knowing where I'll sleep tonight. I take Cade a little ways from the house and we make our own camp—one I'm familiar with.

"Seph?"

I turn to see Avery for a second time tonight. She holds out the blanket I gave her a few days ago. "The Lawmen had a few in their saddlebags," she explains.

I step forward to take it from her. "Avery . . . if you don't want me here, just say so. I can be gone by morning and you'll never see me again."

"What—why are you even asking me? Of course I want you here," she says.

"Does Finn?"

She stops then. Hesitates. "He's not used to being around people he doesn't know. It's been the two of us for years and this is something he has to get used to. He's just worried." Avery steps closer, close enough for us to touch but we don't. "I want you here, Seph. If you decide to ride out tonight while

186

we're sleeping, that's up to you. But you might find me behind you when the sun comes up. That, I can promise you."

At the thought of it being just the two of us again, I feel the side of my mouth come up. "Don't tempt me," I say.

"You'll get used to Finn, I promise. Rami . . . we'll figure him out together."

"*Tolerate* is the word I would use for Finn."

Avery smiles and backs away. "I'll see you in the morning?"

I nod. "Yeah."

Once she's inside, I settle down on my bedroll and pull the blanket over me. I look up at the sky, and seconds before I close my eyes, I swear I see something past the clouds. The bright things in the night sky that I've only heard stories about.

But when I wake in the morning, the sky is still gray and I convince myself it was a dream.

24.

Avery

In the morning, Seph isn't outside. Cade is gone, along with his saddlebags. I'm coming to conclusions and I have to push them away before I do something rash.

Finn is still asleep and I find Rami feeding the horses. He's got one of the Lawmen's pistols buckled around his hips and a gray bandana around his neck. He glances sideways at me.

"Have you seen Seph?" I ask. I keep my voice calm, not wanting to appear concerned, but inside, I'm worried he's left—after everything we've been through, he decided to leave anyway. A quick thought runs through my mind—he has every right to. We've known each other for a week, so why am I freaking out about it?

I know why but I don't want to admit it.

"Yeah, I've seen him," Rami says.

"So where is he?"

He glances again, one side of his mouth turned up. "He's wherever his horse decided to take him."

Seph has gone riding in the morning before, so maybe I'm overthinking it. I take a minute to breathe and convince myself I'm being stupid. Because I am.

To distract myself, I go back inside and pack our things. It doesn't take long since we don't have a lot. Finn sits up in bed, his eyes not completely open. He's never been a morning person and sometimes he can't even think right until after noon. He always had me bring coffee from Kev and I'm wondering how he's faring without it.

I finish packing my saddlebags and stuff my bandana in my back pocket.

"Ave?"

I stop and look up at him.

"I'm sorry about last night," he says. "I just wish we could go home."

I sit next to him on the bed and lean against the wall. "I felt the same way, too," I tell him.

"Felt?"

"I realized we don't need to go home. I know you feel the same. We talked about it the day before Torreck came. We were going to leave anyway."

Finn nods and leans his head against the wall. "I know. It's just . . . it's not what I expected it to be out here. Mom always drilled into our heads to never trust anyone and to never travel into the Wild. And now we're doing both."

"But at least we're doing it together, right?" I try to smile but he isn't taking it.

"I never thought it would be so soon. Leaving sounded fine when we were talking about it, but now that we're actually out here, I—" He struggles to find the words.

"Don't know what to do?"

Finn looks over at me, and for the hundredth time I get this warm feeling in my heart because he's finally here again. Those nights without him, Finn was in my dreams but always too far for me to reach. But those dreams did not become reality.

We have Seph to thank for that, yet I won't bring up his

name again. Even though Finn met him before, he still doesn't trust him—or know him like I do. Without Seph, though, we won't last long out here.

"I hate not knowing where we'll end up," he admits, "or not having control over anything. Out here, it's like nothing from our old life applies anymore." He smiles and says, "And from what you went through, I think you know what I mean. I still can't believe some of it."

"Me either." And he barely knows the half of it. I never told him about Levi.

He pulls something from his pocket and sets the small wooden horse in the palm of my hand. I brush my thumb over it, savoring how familiar it is.

Finn says, "On the days when I knew we were going to be searched, I had to hide it away in my boot."

"After I left, I kept thinking this was the only thing I would go back home for. I'm glad you had it."

Outside, the wind brings the sound of galloping and I slip off the bed. I step out and see Seph riding from the east. Even from this far, I know it's him. The way he rides and holds the reins in one hand. Sometimes I think he and Cade are of the same mind when they ride—so flawless and nothing like I've seen.

Seph slows down when he gets closer. His bandana is down around his neck, so when he smiles I can return it. He dismounts and starts toward me—but stops, his smile slipping as he glances over my shoulder where I feel Finn behind me.

"Are you guys ready to go?" he asks us.

Finn answers, "Whenever you are."

But Seph looks at me when he says, "Then let's go."

About an hour into the ride, I drop back and leave Rami and Finn to lead the way across the flatlands. We've been passing abandoned houses and stone structures all morning but each one is set far apart from each other—places that used to be called farms, where they grew food above the ground instead of under it and used the sun instead of solar lamps.

I try to replace the brown with green and the gray with blue with my imagination, but nothing changes.

I keep pace alongside Seph, and it's so familiar. Even the horses know each other well enough to have the same stride. We're at a good and steady speed, trying to keep the Lawmen behind us if they happen to be following our trail. A few times I catch Seph's eye, then we both look away, probably trying to find words because neither of us knows what to say.

Most of the day passes before we spot a small town on the horizon. Seph suggests we stop for supplies, not knowing when we'll have another chance and I know he's right. Finn argues but Rami agrees—he knows because he's also like Seph. They know the Wild better than we do and I know from experience to listen to them.

"There's always a risk, but it's either that or starve to death," Seph says, looking to the south where the town sits.

Finn is staring at me, and I do everything I can not to look at Seph again since it's impossible to hide anything from him. And I don't trust my face not to give away my thoughts.

"If we're doing this, we'd better go now," Rami says. "There's a storm coming and we won't want to stay here tonight."

Finn hesitates, probably remembering the lessons Mom taught us. I give him a nod, telling him to agree.

"All right fine," he says. "Let's do this."

Wind blows from the north and the clouds are darker. It's the type of wind that might bring a dust storm along with it.

Seph says, "Keep your guns handy. Other than that, just follow my lead."

He kicks Cade ahead and we follow him. The closer we get

to the town, the more I see of it—how run down it is and how half the buildings aren't in use. It's nothing like Stonewall, where we've kept it in good condition and each building has life left in it. These buildings here are from the old days, crumbling away and being picked apart to burn for their fires. Missing parts of buildings are patched up with odd pieces of material and most of the windows are broken.

We walk the horses down the main road. Seph leads us and I try to follow his example—keeping eyes straight ahead and not making eye contact with anyone staring. Because they are. People stand in their doorways and in windows, watching us pass by. I do everything I can to appear like I know what I'm doing. If I'm convincing, I'm not sure.

Seph pulls to stop in front of a building with blacked-out windows. There's a hitching post out front and he dismounts but doesn't loop Cade's reins around it. He digs through the feed bag and pulls out a wad of cash.

Finn dismounts, too, but Rami and I stay put.

"If you see anything," he says, looking straight at me, "don't hesitate to yell for us."

Seph glances at Rami then he and Finn disappear inside. Jack shifts under me and I look both ways down the road, my heart racing. A few people mill around, their eyes glancing at us more often than not, doing nothing to calm my nerves. How does Seph do this all the time?

A rider appears at the end of town but they head south, away from us. It's quiet here. The wind blows a little harder and I look at Rami. He appears as comfortable here as Seph does—like they've done this a million times. I don't know how they do it because a knot is tight in my stomach and my heart can't find a constant beat.

My hands are too tight around the reins, and if I let go, they will shake.

"You're acting like a stray dog waiting for its long-lost master to appear," Rami drawls.

I glare at him. "Then I would have sharp teeth to bite you with."

Rami grins. "I would like that."

After a few slow minutes, Seph and Finn come out with the supplies they've bought. Finn has a feed bag for the horses and Seph has food for us—more ration bars and other things he's managed to get. The rice we had last night was something we won't have again for a long time, and my tongue waters at the memory.

"They say there's a well outside of town where we can fill our canteens," Seph says, closing up his saddlebags. "Let's get it done quick so we can leave."

We find the well as promised, and Rami dismounts to draw the water while the rest of us watch the buildings. A few people are still staring. We hand our canteens down to him one at a time, and I take a drink before stashing it away.

Once Rami has his leg swung over the saddle, we don't waste a second in riding out. The main road leads south, so when we're clear of the buildings, we turn west. The farther we ride from the town, the more my grip loosens on the reins.

Seph falls back next to me and the horses slow to a walk. He's got his ball cap on backwards again and his hair blows across his forehead.

"Are you okay?"

I nod, more to assure myself. "Yeah." I almost don't ask, but I can't help it, "How do you do that?"

"Do what?"

"Go into a strange town so calm, not knowing anything about the people there or what they'll do when they see you. I don't know how you can do it over and over again."

"Trust me, it only comes with practice," Seph says. "I've been doing this my whole life, and it's still not easy."

"You were so confident, though."

"No," he says, looking over, "I *appeared* confident. I know what I'm doing every time I enter a new town, but I never show exactly what I'm feeling. People will take advantage of you if you wear your emotions."

"Rami seems pretty familiar with it, too. I tried, but—"

"—You were great."

I snort. "I could barely breathe."

"But you didn't show it." He nods his head to the side, trying not to smile. "At least most of it."

The corner of my mouth goes up, but I jerk my chin forward, changing the subject. "What do you know about Rami, anyway?"

"Not much. I met him a couple days before Kev, and then again when I was in their prison. He was in a gang before, so I'm sure the Lawmen caught him doing something he shouldn't."

"He was in a gang before?" My voice doesn't hide my doubt about him being here. I don't know why I'm surprised at the fact. A lot of people join gangs when they have nowhere else to go.

"*Was.*" Seph glances again. "I don't know why I let him come with us, but everyone deserves a chance, right?"

"Yeah, I guess. It's just . . . sometimes I look at him and I have no idea what he's thinking. It's unnerving."

I look over to see Seph giving me a look. Like it should be obvious.

"It's the Wild that you see," he says, giving a chance to let the words sink in. "It gets to some people faster than others. Sometimes depending how long they've been out here or what their purpose is. Rami—he's . . . he is who he is. When you see enough things you shouldn't—you can't come back from that.

I can't remember how many times I've come across people who have killed themselves because they couldn't find what they were looking for or they were alone for too long." He shrugs one shoulder. "The Wild is for the people who can stand it the longest. For others, their minds go before their bodies do."

I slow Jack to a stop, not realizing it. Cade stops alongside us. "And what about you?"

His thoughts drift away with his eyes—something I've seen him do a million times but never really thought about.

I can't stop looking at Seph—the pieces finally coming together. Half the time his mind is somewhere else entirely. The way Cade only let me near him when I started talking to him—the same way Seph does because he's used to only having a horse for company. The way he's obsessed with his boots like they're worth more than anything.

The Wild has started getting to him, too, even if he might not realize it. Or maybe he does and he's already embraced it. And I'm only finding out now because besides the small things, he's completely normal. He doesn't have Rami's eyes or the harshness other outlaws have.

I've never met anyone like him. And the weird thing is—it changes nothing about how I feel toward him. With Gage, it was easy. I knew him my whole life and everything was predictable. With Seph, it's different every day and I love who he's become, even if the Wild has become a part of him.

I can't stop thinking about the kiss we had near the river. I want to do it again. My cheeks feel heated but Seph doesn't notice because his mind isn't here.

"Seph."

He blinks and looks at me. "What?"

I shake my head. "Never mind."

Finn and Rami are riding back for us. "What is it?" Finn asks, pulling to a stop.

195

"Sorry," I say, my mind not coming up with an excuse. "It's nothing."

Rami nods behind him. "We'd better keep moving."

On the horizon, the storm draws closer. The wind picks up and dust swirls around the horses' legs. We tie our bandanas around our mouths and pull our goggles over our eyes. Hopefully the rain will come soon or I'll need to take another swim in the river.

We keep riding west and the wind gets stronger. We bend our heads against the dust and the clouds make the sky dark, slowly overcoming us.

Right when the timing couldn't be worse, Jack's gait changes, favoring his left front leg. I fall behind the boys and they ride over the next rise, a wall of dust between me and them. Even if I were to call out, they wouldn't hear me. Jack comes to a stop and I get down to check his hoof, pulling my bandana and goggles down so I can see. It doesn't take long to find the freshly hidden stone, and then I run my hands up his leg, making sure he hasn't strained anything.

A strong gust of wind blows and Jack dances to the side, more skittish of the wind than I've ever seen. He pulls against the reins and his ears twitch. It's almost like—

I turn around seconds too late.

A hand covers my mouth and my arm is twisted behind my back. I fight with everything in me, trying to get free. I'm able to hook my leg behind their knee and we both go down. I hit hard and roll away from my attacker, trying to get my legs beneath me so I can run.

Something hard hits the back of my head and I go down again. My face presses into the dirt and everything spins so fast I don't know which way is up. I'm afraid to close my eyes and give in to the darkness beckoning me.

Someone flips me onto my back, and instead of seeing the

gray sky, four people stare down, their faces hidden behind black cloth.

The edge of my vision goes dark and I shut out the world.

I'm giving in and hate every second of it.

25.

Seph

Avery isn't behind me.

I happened to glance back when she fell behind, and now we've come over a rise and she isn't anywhere. I stop Cade and spin him around, riding back from where we came. The wind is only getting stronger and the dust is making it harder to see.

I stop when I see movement on the rise. First I see Jack, then a second later I realize Avery isn't in the saddle. Nobody is. The horse trots to us, wanting something familiar, but my eyes search everywhere. Seeing nothing but the windblown dirt.

Finn and Rami ride up behind me.

"What's going—" Then Finn sees Jack, riderless. "Where's Avery?" his voice demands and he pulls down his bandana. "Seph, where's Avery?"

I yank my goggles and bandana down, not able to breathe. "I don't know," I snap back.

I kick Cade forward and follow Jack's tracks down the slight hill, where there are more than just his tracks. A lot more. I jump off Cade and kneel, trying to grasp how many there were.

I feel Finn behind me, watching.

My eyes search for clues. I stand and walk over to where there was a struggle, about a half dozen different shoe prints. I need to know what direction they went in, but the wind is making it harder by the second.

Rain starts to fall from the sky. In a matter of minutes, any evidence here will be gone.

"*Shit.*"

I follow the tracks faster until they head south in a straight line. I look up but see nothing on the horizon. The rain makes it hard to see, but I know they're already long gone. I turn and face Finn. Rami stands behind him with the horses.

Finn breathes heavily, looking to me for answers. He was mad a moment ago, but now that the truth has set in and Avery isn't here, he's crumbling. Not knowing what to do.

"We're going to get her back," I say. Finn nods, trying to hold himself together. "Whoever took her went south, but with the rain, we won't have any tracks to follow."

Rami looks up from the ground, his eyes a little less crazy than usual. "Are you sure you wanna do this?" he asks. "You don't know these people like I do."

Then for less than an instant, I see a flash of fear. He hides it quick because he knows how, but now I know a piece of his past he never would have told me. Maybe the very thing that made him the way he is.

I leave Finn standing where he is and approach Rami.

He avoids my eyes.

"Then you know them better than I do," I tell him. "Help me get her back, Rami. Please."

His jaw clenches and unclenches, and after what seems forever, he looks up. "I'll help you find them, but I can't promise much else."

"Then tell me what to do."

Rami swallows and eyes the tracks, which are disappearing

with every drop. "We need to go back to that town," he says. "There's no way in hell it's coincidence they live this close to them. I've seen them do it before—they feed a town and the town tells them when travelers come through. Both benefit from the agreement and the townspeople get to live. We have go back to that shop owner."

"And then what?" Finn asks.

Rami flashes a grin. "Then we make him tell us where they are."

The rain stops before we reach the town. The horses are covered in mud up to their stomachs and our clothes are drenched. It's Cade's instinct to slow down before entering a town, but I nudge his sides to keep going.

Unlike last time, people don't stand outside. I see their faces in the windows, hiding from the storm and maybe us. It's a town ruled by fear. We don't stop until we reach the store. I jump off Cade and Finn stays with the horses this time, leaving Rami and me to do the dirty work.

I unholster my gun and kick the door open.

The shop owner drops a screwdriver at the sight of us, his eyes wide and his mouth not smiling like before. His straggly hair sticks up and he's still wearing an old bow tie. I should have known from how happy he was to see us that something was wrong.

Townies are never happy to see outlaws.

"Wha—what do you want?" he asks, backing away toward the counter.

Rami breezes past me and stops the man with a knife to his side. He gets close to his face and says, "You know what it feels like to drown in your own blood, little man?"

"Rami—"

He looks back, gives me a smile, and moves behind the

man so he has nowhere to go. The man might be nervous, but I'm nervous for him, too. I still remember what it's like to be on the wrong side of Rami.

I stare at the older man, wanting him to fear me as much as he should. We didn't come this far just to be separated again. He knows where Avery is and we need to get to her fast.

"A friend of ours was taken a little while ago," I tell him. "And we need you to tell us where we can find her."

He fakes confusion too late. Maybe he could have fooled someone else. Not me.

"I don't know what you're talking about." The man shakes his head.

"No . . . I think you do." I step forward and stare until he doesn't have a choice but to look at me. "You don't have to die today," I say. "Just tell me where they are. Or my friend will have no problem showing you what he promised."

Another flash of fear crosses his face. His jaw trembles when he opens it, and he manages to say, "You don't want to find them. It's better to leave your friend and escape with your lives while you still have them."

"What I want to do and don't want to do is my business. All you have to do is tell me where to find them."

Rami shifts behind him, maybe hinting with his knife where I can't see. "Southwest of here," he says. "Not far."

I meet Rami's eyes and nod my head toward the door. He hesitates, wanting to kill the shop owner. That's the only life he's known, and I can't help think back to the first day we met. Those people he killed, whose bodies he left under the bridge. I can see him struggling with the change of habit.

"Rami—" His eyes flicker between me and the shopkeeper, fighting with himself. "He isn't the one you want to kill."

After a little while, he lets out a breath and walks past me out the door. I give the shop owner one last look and follow him. Finn is still on his horse, not saying a word and his face void of emotion. Jack stands behind us with an empty saddle and my heart aches to see it.

"It's going to be dark soon," Rami says. He glances at Finn and gives me a pointed look. One that finishes his thought by saying, *We have to go before it's too late.*

I give him a nod.

Finn stares at the ground with his jaw tight.

"Finn." He looks up. "We're going to get her back," I say, trying my best to reassure him.

"And if it wasn't for you, we wouldn't have to."

"What's that supposed to mean?"

"You know what it means. You were riding with her, and it's your fault you didn't notice when she fell behind." His fists tighten around the reins. "You should've been there."

I want to pull him off that horse and show him a side of me he hasn't seen yet. To make my fists bloody and make him take back his words. But I don't. Instead, my finger taps against my leg and I take a breath before I respond.

"Let me know if you feel the same once the day is over."

I pull myself onto Cade and we take off down the road. It's his choice if he wants to follow.

Rami comes up beside us and we take the horses into a new gear. Cade wants to go faster, but the Lawmen horses won't be able to keep up if I let him. I glance back only once to see Finn, making sure he's with us.

After a few miles, we come across a dirt road heading south. It's well used and Rami nods to confirm my thoughts. We follow it and the wind picks up again, drying our damp clothes.

At the point between dusk and night, we slow and stare at the lights flickering on the horizon. A few large shapes of buildings darken the sky against the clouds.

This has to be it.

There's an old silo nearby and I lead us over to it and dismount.

"So what's the plan?" Rami asks.

Inside, I'm relieved—I wasn't sure if Rami would help me. Either way, I'm going, but now the odds are better with him.

"Me and you are going in on foot and doing whatever we have to to get Avery. Finn?" He reluctantly looks at me. "You're going to stay here with the horses, and when you hear the first shot, wait a few minutes, and then haul ass to get us."

"I'm not coming with you?" he dismounts, coming over. "I can shoot."

"I know you can," I say. "But have you ever killed anyone?" Finn hesitates. "Exactly. You won't do Avery any good by dying. If we don't come out alive, at least she'll have you."

He seems to believe me and nods, not having the energy to argue. I need him out of the way. He won't do any good if he can't shoot anyone.

I buckle an ammo belt around my waist and untie the lever-action holster from the saddle to lie across my back in case I need it. Rami has his pistol and knife strapped to his belt. He motions me to the side before we head out, leaving Finn with the horses.

"I still remember how we met," he says, "and I know how you feel about killing. But these people aren't like the others. I need you to know I have every intention of killing all of them."

I manage to smile. "I think today is a good day for rule breaking."

"Does this mean I get to see you kill someone?" He smiles.

I look at the darkening horizon and know Avery is there somewhere, possibly hurt and about to be worse. I remember every single person I've ever killed. All six of them. And I wish there was some way around this.

But I should know I can't live in this world without turning into the person I never wanted to be. It's not giving me a choice.

"Let's go get 'em," I say.

We take off at a jog.

The night swallows us and the only beacon is the fire up ahead. Leading us to a place we don't want to go.

26.

Avery

I wake when my body is dropped on the ground. My eyes don't want to open all the way and my head throbs. Everything is dark except for the bright light of a fire nearby, blinding me when I look at it. There's a pair of horse hooves near my head, and I can only hope they don't step on me.

A hand grabs the back of my shirt and drags me away. My boots make lines in the dirt but I can't make my legs work, let alone my arms. I can barely think straight. The person drags me into the dark and then through a wide doorway of a barn.

The squeak of a metal door hurts my ears and they throw me inside a room with bars and lock the door. I try to push myself up, but my arms are too weak and something keeps my wrists together.

I take a second to breathe, in and out until the pounding in my head lessens, then I push myself into a sitting position with my eyes closed to keep the world from turning, my wrists locked together with a pair of metal cuffs. After a couple minutes, I crack my eyes open. The dizziness is gone now but nothing else has changed.

Other people are in here with me—huddled in the corner like maybe they'll be forgotten if they're hard to see. Five total, not including myself. The barn doors are left open, and there's a large fire burning close enough for me to smell the smoke. Close enough for them to keep an eye on us. There're only a few of them out there, keeping warm by the flames.

The sky is dark. The last thing I remember is the dust storm and Jack being spooked by something. An hour or two must have passed from then until now. I tuck my hands into my legs to keep them from shaking, but the cold seeps deeper with every minute.

Another hour or so passes and I haven't moved. Through the barn door, I can see the men around the fire, drinking but not yet drunk. They laugh and make gestures with their hands, telling stories I don't want to hear. I'm staring into nothing, trying not to think much to keep the nerves down, when I hear a voice I never thought I'd hear again. My head snaps up and so do the others, recognizing him as I do.

The two men around the fire stand, the smiles now gone from their faces.

"Donald wants another one," a man says, somewhere out of view. He joins those by the fire with another man next to him—shorter and older by the way he holds himself. The one whose voice I recognized.

"Does he have a preference this time?" But he says it like a joke.

"Just go and get one."

The two men start toward the barn, but the man—someone who must be in charge—calls out again. "And bring the one you brought in tonight. I want to get a look at her."

Even though I want to, I can't move. My heart pounds unevenly against my chest, begging me to move.

I want to wake up and have this all be a dream. Seph and I would still be riding side by side and he would finally tell me what he's looking for. Getting to know Seph might be the only good thing coming out of all this, but I would do it all over again and not change a thing, even what's about to happen now.

The two outlaws come inside the barn and open the cell door. They go for a man in the corner, who tries to plead with them, begging them to let him go. Even in the dark and without being able to see him, I know he's crying.

The last time I saw a grown man cry was almost a year ago when Mr. Santana's son died in the mine. It was December and it was cold, snow settling in our hair. He stood there for hours while the other miners tried to get to him. And when they did, it was too late.

One of them grabs my arm and hauls me to my feet, shoving the thoughts of home a long ways from here. I don't fight him because I can't. I'm staring fear in the eye and can barely make my legs work properly. We walk out of the barn. I can see my breath.

The man is dragged away toward one of the nearby buildings—a one-level with a large sliding door. It's only cracked open, enough to fit a person through, letting light into the night. The man starts to fight the closer they get. I force myself to look away, trying to ignore his pleas even when there's nothing else to fill the air.

The outlaw clings to my arm and we face the man I hoped to never see again. He doesn't recognize me at first, but when something clicks, he pushes past the younger man to get a better look.

"Well if it isn't the girlie who broke my window and stole my rifle," Levi says. He steps closer and I can smell his breath— worse than my horse's breath has ever been. "To be fully honest, I never thought I would see you again."

The man behind him says, "This is the girl you were telling me about?"

"Sure is," he says. "I sent Reynolds and his crew after her, but they never came back."

My braid hangs over my shoulder and Levi touches the end of it. I try to swallow, but it's hard. I want to vomit, or cry, or maybe both at once.

I don't know how my legs are keeping me upright.

"Guess your luck ran out, didn't it?" he asks.

I take a shallow breath and say, "The night isn't over yet."

He laughs once, and then again, finally backing away. "You'll want to get rid of this one fast, Johnson," Levi says to the man next to him. "She's nothing but trouble."

"I don't know," Johnson says, staring at me. "Maybe I'll keep her around for morale."

Levi laughs again, but it's cut off when a gunshot echoes somewhere nearby. We listen for another one, and it comes exactly ten seconds later. People shout and more shots disrupt the night.

Another goes off behind the barn, in the opposite direction, and Levi grabs my arm, pushing the younger outlaw out of the way. "Go see what's going on."

"But—"

"*Go.*"

He runs off in the direction of the first shots, and the moment he's gone, three more follow. There's more shouting not far off, and Johnson pulls out his own pistol the closer they get. The only light comes from the fire and the building where the other prisoner disappeared into, masking the rest of the world around us in black. My eyes search but see nothing. My breathing is less than shallow.

Then everything goes silent. No shouting and no gunshots. Just the night pressing in around us. There's a click of a gun behind me and I look down to see one in Levi's hand. The old man can barely see but I'll bet my life he can shoot.

Johnson takes one step forward toward the dark, unsure, and then commits. He's three steps from the edge of the light when a shot goes off, close enough to make me jump. Johnson falls, his body already limp when he hits the ground, his head making a sickening thump.

Someone steps from the shadows with a pistol in their hand, which is hanging at their side. His head is bent, looking down at Johnson, and then Seph looks up at me and it's like I don't know him. His eyes are hard and there's blood splattered across his shirt and neck.

Seph's gun hangs loose and I feel Levi's pressed against my head—the metal barrel cold as the death it'll carry. But Seph doesn't seem to care, like he doesn't even see it. He walks toward us without a thought, no hesitation.

Levi shifts behind me and says, "Don't come any closer or I'll—"

Seph lifts his gun, not stopping, and pulls the trigger. Levi falls away and I don't realize I'm shaking until Seph stops before me, so calm and together. I've held everything in this long and I can't do it anymore. Seph holsters his gun and takes a pair of keys from Levi's belt to unlock my wrists. He throws the cuffs into the fire and reaches for me but stops halfway.

I feel tears in my eyes and nothing else. A minute ago, I was as close to death as I've ever been. I can't. I think. I don't know . . . I—

I can't breathe.

I can't breathe.

Seph steps closer and wraps his arms around me, pulling me into him.

"Just breathe," he says.

I press my face into his shoulder and let his warmth bring my heart rate down. His scent fills me, helping me breathe deeper. I listen to his heart, confirming he's really here. He's here and I'm not dead.

"You're safe now," he whispers.

Every second that passes, I feel myself shaking less and my breathing become steadier. Seph pulls away enough to put his hands on either side of my face. His eyes are normal again—soft and green and everything I remember. Not like before when I hardly recognized him.

"Are you okay?"

"I think so."

Seph turns when the door of the building slides open. He touches his gun until he sees that it's Rami, and he lets out a breath. Following on his heels is the other prisoner, who runs off without another word, the dark erasing him as fast as it brought Seph here.

"Have you seen anyone else?" Seph asks him.

Rami shakes his head, for once not grinning or making some weird comment. A long knife is in his hand, red with blood. He pushes himself off the door and goes up to the fire, taking a long branch that's already half burnt. Without a word, he backtracks and throws the branch into the building, and when it lands somewhere inside, more flames erupt.

"There are others," I tell Rami as he walks up. I point to the barn. "In there."

He nods, understanding.

Seph steps away once Rami is gone and reloads his gun. The lever-action sits on his back unused, and there's an ammo belt along with his holster on his hips. His hat and bandana are missing tonight, leaving him bare. He came thinking there were going to be more to kill.

"You came for me," I say, stating the obvious.

Seph looks up, hands paused over his gun. "Of course I did." He searches me for a moment and says, "Avery, I—"

At the sounds of horses, he looks over his shoulder. A second later, Finn rides out of the darkness, followed by Cade and Jack and Rami's horse. He jumps off before the horse has even stopped and throws his arms around me. This is the second time we've been separated. I never want it to happen again.

The people who were locked in the barn come out and scatter in different directions. Rami has his knife holstered now and heads for the horses, not wasting any time. And he's right, because we shouldn't. Another crew could show up at any minute.

"Let's get out of here," Rami says.

Finn reluctantly lets go of my hand and Jack greets me by pressing his head into my chest. I give him a quick rub and pull myself into the saddle. My legs are still weak and my hands won't stop shaking, but I gather the reins and take one more look at the burning building. Then I follow them into the night, the wind drying my tears. I have another chance to live.

27.

Seph

When Rami comes to get me in the early hours of the morning for my watch, I'm still awake. I let him take my bedroll and settle my back against one of boulders facing east in case someone happens to be following us.

It's doubtful. The gang's settlement burned into the night behind us until we were too far to see it. We rode away with nobody left alive to follow.

But I lost myself tonight.

Maybe for a minute. Maybe two. But it happened, and it scares me to think it'll happen again.

I look down to see dried blood on my shirt. I can't feel it on my skin but I know it's still there, a mark I'll have to carry even after it's washed away. I killed more people tonight than I ever have. And the thing that scares me most is that I didn't have a problem with it. I shot them all without hesitation or regret, because I knew who they were and what they've done—what they were going to do with Avery and those other prisoners.

I never wanted to become that person. The person who Torreck saw in me and who everyone thinks I am when they find out I'm an outlaw.

Maybe I was always that person but haven't realized it until now.

Someone comes around the boulder, and I look up to see Avery hesitating to get closer. She sits down down next to me only after I give her a smile, like she needed permission.

"Are you all right?" I ask.

Avery nods and shrugs at the same time. "Couldn't sleep." She looks out over the flatlands, holding everything in as though I can't see it.

"You don't have to pretend you're okay," I say. "This isn't something that happens and you get over it in a day."

"And you would know?" she asks.

I don't say anything at first, not sure if I want to go there. But she obviously needs to hear it, and I wish I had someone to tell me when I was in her shoes.

So I tell her.

"When I was thirteen, I came across this really bad gang up near the border of Canada. It was cold and the winter was never going to stop. They played nice at first, letting me give them my trust, even though I knew I shouldn't. But I was hungry and they had a little food to share." Avery looks over at me and I continue. "I fell asleep not thinking anything would happen, and I woke with my arms and legs tied together and heard them arguing about which way to kill me. They had the fire high and they were drunk. I really thought I was going to die that night."

"How did you escape?"

"I was able to get a knife without them noticing. They turned on each other and it gave me enough time to slip away. But I'll never forget those few minutes when I was sure they were going to kill me. You feel helpless and scared, and—" I stop and really look at her. "And it's not something you can pretend never happened."

213

"Even if you want to?" she asks, her eyes pleading. "Because right now, every time I think about it, I can't breathe."

I move closer and interlace my fingers with hers. It makes my heart jump, but I try not to let her see. Then I kiss the back of her hand, not taking my eyes off hers. "And what about now?" I ask.

Avery gives me a faint smile. "Better."

"When you focus on the good, the bad doesn't seem so terrible."

"Is that your logic of the day?"

"I have more where that came from, if you want to hear it."

Avery turns my hand over in hers, tracing a scar across my palm. I'm surprised she even saw it in this light, even though the sky is slowly beginning to brighten with dawn. Her skin is soft against mine, only urging me to move closer to her.

"Where is this from?" she asks, looking up.

I know she asked a question, but the words get mixed in my head and I can't think straight. I know this night can't last forever, even though I want it to. Never in my life have I wanted to travel with anyone or *be* with anyone.

Avery makes me want those things.

I know the Wild better than anyone, and I have to take this moment before it's gone.

"It's from a couple years ago." I clear my throat and straighten my thoughts. "Cade and I ran into a storm and we came across this abandoned barn. It was locked and I used this piece of metal to break the lock. But it was raining and my hand slipped. It actually got infected," I say, remembering. "It wasn't bad, but it could have turned into something worse if I hadn't been lucky."

A lot of things could've been worse than they were. Sometimes it's hard to believe I'm alive after everything.

I find myself looking south, knowing the ocean is close but

214

not wanting to leave. Gangs have ruled the territories around every coast I've tried to get to, so I wouldn't risk taking her with me in case they're here, too. I'll have to wait it out until the right time.

So close yet so far.

"Seph."

I blink and look at her. She rests her head against the boulder, tilted toward me. "What's south?"

"What?" I heard her but I don't understand what she's asking.

"You've been wanting to go south since I've known you."

I shrug, trying to act like it's nothing. "No reason."

"Seph," Avery says, "I'm not blind. What are you trying to find?"

"It's stupid." I look away.

"Even if it keeps you alive?" she asks. "Mom told us stories of people coming through town, trying to find the sky or something else they thought still exists. Even you said it yourself. People don't last long out here if they don't know what they want. Or sometimes they do but go crazy never able to find it."

"And what makes you think I'm not one of those people?" I ask.

"Because you're not like them."

"Like who?"

"People like Rami. Outlaws that the Wild has turned into someone else." She shakes her head and says, "You're just you. And you've survived this long because of it."

I wish it were true, but she doesn't know how wrong she is. She didn't see me last night or too much of what I did.

I keep my jaw clenched until I find the words to say.

"If I'm still myself, then why have I killed so many people?"

Avery lifts her head off the rock, and after a long moment,

215

leans closer. "You killed those people because if you didn't, they would've killed you. And they would have killed me and whoever else they could get. And I know for the handful of people you have killed, there are hundreds that you didn't but could have. You don't kill people, Seph," she says, "you save them."

I want to believe her. I do. So much that it hurts. Even if what she says is true, it doesn't change one thing. "But I know it'll happen again," I admit, "and I don't know if I can stop myself."

"You're making yourself out to be someone you're not," she argues.

"And you're not the one who has lived in the Wild their whole life, slowly realizing you're losing yourself," I say. "It creeps up on me whether I like it or not, no matter my reasons. I've gone weeks without seeing another human being, let alone talking to anyone. I find myself talking to Cade like he can talk back, because that's the only company I've ever had." I hesitate but say it anyway: "Sometimes I envy those people who gave up, knowing I can't do the same because I don't have the guts."

"Seph—"

I shake my head and stand. I start walking, needing more air than the world can give me.

"Stop," Avery says behind me.

My legs slow down, betraying me.

I love the Wild but I also hate it.

It lures me in, and even though I fight it, I can't do it forever. I'm like the ground, turning into dust for the winds to take away.

"Turn around," she says, right behind me.

I do, keeping my face blank.

"You don't mean what you just said." She steps closer.

216

"And how would you know that?" I challenge.

"Because you're still here." She lets out a breath, almost angry, and turns away and comes back all in the same second. "Just stop thinking so damn much and live. You're here, aren't you? If you wanted to die, you wouldn't try so hard. You wouldn't have Cade, and you certainly wouldn't be alive right now. But you *are*. We both are," she says quieter.

"But we might not always be," I say. "I'm not going to lie—I'm afraid of what is to come of me, because I feel it coming one way or the other. But I'm more afraid of something happening to you before I can stop it. It's too late for me, but you still have a chance to have a normal life."

"It's only too late for you because you're accepting it," she says. "You don't see yourself like I do. You need to stop thinking so much and just be. So would you do me a favor and trust me when I say this?" She puts a hand on my chest, searching my eyes. "I've never met anyone as good as you, Seph. You might zone out once in a while and think of Cade as a human, but I wouldn't have you any other way."

Avery's eyes are as fierce now as they were the day in Houston when the gang members tried to take us alive. But this time they're focused on me.

And I realize how lucky I am that they are.

"Are you sure?" I ask, really needing to know. "Because if you aren't, I can leave. I can—" I look south, torn. "I can leave before things get worse."

"Things aren't going to get worse."

"How do you know that?"

Avery leans in closer, bringing her lips to my ear, and whispers, "Because you aren't alone anymore."

The wind blows through us, reminding me to breathe. It takes me a few moments to realize she's right. If I decide to stay with her, this will be the first time since Dad died that I haven't been by myself. But is that such a bad thing? My mind automatically begins to weigh the risks and puts variables in place.

I'm doing exactly what Avery told me to stop doing—thinking too much.

I'm done fighting myself to make the right choice. Avery's right—I'm not alone anymore. I hold her closer so the wind can't push us apart.

I whisper, "And I don't want to be."

Because sometimes, I need to take a chance.

28.

Avery

"I don't think I've been more scared in my whole life than I was last night," Finn says, after not speaking for almost an hour.

We walk side by side, as we have been the whole morning, resting the horses after the long miles they've put in before now. It actually feels good to walk after all those hours in the saddle, but Jack keeps nudging me in the shoulder—bored with the slow pace.

I finally say to Finn, "Me too." But I stop it there, not wanting to think of it more. Maybe in a week I'll be able to speak freely about it but not when it was only hours ago.

Finn and I trail behind Seph and Rami, just out of earshot. Rami talks to Seph and I can only catch a few words when the wind blows right. I've almost memorized Seph by now. From the way he walks, anyone can tell he grew up in a saddle. Every few minutes, he turns to talk to Rami and I see his profile against the horizon.

Finn stops me with a hand on my arm, already giving me a look I've seen countless times. "I'm sorry for acting the way I've been the last couple days," he says. "I miss home, I miss Axel, and I miss what we had, but there's no excuse for the way I acted."

"I don't think I'm the one you need to apologize to."

He nods. "I know, but I owe it to both of you. We're all in this together, right? I've been thinking a lot about this place we're trying to find," he says. "If these people are anything like the Lawmen or the gangs we've come across, we have to keep going. Even though I hate to say it."

"Trust me, you're not the only one who feels that way," I agree. "But let's get there first and then we'll figure it out."

Finn gives me a trying smile. "Whenever that will be."

"Why, don't you like wandering around in the Wild?"

"It wasn't on my list of things to do," he smirks.

I shove him in the shoulder.

"Oh, so it's gonna be like that?" he asks, shoving me back.

"Only if you don't start crying over it." Before he can grab me, I take off running. I glance back to see him leaving his horse behind with Jack, sprinting to catch up with me. Unfortunately, Finn has always been the fast one. He catches me around the waist and drags me down to the ground.

In seconds I'm on my back with him sitting on top of me. "If you don't let me up I'm going to punch you in the face," I say, trying to sound serious.

"You couldn't even if you wanted to, little sis." His smile is cut off when he sees my face. I swing my legs up and pull him backward. He's able to get free, but when he tries to back away, I trip him and he goes down hard. I scramble to my feet but he sees me coming. I tackle him before he's up and we're both in the dirt a few seconds later, on our backs and breathing hard.

"I feel old," he says, trying to catch his breath.

"Or maybe weak, because your *older* sister can still kick your ass."

He laughs. "Wish on. I was going easy on you."

Seph and Rami appear above us, both with different shades of curiosity on their faces.

"Do we need to break something up?" Seph asks.

"You might need to if he calls me his little sister again," I say.

Seph gives me a hand up. I flip my braid over my shoulder and shake the dust out of it.

"So you're the older one?" Rami asks me.

Finn gets up and brushes the dirt off his jeans, giving him a pointed look. "No, she isn't."

Seph looks between us, his gaze landing on Finn. "So, you are?"

"*No,*" I growl.

"I'm confused."

"We don't—" I stop and clear my throat. "We don't know who is older."

Finn and I stare at each other while Rami and Seph try not to laugh. It's almost the only thing we end up fighting over, because it bothers us both the same.

"How is that even possible?" Rami asks.

Finn shakes his head and gives me a smile. "We never wanted to know until about a year ago, but by then it was too late to ask."

Rami laughs with an exhale and turns his horse around, heading west again, shaking his head. Finn whistles for the horses and takes both, following after Rami and leaving Seph and I alone. He gives me his best impression of a dirty look over his shoulder.

"Is it really that big of a deal?" Seph asks.

We start walking with Cade between us. "No, but it's an ongoing argument. And I can't let him get away with thinking he's the older one."

"I guess the sibling thing is something I'll never understand."

"Some days it's great and then some days it's . . ." I throw

221

my hand toward Finn. "Stupid stuff that makes me want to punch him."

Seph shrugs. "I wouldn't mind seeing that."

"Maybe you will." I grin.

"What was it like, with you guys living alone after your mom died?"

I chew my inner cheek and think of how to describe it. "It wasn't something we were ready for. We turned to her for everything, so after she was gone, we were suddenly at a loss of what to do." I turn to see Seph looking at me. "It was really hard for the first few months, trying to figure what to eat at night and what to do for extra money. The simplest things that became the hardest—things we never noticed because she always did them."

Then I ask, "What was it like for you?"

His eyebrows go up, and he looks away—like he's never thought about it. "I don't know," he says. "One day he was there and the next he wasn't. I had no choice but to deal with it. He made sure I knew how to survive on my own. He taught me how to shoot and how to hunt—when there were still animals around anyway. It's like he wanted me to be ready because he knew that day would come eventually." He thinks about something and says, "But mostly I just felt alone. I was by myself for a long time, and it wasn't until a few years later when I came across Cade."

"I was lucky to have Finn," I say. "I miss Mom every day, but at least I still have him. Because I couldn't imagine doing any of this by myself. Let alone face the Wild."

"You don't think you could do it?"

I snort once and shake my head. "I wouldn't even know where to go. My first night in the Wild, I couldn't tell which way was north." I look to the sky and admit, "Even during the day I still have trouble sometimes."

Seph looks up, showing a ghost of a smile. "Once you know the sky like the palm of your hand, it gets easier."

"Do you always know where you're going?"

He takes his eyes from the sky and gives me a long look. "Almost always. Sometimes it's as easy as going west or north, and sometimes I hear rumors of a certain town in the mountains that I go looking for." He nods and rubs his hand down Cade's head. "But some days I let the wind take us wherever it's going."

I look at them both, wondering where I would be if I never came across either of them. Not here, certainly. Probably nowhere.

"Hey, guys!" We look ahead where Rami and Finn are stopped, looking at something in the distance. We catch up, squinting to see what caught their eye.

"What do you think it is?" Rami asks. He's chewing something in his mouth, making his words sound funny.

We all stand and stare at the shape in the distance. It's something big with a thick pole sticking out the middle, half buried in the ground. Eventually, everything from the past becomes buried; it just depends how long it's been there.

Seph pulls himself on Cade and says, "Let's go check it out."

We ride the last half mile and pull up to examine whatever it is. It sits next to a wide river that isn't as deep as it used to be, judging from the size of the banks. Seph dismounts, never taking his eyes off it. He walks a few steps, then turns around smiling.

"It's a boat," he says, unable to hide his excitement.

I slide off Jack, trying to remember an old picture Mom had of a boat on the ocean, the waves tall around it. It didn't look anything like this, but maybe it's a different kind.

"It doesn't look like a boat," Finn voices.

"It's a sailboat," Seph answers. "See the mast coming out of the middle? That's where the sail is supposed to hang from."

I look back and Finn gives me a shrug but he's smiling. Rami looks slightly bored, but he kicks his horse to go take a closer look. Finn follows him, and when I look at Seph next to me, I've never seen him so fascinated about something before. He looks at the ship like how I would imagine people would look at the sun if they ever found it.

"It's amazing, isn't it?" he says.

I watch as Finn and Rami trek up the a mound formed where the wind had pushed the dirt against the boat, burying most of the front end. With them next to it, the boat seems bigger than before.

"But where did it come from?" I ask.

Seph thinks about it and looks south. "If I had to guess, they came from the ocean and tried coming up the river at some point, probably years ago when the river was still full. Because this isn't just some riverboat. It's made for bigger waters. Or maybe it got washed in from sea from one of those killer storms."

"Come on then," I say, starting toward it. "Let's go check it out."

We leave the horses and climb up to the boat. The wooden deck is covered in a thin layer of dirt and old rope hangs from what Seph called the mast. There's no sign of the sail, but it's easy to guess that the wind took it away long ago. Now that we're up here, I can see it's got to be at least seventy-five feet long—bigger than anything I've ever stood on.

Rami and Finn appear from a set of stairs that disappear underneath.

"It's not too bad in there," Finn says. "A lot of dirt, but nothing that can't be cleaned out. And it's bigger than our old house."

"Are you trying to suggest something?" I ask, one eyebrow raised.

He shrugs. "We could always stay here the night. The horses could use the long rest and this guy needs to take a dip in the river." He jabs his thumb at Rami.

The outlaw gives him his creepy smile. "Careful what you wish for."

Seph laughs once and then nods. "It's a good idea. I think we'd know if someone was following us by now."

Rami punches Finn in the shoulder and says, "Let's go get the stuff inside so I can drown you in the river."

"Can't wait," he says, following him.

I sit on the side of the boat and watch as Seph walks around, taking it all in.

"Isn't it amazing to think that this used to sail across the ocean?" he says, looking up at the mast. "I can't imagine what that must feel like."

"Probably really dull," I say.

Seph looks at me. "Why do you say that?"

"Being surrounded by water isn't something I would want. You can't ride horses on water."

Seph sits next to me. "It's not just being surrounded by water," he says. "It's the ocean. One day it could be calm and the next it could be storming, and you can go wherever you want. No borders, no bridges, no walls you can't cross. I guess the only thing you have to look out for is pirates."

"Pirates? You mean like, in those stories about men with parrots on their shoulders and wooden legs?"

"Those stories are only told by parents who don't want to scare their kids. I'm talking about real pirates. Men who live on the water and will kill anyone who crosses paths with them. They raid oceanside towns and take prisoners to sell as slaves in different countries." He smiles. "Those are the real pirates."

"You seem to know a lot about this stuff."

Seph shakes his head. "I've just heard a lot different people talk about it. Some stuff sticks with me and other things don't."

We sit for a while, letting the wind brush against us from the north. I let Seph wander in his own mind again. From this high up, I can see as far as my eyes will let me. To the south, the land rises into a small hill and what's beyond that isn't hard to guess. More nothing like everywhere else.

"You know," he says, "this is the first place I've been to that I could see myself staying for a while."

"Here?"

He looks over and nods. "Right here."

"It's not very practical."

"Does life have to be?"

"If you want to survive, yes. You should know that better than anyone."

"I suppose. But what if it's only for a few days?"

I think about it, because right now—after all those days of riding—staying in one place can't sound any better. "I think a few days would be fine."

"Are you sure?" His green eyes bore into me.

"I'm sure. A townie like me knows what it's like to stay in one place. You'll be out of your element for a little while."

Seph smiles at that and says, "Well if you're such an expert on this stuff, what should I do next?"

"You promise not to think about it too long?"

His smile widens. "I promise."

My heart kicks. "Well then . . . I think you should kiss me," I say, looking down at my feet. "And be quick about it because Finn will be back any—"

When I look back up, he's already there to cut off my words.

29.

Seph

Ever since Avery brought up my father, I can't stop thinking about him.

I stand up to my knees in the river, remembering every moment he watched me from the bank and let me be who I wanted to be. I hope I've become someone he would be proud of. After last night, I'm still not sure. I finger the cloth around my wrist, wondering what he meant for me.

Cade stands beside me, his legs and belly wet and dark. A little more than a week ago, we would have been standing in a river alone. Just the two of us.

Now we watch the others and listen to the snippets of banter. It's a change I never thought I would be okay with. A change I never thought I would like. Somewhere inside me, I'm excited for what's to come. Because for once, I don't know what it holds.

"Can I talk to you for a minute?"

I turn to see Finn behind me, his pants rolled up to his knees even though they're totally soaked.

"Sure, what's up?"

He stands a few feet away like there's a barrier between us—and there has been. In the Lawmen's prison, we might have been as close to friends as I've ever been, though since then it's been backwards, like none of it ever happened.

Finn digs his hands deep into his pockets and finally looks at me.

"I wanted to say thank you," he says. "For keeping Avery safe while I wasn't around, and for what you did last night."

"It's really nothing, I—"

"No, but it is. She could've come across anyone out there, and if she did, she wouldn't be here right now. Neither would I." He glances down the river where Avery washes a pair of clothes. Rami is a little ways out, floating on his back with his eyes closed. "I'm sorry," Finn says, turning back, "for being an ass these past few days. I could list excuses and try to explain why but none of it matters. The fact is, Avery was lucky to have you and I'm grateful for it. I want you to know that we're good. There's nobody else in the world I would trust her with more than myself."

"The thing is," I say, "I probably wouldn't be here either if it wasn't for her. She's the toughest girl I've ever met."

Finn smiles and says, "Yeah, she is."

He holds out his hand for me to shake and I take it. I want to say something, but I don't know what. But he seems satisfied with me saying nothing and leaves to rejoin his sister.

"People are complicated sometimes," I say to Cade.

He blows air from his nose in response.

Despite my protests, Rami and Finn make a fire using broken scraps from the boat. Not because I'm afraid of someone seeing the flames, but because I don't want them chopping up this boat for one night's worth of heat. Some part of me feels protective over it.

Night falls and we sit around the fire. Our wet clothes hang from a rope tied to the mast and the horses make familiar

228

noises down near the water. The collar of my jacket is popped up against the cold breeze. It's the first time I've needed to wear it in months.

I chew on my ration bar and try not to look at the fire. I don't like the way it blinds me when I look away from it, leaving me vulnerable. Avery and Finn sit across from me and Rami sits between us, smoking a rare cigarette—the paper almost a brown color after so many years of sitting. I can't imagine it tastes very good.

I catch Avery's eye over the flames and she gives me a smile, one that Finn doesn't see. The night is not as cold because of it.

"So I was thinking," she starts. Finn stops eating. "Maybe we could stay here for a few days."

"What for?" he asks. "There's nothing here."

"Because these last two weeks haven't been what I call easy," she says. "I just—" she glances at me quick, "—I thought it would be a nice break."

"I wouldn't call this place *nice*," Rami adds, talking even slower while smoking.

Finn laughs once in response and I don't say anything. Even though Finn and I are on neutral ground now, I have a feeling he would argue against Avery more if I were on her side. She knows it, too—not looking at me or asking for any comment. She knows her brother better than anyone.

"Look," Finn says. "Rami says the settlement shouldn't be much farther from what he's heard. Maybe even less than a day's ride from here if we're lucky."

Avery jumps on it before he can think more. "Well that's perfect then. You guys can go out in the morning, and if you don't come across anything by midday, come back and we'll go back out together. Jack needs more than a day's rest. He's been riding steady for a week."

"I won't let you stay here alone—no way in hell."

Seeing my opportunity, I decide to interject. "I'll stay with her. Cade could use a break, as well."

He doesn't need a break—Cade's been riding like this his whole life, but he doesn't need to know that.

Finn looks unsure. Rami shrugs.

"You sure you want to?" Finn asks his sister.

"Yes, I'm sure. You guys head out in the morning and see what you can find. We'll be here when you get back."

Finn doesn't look totally sold, but he nods anyway. I feel his eyes on me and I do my best to look emotionless, even when I want to look at Avery and flash her a smile nobody else will see. We haven't been truly alone since the train rescue.

After a while, they each disappear beneath the boat, Rami being the last one to go. The fire is almost down to coals, and after I put it out, I lean back and stare up at the sky. Sometimes if I look long enough, I can see something glowing behind the clouds. The moon I've never seen. I can lay awake for hours hoping I will until my eyes become too heavy to keep open. My hope diminishes with the night.

Sometimes I want to see the moon as much as the ocean. With everyone down below for the night, I can almost hear it if I try hard enough—my imagination getting the better of me.

Someone comes up on the deck, and I know it's Avery from her light footsteps. I sit up and she stands over me, her arms crossed from the cold.

"Will you come down to sleep tonight?"

"I wasn't planning on it," I admit.

"Seph—"

"I can't," I tell her. I look away and she sits down next to me, close enough for her arm to brush against mine. I feel the warmth through my coat. "I can't sleep with something over me," I say. "Sometimes I have to when it's storming but I don't sleep long on those nights. Sometimes not at all."

"What did you do in prison?"

"I only slept when I was too exhausted not to," I say. "Sometimes when it's bad, I can't even breathe. It's like everything is closing in around me, crushing me."

Avery leans closer and says, "Some men who went into the mines felt the same way, and they couldn't work down there because of it. But when I'm inside, I feel safer. The roof over my head protects me from the outside, and the walls hide me when I don't want to be seen." She pauses and then continues, "You don't have to be afraid of something you're not used to. My first real night in the Wild, I barely slept at all. But I got used to it—something I never thought would happen."

"Are you trying to tell me something?"

"I think you already know."

I let out a slow breath. "It's not something that's going to change overnight."

"I don't expect it to." Avery stands up and holds her hand down for me. "Sometimes it's easier to sleep when you're near people you care about."

"I wouldn't know."

"You're about to."

I take her hand and she leads me below where Finn and Rami are already asleep. It's dark down here, the night barely coming through the broken windows. My eyes adjust more, making out the shapes of things from the old world, things I don't know names of—covered in layers of dirt and dust and long forgotten.

My bedroll is next to hers and I glance at Finn again, wondering what he'll do when he wakes up to find me next to her.

"Are you sure this is okay?" I whisper.

Avery leans close and brushes her lips on my cheek. "Yes." It makes me warm all over, and she leaves me to settle under her own blanket. I pull off my boots and jacket and crawl into my own bed.

I lie on my back with my blanket up to my chin, staring at the underside of the deck and wishing it to be clouds. The air seems thin in here. I have to take shallow breaths while my heart pounds.

"Seph." Avery's whispering voice makes me turn my head. She's lying on her side facing me, using her saddlebags as a pillow. What little light comes through the window shines between us. I turn on my side, never taking my eyes off her.

"Just don't think about it," she says.

I can't stop. I feel it over me and around me—everything in me yearns to be outside. Under the clouds and where the wind can still find me. "Tell me about where you used to live," I say, on the edge of somewhere I don't want to be.

"Our house?"

I nod.

"Well it was nothing really special, but it was home. It sits on the outskirts of town, a long dirt path leading to it but still in earshot of the mine's sirens. It only has two bedrooms—one for our parents and one for us, though Dad died when we were young. We never had much, but Mom always had something for dinner every night, no matter the season."

"How did your father die?" I ask.

"The mine," she says. "I don't remember much of that day—just that Mom wouldn't let us see her cry."

I can't imagine dying like that—in a dark, enclosed space where the air barely touches. When I die, I want to be under the sky—the wind on my face and the ground beneath me.

Avery reaches into her saddlebags and takes out something small. She looks at it for a moment then sets it between us, where the dim light shines on it.

It's the small wooden horse I've seen her look at before and that Finn had in prison.

"This is the only thing we have left of our father. He made it for us when we were young and told us we had to share it." Avery smiles at the thought.

"My dad didn't leave me with anything but knowledge and a red cloth to remember him by. I guess I turned out okay nonetheless."

"To say the least." She laughs, careful not to wake the others.

We lie in silence, listening to the wind outside with the little horse between us. My heart is somehow beating steady now, like there's no longer a roof over me. Sleep creeps into my eyes.

Avery sees it too because she smiles and whispers, "Good night, Seph."

"Good night, Avery."

The next time I open my eyes, gray daylight comes through the boat's windows and I'm alone. I sit up fast, seeing the empty beds around me. The immediate thought something is wrong runs through my head, until I hear Avery's laugh somewhere outside. I take a deep breath and dig the heels of my hands into my eyes. I haven't slept past dawn in years.

I find my boots and pull them on with numb fingers. The morning is cold, but I leave my jacket inside as I climb the steps leading out onto the deck to find the clouds low, riding the wind high above us like they want to go somewhere. I scan the horizon out of habit. Avery stands on the shore of the river with Jack, trying to brush his coat as he nibbles her shoulder.

When she sees me standing on the boat, she gives a small wave and starts toward me. Cade stands nearby, flicking his tail and waiting for any signal from me. For now, I give him none.

Avery climbs up onto the boat and joins me on the stern. When she sits down, her leg presses against mine. My muscles tense without me telling them to and my stomach does a flip.

"How did you sleep?" She looks over with a smile.

I return it with a small one and admit, "I don't remember the last time I slept like that. Especially indoors." Then I ask, "Where's Finn and Rami?"

"They left after the sun came up. I didn't want to wake you."

"Usually Cade is the one who does that, so I wouldn't have complained if today was different."

Avery doesn't look away and says, "But today is already different."

I counter with, "The past week has been different."

"Have you ever had different before now?"

I narrow my eyes and dare to ask, "Are you asking if I've kissed anyone?"

A touch of color adds to her cheeks. "Maybe."

"Well—" I pretend to think about it. "Not too long ago, I kissed this girl next to a river. It was raining and she was mad at me for some reason. But before then, no." I look over and Avery has a look on her face I've seen only a handful of times. A look she only gives me. "Do you want to go riding with me?"

"But you always go alone in the morning."

"Like you said, today is different."

She smiles again and we climb down from the boat. Cade and Jack already wait for us next to our gear where we stowed it for the night. I put on his bridle and pull myself up, riding bareback. Avery does the same and gives me a grin before pressing her heels into Jack's sides. They take off and Cade throws his head to follow them.

After a couple seconds, I let him. His stride is long and his ears are forward, loving the chase after a day's rest. We come up next to them and he slows down to keep pace. I don't know which way we're riding, and I don't care. I love the feeling of Cade beneath me with no saddle between us and the wind rushing past.

We slow down gradually, coming to a stop on a small rise. This is one of the flatter states I've been in—in some places you can see for miles or as far as your eyes will allow. Once in a while, an old building will dot the horizon.

"It's odd to think that this was all different before we were born," Avery says. "Things in pictures never look the same in real life, so it's hard to imagine. Do you think we'll see it that way again?"

I turn toward her and say, "I do. If the earth is really healing itself like some people say, it has to be done at some point, right? The sun has to shine again and let things grow. If it doesn't, I'm not sure how long we can survive."

"We've made it this far, haven't we?"

"And hopefully a little farther." I close the gap between us and kiss her, the wind tossing her hair against my neck.

Cade throws his head and dances aside, breaking us apart too soon. And I'm smiling because of it until I catch sight of dust over Avery's shoulder. My hearts jolts into my ribs and I now know why Cade won't stay still.

A half dozen riders are closing in on us.

Avery glances over her shoulder and looks back to me with a changed face—one I last saw the night she almost died and one I'd hoped never to see again.

My hand reflectively goes to my side, where my gun should be sitting. There's nothing there. I forgot to bring it.

"Seph—"

"Come on!"

We take off fast, heading west and back to the boat. If we get our guns, we can defend ourselves on high ground. When

I look back, I expect them to be farther behind—gang horses never have the endurance for a chase, especially against animals like Cade and Jack.

But if anything, they're gaining on us. And when I catch sight of the white bands around their arms, I understand why. Somewhere in me, I find myself more afraid of that fact. Gangs I've dealt with my whole life. They're predictable and unorganized. Half the men can't even shoot straight.

The Lawmen are everything the other gangs aren't and more of what I am.

I push Cade to keep going, but he can't give everything he has without leaving Avery and Jack behind. The boat is in view now, slowly growing bigger. I can hear the other horses behind us.

I don't want to look back—afraid of who I'll see riding with them.

We're less than a quarter mile away now.

A slick sheen of sweat coats Jack's neck and he's beginning to slow. We won't make it in time with his speed.

I have to do something.

Without thinking, I swing behind them and slap Jack in the rear, giving him one more burst of speed. Then I pull hard on Cade's reins, immersing us into dust and horses as he comes to a quick stop. A hand grabs the back of my shirt and pulls me off Cade before I have the chance to hang on. I hit the ground hard. Through the dust and legs of horses, I see the boat and Avery being dragged off her horse by another Lawman soldier. My saddlebags and gun lay fewer than a hundred feet away.

Someone hauls me to my knees, keeping their hand fisted into the back of my shirt. I cough the dust from my lungs and try to ignore the ache in my ribs. A man dismounts and walks toward me, but I only stare at his boots, wishing I didn't recognize them and wishing I had killed him when I had the chance.

The barrel of a rifle settles beneath my jaw, forcing my head up to see Torreck standing over me.

He takes a long look and makes a disappointed sound before letting my head drop again. Torreck walks away somewhere behind me and it gives me enough time to locate Avery. A soldier has a gun to her head and the rest of his comrades stand between us. I taste blood in my mouth from when I fell and I spit it out, the dust swallowing it greedily.

I glance at Avery again, trying to find some way out of this.

Because getting out of things is what I'm good at. This isn't the first time I've been surrounded by people who would like nothing more than to kill me, or have a gun to my head, being told to say my final words.

Through all of that, I'm still here, and I still plan to be here tomorrow. I ignore all the whispers that say otherwise.

"To tell you the truth," Torreck says, somewhere behind me, "I wasn't sure if I would find you. And if I did, I hoped you would've put up more of a fight. This is a bit disappointing."

He comes around to face me again, this time without his rifle and just his pistol on his hip. It's the same one he used to kill my dad. The sight of it creates something hard in my heart. Something dark.

"If it's a fight you want, I'll give you one," I say.

He smiles but changes the subject. "Where are the prisoners you helped escape?"

"Not here."

"If you don't answer me, maybe I'll question her instead," he says, pointing back at Avery. "It is her brother after all, isn't it? And whatever I do to her, you will be forced to watch every second of it."

"They aren't here," I repeat, firmer this time. "They rode on ahead of us."

Torreck doesn't take his eyes off me. "You lie as well as your old man," he says.

I swallow, finding my throat tight. "I'm not lying." Then I dare to say, "And even if I am, will you give me the same fate as him?"

"Not yet I won't," Torreck says. He looks away for a moment, thinking about something with his hands on his hips. "To tell you the truth, I don't care where they are. I didn't track you down to find a couple of runaway prisoners."

"Then why did you?"

"To teach you a lesson," he steps forward, bending over to make sure I see him. "You don't cross me and get away with it. Especially outlaws like you who need to learn their place in this world. It's not something I take lightly."

Torreck gives a single nod to the man behind me and something hard hits the side of my head. A boot kicks my ribs and then my stomach when I try to roll over. I hear Avery screaming my name, but I can't answer her through the blows, trying to cover my head with my arms. After a few more kicks, they back away.

Blood pounds through my head and I force my eyes open. "This is how you're going to do it then?" I ask him, struggling to sit up. "I know you take pleasure in taking advantage of unarmed people, but it really makes me realize how much of a piece of shit you are. You're a coward."

"And you're someone who I never should've let live," he admits.

His hand rests over his pistol, probably moments away from killing me.

Before he can make a move, I say one last thing.

"If you want proof of who I've become—who you hoped I would be—then let me show you. Or are you not man enough to face me?"

The rest of his men turn to look at him, waiting for his response. If he kills me now, he'll lose the respect of his men.

I stare back hard, praying he'll agree. It's the only chance I have. My ribs ache and blood runs down the side of my face from being hit. But I can still stand and I can still shoot.

I can always shoot.

"You want to take your chances with me, boy?"

I say, "Skill isn't chance."

He smiles. "You've got that right." Without turning to anyone particular, he says, "Someone go get his gun."

They pull me to my feet and someone returns with my gun and belt. They back away from me as I buckle it around my hips. My middle finger wants to tap but I don't let it. The soldiers gather around us, Avery among them and unable to do anything but watch. I don't like the worry in her eyes. To try to take it away, I give her a slight smile, something that's hard to do moments before a standoff. My nerves are high, but just like Dad taught me, I use my fear to make my hands steady and trust myself.

Torreck inspects his gun and seeing it reminds me of Dad's last moments. For the first time in my life, I feel a real anger toward him. Up until now, I was living my life as best I could, trying to forget the man. Any other person would have wanted revenge.

I ask, "Do you remember what you told me all those years ago?"

He nods. "I said you'd thank me one day for doing what I did. By killing your father, I made you strong enough to survive this world. Do you deny it? You'd be dead if it weren't for me."

"No." I shake my head and say, "If it weren't for you, my father would still be alive. If it weren't for you, I wouldn't have killed someone for the first time when I was *eleven*. I wouldn't have to dig through someone's garbage to find something to eat, or hear a girl get raped by a gang while I hid in a pipeline, too young and weak to help or understand but know in my soul whatever it was happening wasn't right. Everything comes down to you and what you did. You can't try and make it out to be right."

"Because of me," he says, "you're strong. You cannot say that isn't true."

"My father made me strong, not you. Never you."

He finally says, "I guess we'll see who the real survivor is."

My heart won't stop pounding in my throat. One false move and I could be dead in seconds. I have to trust myself. Trust what I can do. What I'm capable of. Despite all that, sweat beads along my forehead.

To my left, nobody says a word. They're silent watchers of a death today. The wind prods at my back and the sound of the ocean comes with it, maybe reminding me I can't die until I see it.

I wait on Torreck, because I never make the first move.

Maybe he doesn't either and we'll be here forever, growing old with the dust slowly covering our feet.

Then it happens.

His eye twitches, giving him away, and then his hand, going for his gun. I go for mine. Somehow—maybe because I wasn't fast enough or he's just as good as I am—he's able to pull the trigger. Both guns go off at the same time and my bullet hits its mark with that sickening *thunk* I've come to know too well.

Torreck staggers back and looks down, blood spreading from the hole in his chest, right where his heart should be. I feel something stinging on my side, but I keep my gun up, making sure he's going down before he can take another shot. His face twists in an angry way—one I've seen before, knowing what he's going to do. He raises his gun to take another shot, but I pull the trigger again before he's able to.

Torreck looks at me, his face growing white. His mouth opens, but no words come out. Then he falls to his knees, and seconds later he tips over with a cloud of dust. His body lies motionless on the ground, yet I have this horrible fear he's going to get up and finish the job. After so long, how could it be so easy to kill him? Even though I've made him out to be this unkillable monster my whole life—one that I never wanted to chase—he's human just like everyone else. Just like me.

I lower my gun and look down where his bullet got me. It's low on my right side, just above my hip. I want it to be a flesh wound. I pray for it to be. But nothing will change what happened. I holster my gun and put my hand over it, somehow thinking I can keep the blood in. It's starting to ache now, my adrenaline wearing off and my body figuring out something is wrong.

I'm calm and that scares me. I've been shot before. But never in a place where it could kill me.

A Lawman soldier inspects Torreck, pressing two fingers to the side of his neck. We wait for his fate, and after a moment seeming to last forever, he stands up and shakes his head.

"He's dead."

The others shift and voices call out, now without their leader.

"So what do we do now?"

"Do we let them go?"

"Good riddance."

I don't listen or look to them. My eyes are on only Avery and I try to give her a smile. The relief on her face tells me she doesn't know I'm shot. From where she stands, she can't see the blood soaking into my white shirt. The shirt Marshall gave me days ago. It seems more like weeks.

She doesn't know I'll probably be dead within the hour. I've seen this type of gut shot before and it's never ended well. It's the type of wound that makes you think you're going to be fine but slowly kills you.

Something changes and I realize it's the silence. The voices have stopped and every person is looking at something above me. Even Avery follows their gaze and locks her eyes on something I don't see. I'm hesitant, and then I look up—

And see blue. Through the gray clouds, there's a break. It almost doesn't look real. Too good to be true. I can see the layers of clouds and then the blue just above it, mocking us way down here.

The first wave of pain rolls through me, forcing my eyes off the sky. My legs threaten to buckle and I stagger to stay upright. Right now, nobody sees me. Except Cade. He waits for me and I look to the south, knowing what I have to do.

So I turn away from the first glimpse of sky and go toward the only thing I want to see.

30.

Avery

I only tear my eyes from the sky when I hear a horse galloping away. I turn and see Seph and Cade heading south, and I wonder why and where he would be going. I look back at the sky. I'm afraid this is a dream and I'll wake up and not remember it or have it all be fake. I wish Finn were here to see it, and then I remember I'm not surrounded by friends.

The Lawmen soldiers talk around me like I'm not there—about heading back to Kev to tell the Sheriff what they found.

"But what about them?" someone asks.

"It doesn't matter—the boy is as good as dead anyway. Once we come with the news, he won't even remember why we were out here in the first place. And unlike Torreck, I'm not in the business to kill kids."

His words run through my head again and I'm slow to realize what he said. Was Seph shot? I never saw any blood and he was well enough to ride away. But why would they say that? My heart pounds for me to do something.

The sky forgotten, I frantically look for Jack and leave the soldiers behind. Like a ghost to them, I ride away with nobody following me, something I wasn't sure would happen a few moments ago. I follow his trail south for a good mile until I come to a rise where Cade stands alone near the top—his reins hanging loose and something dark smeared over his shoulder. I dismount and start up the hill.

When I get close enough, my legs stop working and I stare at Cade, trying to understand what I'm seeing while everything in me wants to deny it. I step closer with my fingers outstretched. My breath is shallow but my heart pounds fast.

I touch Cade's shoulder and my fingers come away red. Once my mind makes the connection, they shake. The blood starts at his back and runs down to his leg. But Cade's not hurt.

The blood isn't his.

I leave the horses and continue on. The dirt is different here—it's too fine and my boots sink into it, making it hard for me to walk.

At the top of the hill, a gust of wind pushes the loose hair away from my face and for the second time today, I stop and stare at something I've never before seen.

For as long as I can remember, we've had a picture of the ocean in our house. Mom always said it was our grandmother's, who used to live near it where she could watch the storms roll in and the wind could toss her hair. Whenever she told that story, she would always smile, like that's the way she would always remember her mother.

I never thought I would see it in person. I never thought I would leave home or travel this far or ever see a piece of the sky.

But now I'm standing here, looking out over a stretch of water that never ends. Waves roll inland, making a sound so unfamiliar but comforting. The sky is here, too. Patches of it break away the clouds I've lived under my whole life. I can't see the sun but streams of light shine down, making rays in the sky and touching the water.

If things were different, I could stare at it all day.

But instead I search for Seph and spot him instantly. He sits against a boulder and faces the ocean. His gun belt is coiled at his feet and his right hand rests over his side, where his fingers hold nothing in.

The horses have followed me and Cade stands behind me, his ears forward like he doesn't know what's happening. I leave him and drop down next to Seph, facing him instead of the sky and ocean behind me. His eyes—even greener now that the gray sky is gone—stare out across the water. I was stupid to never realize why he wanted to go south until now.

He wanted to see the ocean.

For someone who has traveled as much as he does, I don't understand why he hasn't before now, but I know it to be true from the way he's looking at it. It's the same way those soldiers looked at the sky, because that's what everyone is always looking for.

But all Seph wanted was to see this, not the sky. Something so simple.

"It's better than I thought it would be," he says. "But I never thought I would see it like this."

I look down at his side again, not knowing what to do. I know people who have been shot there. I don't want to think about what happened to them. Finn and Rami will come back soon—and then what? Will they know what to do when I don't?

My eyes burn and my throat is so swollen I can barely breathe.

"Avery." Seph looks over, and I have the hardest time meeting his eyes. "It's okay," he says. "It's going to be okay."

I shake my head and swipe at my eyes. "It's not okay. Nothing about this is okay. We're too far from a town and I know nothing about . . . about this." I shake my head. "And you shouldn't be the one comforting me. I should be the one—"

My throat tightens and I can't finish the sentence. I'm breathing too fast.

Seph stares, his face relaxed in a weird way with his eyes still bright. Maybe if I sit here long enough and only gaze into his eyes, I can believe nothing is wrong with him.

I feel every warning about the Wild behind me, whispering into my ear, *I told you so.*

"I have something for you," he says.

I will my eyes to stay dry and I watch as Seph pulls something from his pocket, like he's had it this whole time but never knew when to give it to me. He places it in my palm and I look down to see a compass.

"Now you don't have to go asking old men for directions," he says.

I look up to see him smiling. He's bleeding and dying and trying to make a joke. But despite everything, I smile back.

"Seph, I don't . . ."

"You can," he says. "You were strong before I met you, and this right here," he closes my hand around the compass, "will give you that piece of me you didn't have before."

"I don't want a compass," I tell him, half whispering. "I want you. Just you."

"You don't need me—"

"But I do," I argue.

All I can think about are those first moments with Seph, and all the others after. The first time I saw him, his hands were cuffed and he was a prisoner charged with murder. The second time, he stood knee-deep in a river with a stupid smile on his face, like a kid swimming for the first time.

I want to scream until my voice goes hoarse because none of this is right.

Seph turns away, closing his eyes. His jaw clenches in pain and his skin is paler than it was a minute ago. I thread my fingers through his cold ones, somehow thinking it'll help.

"I didn't think this would happen so soon," he whispers, opening his eyes again. I see the fear in them—the uncertainty and doubt I've never seen him have. "But I guess that's the risk of living in the Wild. Someday, it always catches up to you."

"Seph." He looks at me. "Remember the first time we met?" He nods and I continue. "Even though they told me you killed a man, I didn't believe them. One look in your eyes and I didn't understand why you were there. And somewhere in me, I knew I wanted to help you, even though I had no way to and didn't know why."

"You were the first person I had a hard time reading," he says, his words becoming slower. "And it annoyed me, because I wanted to know more than anything."

"It seems like a lifetime ago."

"Then we were lucky to have a lifetime together," he says, more serious than I've ever heard him say anything. "Promise me you'll take care of Cade," he says, his voice cracking.

"Seph—"

"Please, Avery."

I nod with the words choking me. "Of course."

With that, he looks over the ocean again, his chest rising and dropping slowly. "I didn't think it would end like this," he says, his eyes narrowing. "And I don't want it to. I wish . . . wishing is stupid, but I wish it didn't have to be this way."

The wind brushes against my cheeks to make it clear how wet they are. Then something clicks in my mind—a miner came out still alive but hurt, and everyone did what they could to save him. That's what I should be doing—saving him, not sitting here and watching him die.

I hear myself say, "It's not going to end this way."

My hands start working, somehow knowing what to do. I

unbuckle my belt and loop it around Seph's middle with my bandana over his wound. When I tighten it, he sucks in a gasp.

"What are you doing?"

"I'm trying to save your life, idiot. Sure, I could survive this world without you, but I don't *want* to. Is that okay with you?"

Seph hesitates, then nods. "I'm okay with that."

"Good." I lead Cade over to Seph and wonder how I'm going to get him on his back.

"Avery." His voice is weak and the wind almost carries it away.

"What?"

"Tap on the back of his leg."

I look between him and Cade, wondering how he ever taught him this. After I do what he says, Cade lowers himself down next to Seph, his coat still stained with blood. I help Seph onto his back, using most of my weight so he doesn't have to. Cade stands up with Seph laid out on him, his fists knotted in his mane. I grab his holster and belt off the ground and buckle it around my hips.

"Hold on tight," I tell him. "And don't die on me."

"I'll try."

I don't know where we're going, but I know we have to go somewhere. Anywhere. I point Jack west, down the coast where we might be lucky, and Cade follows us, his rider dying on his back.

31.

Seph

I don't want to die. I'm sure everyone thinks that when they're facing death, but no matter how hard I try to deny it, it's true.

I want to ride Cade until I'm too old to sit up. And I want to wake up every day and see Avery next to me, however bizarre it is to admit. Because before I met her, I was sure I would die alone.

I don't want to die today. Because these last few days really made me realize how good life can be. And how unpredictable.

I'm afraid to close my eyes, knowing once I do, I'll never open them again. As Avery takes us more inland, where the ground is harder and horses can run faster, I look at the ocean one last time and try to memorize it.

If I am to die, I'm lucky to be here where I love it most—the Wild—where I grew up and lived my whole life. It's where I found Cade and Avery and learned how to live with being alone.

Do pirates ever get lonely? They must, being out at sea all the time.

For once, I don't want to think about pirates and boots or anything else. I don't want to think at all.

I rest my head against Cade's neck while he runs, watching his legs move faster and faster. With each step, they become more red.

32.

Avery

I don't want to glance back at Seph because I'm afraid of what I'll see. So I keep pushing Jack forward, over every rise and hoping the next will have something there. The horses are lathered in sweat and won't be able to go on much longer. There's a small river up ahead, snaking around the low hills, and I let Jack slow to stop. When he lowers his head to the water, I slide off his back, my legs shaking with fatigue.

I finally turn and face Cade and the still rider on his back. Seph's hands are knotted in his mane with his cheek resting on his neck. His eyes are half closed, staring into the distance.

"Come on, Cade." I take his loose reins and lead him to the water. His nostrils flare with the smell of Seph's blood, but he drinks because he needs to. I step closer to Seph and put my hand on his, feeling how cold it is.

"Not too much longer now," I tell him.

"Avery," he says, just over a whisper.

"Yeah?"

"There's someone over there."

I turn quickly, catching sight of a horse and rider on the hill across the river. They wear a wide-brimmed hat and long coat, reminding me of the Lawmen. They start down the hill and my hand reaches for Seph's pistol at my hip. It's out by the time they reach the bottom, but Seph would probably laugh at how slow I am.

The rider stops at the edge of the river and dismounts, pulling off his hat so I can see his face and dark hair. He looks familiar, but wears no white band.

"I don't mean you any harm," he says, holding out his hands. "If your friend is wounded, I can help."

"The last few people we've come across haven't exactly been friendly, so if it's the same to you, I'll keep my gun out."

He smiles and says, "Fair enough."

The river only comes up to his ankles and his horse follows behind, flicking his ears at Jack and Cade. When the stranger gets close, his forehead creases and he says, "Seph?"

"You know him?" I ask.

"I helped him escape from Kev."

Marshall—Seph told me how someone from the Lawmen turned and helped him escape. But what is he doing here?

He approaches Seph, trying to see where he was shot. Seph doesn't say anything and I lower the gun, recognizing the look in his eyes.

"I get you out of trouble once, and now you're back for more," Marshall says, and then turns to me. "We have to get him to Radnor. He's lost a lot of blood and I can help him there."

"Where is it?"

"Just over the hill. But we have to hurry."

I mount Jack again and whistle for Cade to follow. The river splashes my boots and I follow Marshall up the hill. We're almost there. About a half mile across a flat plain, the town sits next to the ocean, a stone wall surrounding it and stretching inland. Some of the buildings are taller in the center, making it look like it's on top of a hill. With splashes of sunlight on the stone, it's the most beautiful town I've ever seen.

We follow Marshall across the plain, and I silently tell Seph to hold on a little longer. I wonder how long it's already been. One, two hours? Less? Even though it feels like a whole day. The town gets larger and larger, bigger than Kev, and then we're at the gates. Marshall dismounts and shouts to the people to let us in. He pushes back his coat sleeve and holds up his arm, revealing a red cloth around his wrist. It looks exactly like Seph's except not as old.

When the gates open, a couple of people run out with a stretcher between them. Marshall shouts orders and they pry Seph's hands from his horse's mane, trying to get him on the stretcher without moving him too much. I jump off Jack and go to his side. I just want him to look at me again, however selfish that may be.

"Seph."

And he does, looking at me for a long time before he says, "Ride on, Avery."

It's the good-bye someone says when you won't ever see them again. Words I never wanted to hear come from his mouth. They take him away before I can say anything, possibly leaving me with his last words.

"Are you coming in, girl?" The man at the gate waits, ready to shut the doors.

I shake my head. "Not yet."

His shoulders shrug as if saying, *Suit yourself.* I don't linger—I don't give myself enough time to think about what's happening on the other side of the wall or if Seph will make it. I remount Jack and whistle for Cade. He hesitates before trusting me enough to follow. We go south along the wall until it ends and then a little farther to the ocean. The sun is setting, now breaking through the clouds. The blue has gone and is replaced by more colors than I can name.

I leave Jack on the beach and lead Cade into the water until

252

it comes up to his knees, and he's uneasy about the waves. It's cold and sand shifts under my feet. I start with his legs—cupping the water with my hands to wash away the blood. It comes away too easy. Like Seph was never here.

33.

Avery

"Avery."

I turn. Finn stands on the beach, worry etched into his face. He always reminds me of Mom when he gets this look. Rami is beside him with eyes for only the sky and sun. Finn wades into the water and joins me next to Cade, brushing a tear from my cheek.

"Marshall found us while we were out looking for this place and said he would go back out to find you guys," he says. "I saw Seph earlier but not you. Are you okay?"

"I think that's a relative term."

He pulls me to him. "He's going to be fine."

If only he could be sure.

Finn helps me clean the rest of the blood off Cade and then we head back to the city. We've been assigned a couple rooms in one of the buildings overlooking the ocean. A man says they've already sent someone to get the rest of our things at the boat where we spent the previous night.

Everyone here has red cloths tied around their wrists. I would ask about them, but I don't feel like talking to anyone, even though they seem friendly enough. Once we're left alone in our rooms, Finn says he's going to check on the horses, but I know it's an excuse to explore.

Hours drag on with no news of Seph. I sit on the sill to watch the moon rise over the ocean. Countless times, I've imagined what it would look like, but nothing has ever come close. The only thing left to see are the stars—something Seph has always talked about, and it doesn't feel right to see them for the first time without him.

So I decide to wait, convincing myself he's going to survive the night.

34.

Seph

I want more than anything to pass out. With the amount of blood I've lost, I should be sleeping so deep that I won't feel anything as Marshall digs the bullet out. He keeps saying how lucky I am. Lucky that it didn't pass through or I'd be dead. Lucky because if it were two inches higher, I'd be dead.

Honestly, I thought I would be dead by now either way.

Two men hold me down, and after another shot of pain, Marshall holds the bullet up for me to see. There's a man sitting next to me with a thin red tube connecting our arms, replacing what was lost, and I find the window behind him. I can hear the ocean but can't see it. I want to see it.

"Seph." I move my eyes until I see Marshall. The men holding me are gone even though I don't remember them leaving. "The worst part is over. I'm going to clean the wound and stitch you up. Shouldn't be much longer."

"I'm cold." My mouth is dry, but I don't know if I can say anything else.

His eyebrows draw together and then he touches my forehead. Cursing, he turns to someone behind him. "Go get Drews. Tell him it's urgent."

I go back to looking out the window, focusing on the sliver

of blue and some other color I can't put a name to. I didn't know the sky could be anything else.

"You're running a bit of a fever, Seph, but it's nothing to worry about yet. We have good people who probably know more than I do."

"Then why are you here and not them?"

I look in time to see Marshall smile. "Because I insisted. You are my patient after all." I return my attention to the window and he says. "It started a few days ago." I glance long enough to see him nod to the sky. "Seems like it's becoming a little more every day, stretching inland."

"You think it's gonna keep going?"

"I think there's a good chance."

Maybe Avery will finally see the world of her mother's pictures.

After a while, the sky turns dark and I drift in and out of sleep. Sometimes hot and sometimes cold, and then I finally sleep for a long time. When I wake, the tube giving me blood is gone and my body doesn't feel like lead anymore. I lie for a moment, studying the ceiling with wooden beams, dresser in the corner, and then the window. The sky is bright today—brighter than I've seen in my whole life.

The window is big enough to hold the walls back and keeps the ceiling from coming down on top of me. For once, I'm actually okay with being inside.

The ocean sounds call me up and out of bed. My legs are steady enough to hold my weight, but I use the wall for support. My torso is bare and a white cloth has been wrapped tight around the middle. I resist touching where I was shot. Only a few feet are between me and the window, and before I get any weaker, I take the unassisted steps and grab the window frame.

Some of the city is laid out below me, narrow streets made

of stone and houses pressed up against each other, and then a wall keeping it all together. It's nothing like the towns I've passed through or the old cities people tried to rebuild—it's something totally new. And just beyond the wall is the ocean. It's calm today—not like the day I sat on the beach to wait for death—the ripples of waves wash up onto the sand and disappear, making just enough sound to reach my ears.

The sky above is blue and bright, with the sun high. White clouds are drifting by.

I wonder if it's real at all or if my mind has finally broken.

It feels real, at least. I taste the salt from the ocean and feel the breeze on my face.

The door creaks open and I look over my shoulder. Avery stands there, pausing halfway through the door, her eyes taking me all in. "I wasn't sure if you were awake yet."

"I don't want to sleep anymore."

Avery shuts the door behind her, stopping next to me and only glancing once outside. "Marshall told them to give you a room with a big window facing the ocean."

"Marshall did?"

"Okay, I may have hinted at it."

I rest my hand over hers on the windowsill, curling my fingers around hers. "Thank you. It helps more than you know."

We both look over the ocean and the sky above, and Avery says, "I didn't think it would be this beautiful. Pictures never did it justice."

"The sky or the ocean?"

"Both."

Avery then looks at me with a mix of emotions, pulling her hand from mine and leaving me cold. A list of possibilities run through my mind—most of them having to do with Finn and Rami, and then Cade.

"What is it?"

She takes a slow breath and says, "You almost died."

"Yeah, but I didn't." I take her hand again and pull her toward me. Her fingers carefully touch the cloth around my middle, making small bumps appear along my arms as my heart beats a bit faster. "And it's because of you."

She looks up. "I guess your trigger finger isn't as fast as you thought it was."

"It's fast enough." I try to hide my smile but she's already seen it. A wave of dizziness comes over me and I lean on the sill for support. "Maybe not right now, but it will be again."

Avery helps me back to the bed, where we sit on the edge with our legs touching.

"What do you think you'll do once you're well?"

I honestly haven't thought about it yet. Now that I've seen the ocean and found the place my father may or may not have known about, I don't feel the need to do anything. Not yet.

"I don't know . . . maybe go look for pirates?"

Avery laughs. "Pirates?"

"Yeah, I'll go fix that boat and we'll sail away until we find something new."

"We?"

I take a moment and nod. "We."

Then I kiss her with the sound of the ocean and laughter coming from somewhere below, promising our future with something good.

Just after dusk, when the sky is a deep red turning into black, someone knocks once on my door and doesn't wait for a response before entering. An older woman comes in, gray streaking her hair—something I'm always surprised to see. People are always lucky to live that long.

"I hope I'm not interrupting," she says, shutting the door.

I shake my head and try to sit up in bed—try because I can

only get halfway, so I settle against the headboard. She takes the seat facing me, the same one Marshall left not too long ago. Before he did, he moved my bed next to the window and it's made everything so much better. The only thing I'm missing is Cade.

I'm fairly certain I've never met her before, but she's not looking at me like I'm a stranger. She finally starts, "My name is Amira, and this might sound odd, but I think I knew your father."

My breath hitches. "What?"

"When I heard a boy named Seph was brought in, there was nobody else I could think of. I knew a man once, his name was Joseph, and he had a son with your name. He always said he didn't want you to have his name, so he chose the closest thing to it."

"He didn't want me to be a Junior." Amira smiles like she knows the joke and I have no doubt she's telling the truth. Nobody else would know that. "How did you know him?"

"There was a group of us that kept in contact back when the radios still worked. We all knew each other from before, when we were in the military." She touches my wrist and asks, "Was this his?"

I nod. "He never told me what it meant. I just wore it because it was his and it was something to remember him by."

"We started wearing them to recognize others like us, then it became something more. We wear them now to let people know there is still good in the world. That there are still safe and free places to live."

"How many settlements do you have?"

Amira sits backs and thinks about it. "Oh, I think there are about a dozen these days. I'm surprised you haven't come across one of them before now."

"I tend to avoid people if I can."

She shows me a small smile. "That's the other thing I wanted to talk to you about. I know your lifestyle is different than ours, but if you want a place here, it's yours. Your father was a good man and I can see that you are, too, and we could always use someone with your skills."

I don't know how I feel about that, and she notices the discomfort on my face—I don't even try to hide it. I've done things she wouldn't even want to know about, but haven't we all? Would these people really welcome me here? Have I ever had the option?

"You can think about it." She stands to leave but pauses at the door. "Your father would've been proud of who you've become."

After she's gone, I watch the sky for the longest time, trying to decide if she's right.

35.

Avery

I double-check my room, making sure I haven't left anything I'm going to need—it's not like I had much to begin with. Finn sits on his bed and watches me empty one half of our room, wanting to say something for the last hour.

"I think I've got everything," I say, mostly to myself because I know Finn won't respond. He hasn't said much over the last week—not since he found out Seph and I were planning to leave again. We've been together our whole lives, but he must've known we would part ways at some point. Or maybe not, because I didn't even think about it until the opportunity arose.

I set my bag next to the door and finally face him. His hands are tight on the edge of the mattress and he studies the dresser between our beds, where our wooden horse sits on top. After another minute of total silence, I walk over and grab it and then sit down next to him.

"You know it's not permanent," I say.

"It feels like it is. You don't know when you'll be back and anything could happen while you're out there."

"Seph says he wants to be back by spring."

"Is this what you want?" Finn turns and focuses on me,

his eyes begging me to stay. "Really? You don't have to go just because he asked you to."

I rub my thumb down the horse's neck, place it in Finn's hand, and fold his fingers over it. "We've been together our whole lives. I wouldn't leave if I didn't really want to. You know that."

"I do . . . it doesn't mean I like it."

"I can't lie and say it's safe. Even with the sky clearing and more green showing every day, it's still the world we're from. But I'm not that same girl and I'm not going to be alone."

"It's not that I'm worried you'll get hurt. Even though there's a good chance you will."

"Hey." I shove him in the shoulder.

Finn smiles. "It's mostly because I'll miss you. More than ever before."

"Finn . . ." I wrap my arms around him and he leans his head on mine. "I'll miss you, too. But I promise I'll be back."

Finn straightens again and places the horse back in my hands and says, "You need this more than I do."

I smile, trying to hold something back. "I was hoping you would say that."

He nods. "I know. Come on. I'll walk you down."

He leads the way down the main staircase and winding halls until we're out on the streets. The cobblestones are uneven in some parts and the buildings are pressed tightly together, making the city a giant maze if you didn't already know the way. People recognize our faces—waving with silent hellos and smiling as we pass. To them, we were the ones who came right after the sun and remind them of something good.

Even though we haven't been here very long, this place already feels like home. They expand the settlement farther inland every year, making more space for any newcomers that happen to arrive here. There are people who have died of old age here and they have medicine for when someone gets sick.

When we get to the gates, they're already open. Seph and Marshall are talking near Cade, Amira stands between them, silently waiting, and Rami has Jack, all saddled and ready to go for me. He smiles his lazy, crooked smile when I come over, strapping my pack to my saddlebags.

"Has Marshall found you a job yet?" I ask.

His shakes his head, still rubbing Jack's head. "Not yet. Don't know if it's ever gonna happen."

And he might be right. Rami is a former gang member and murderer, trying to do good again but occasionally forgetting how.

"You'll figure out something—I'm sure."

He hands me the reins. "I think you're right. Good luck out there."

"You both ready to go then?" Amira asks, looking at both of us in turn.

I finally meet Seph's gaze, remembering to nod. "I'm ready."

"Me too."

Amira turns to me. "Then there's one last thing I need to give you." She holds out her hand, showing me a piece of red cloth. Over her shoulder, Seph nods and Finn gives the slightest smile, still not ready for me to go but accepting it all the same.

I step forward and hold out my wrist to let Amira tie it around. "We trust you to help those in need, to point them in the right direction, and to never take it upon yourself to become the law. Do you promise this in return?"

"I promise."

"Then don't let us down." Then she turns, raising her voice so the others can hear. "I wish you both the best of luck. This is the first time we've sent out people to bring others in, and hopefully this is the start of something good. I can't think of two people more suited for the job."

I look at Seph, thinking of a conversation we had a few weeks prior. When I couldn't find him indoors or anywhere in the city, I always knew he would be at the beach. He was alone that day—usually he was with Cade and sometimes Rami—and I sat next to him, close to touching.

"I want to ask you about something," he said. "It might sound crazy, but there's reason behind it."

"Okay."

I knew what he was going to say. For the last couple weeks, after he was fully healed, Seph had been restless. He had never stayed in one place for so long and still had trouble sleeping indoors. Out of all of us, Seph was having the most trouble adjusting.

Finn quickly took to the farms they had outside the city walls. Dozens of greenhouses had been half-buried in the earth, growing things we'd never seen before. Even as a kid, Finn was most happy when he had a job to do, and he finally found one that would never go away. I hadn't found anything yet, but I helped with horses when they needed it and whatever else they asked of me. But I knew Seph would never find anything here.

"I'm leaving again," he said.

"You mean . . . back out in the Wild?"

Seph nodded, confirming my thoughts.

"Why?"

"Amira has a job for me, and I know I'm the right person for it. There're a lot of people out there who don't have a home—like you and Finn after the Lawmen came to your town—and most of them don't know where they're going, making them easy prey to gangs still roaming out there. And I can be the one to point them in the right direction. To here, where it's safe."

I couldn't argue with him. For Seph, there couldn't be a better job—or a better person for it. Even Cade wanted to get back out there. But for everything telling me the good of it, I didn't want him to leave. Even though Finn was here, it wouldn't be the same.

"You said you wanted to ask me something," I said, ready for whatever he had to say but hoping for something specific.

"I wanted to ask if you would come with me."

And there it was. I'd started out dreading the Wild, but truth be told, I missed it now. "Of course I'll come with you."

"Really?" He genuinely seemed surprised.

"I want to be wherever you are."

So here we were—two weeks later and about to leave to go to unknown places to meet unknown people. My stomach twists with anticipation and fear all at once, but maybe not as much fear as I expected.

Marshall and Rami say their quick good-byes, and then it's just me and Finn, a foot between us that we have a hard time breaking.

"If you don't come back by spring, I'm coming to look for you," he says, hands deep in his pockets and his jacket collar high on his neck. Winter is coming fast even with the sun. I wonder if they get any snow here on the coast and what spring will be like when we get back.

"You won't have to come looking for me," I tell him. "I'll see you in a couple months."

Finn pulls me into a hug, lasting longer than ever. I memorize his scent and the feel of his arms around me. This time we're parting on our own terms, but it doesn't make it any easier.

In no time at all, I'm on Jack and riding with the city to my back, my heart torn between Seph and Finn and the Wild and safety. After a little ways, I stop Jack and turn around. Finn lifts his hand in good-bye and I do the same, missing him but eager to be doing something new and on my own without him.

Seph asks beside me, "Are you okay?"

I turn away from my brother and toward the Wild, which waits with the unknown. With Seph beside me, I feel like we can do anything.

"I'm more than okay."

Seph really smiles then and leans over to kiss me, the wind brushing his bandana against my neck. I never want to let him go. Even though I'm leaving my brother and a city that offers safety, and going into the Wild where there no rules, I can't be happier.

Seph breaks away and says, "Let's get out of here. I know the perfect place to spend the night."

Cade shoots forward and Jack is eager for a chase. We ride after them, knowing we're going to find new places but never knowing what to expect.

I'll always be a townie at heart, but I can't live in the city knowing the Wild is still out here—some parts of sky showing and some not—calling me the way it calls to Seph. Something I never thought would happen. A piece of him is always out here and because of that, so is a piece of me.

The Wild may not have always been in me, but now it's a part I can never live without.

36.

Seph

Tonight we sleep under the stars on the deck of the sailboat, Avery pressed close to me and staring up. The moment I was out of those gates today, it was like I could breathe again. Not only that, but now I have an actual purpose—more fueled than ever before.

I break the silence. "I think I want our first stop to be your old town."

Avery lifts her head and looks at me. "Really?" Her tone tells me that's exactly what she was hoping to hear. "I wasn't sure if you wanted to get that close to Kev."

"We can't ignore it forever, and we know for a fact a lot of people are there needing somewhere to go."

"And this time we know to avoid Houston."

"You don't want to run into Craig and Gerard again?"

Avery laughs. "I can't believe his name was actually Craig." She puts her head down on my arm and sighs. "I hope there are still people there."

"There will be."

"Can I ask you something?" She hesitates. "But you don't have to answer if you don't want to."

"What is it?" She fidgets more, making me curious. "Avery, just ask me."

"What would you have done if I said no to coming with you?"

I smile up at the sky, already knowing the answer to that. "I would've left anyway." Avery sits up and I laugh. "Just let me finish. I would've left, but only for a day . . . maybe two. I probably would've gone as far as this boat before I realized I can't go back to the life I had before."

"Why is that?"

I sit up so I can really look at her. "Because I don't want to be alone anymore. Because you showed me something better. You're the first person I've ever met who I actually *want* to be around, and I can't let that go . . . I can't let you go."

"I think that's the second best thing I've heard today," she says.

The side of my mouth goes up. "What's the first?"

"Your laugh—I'll never get sick of it."

I can't hold my smile anymore. Then I say, "There's not a lot to laugh about out here, but I never smiled much before you came around. So maybe that's a start."

"It's probably my fault—I'm not very funny." Avery smirks and I pull her down to our bed.

"I don't need you to be funny," I say.

"Not even a little?"

"No. Just you being here is all I need."

Her lips are warm on this cold night, and she eventually falls asleep on my shoulder. The stars look down on us from above without a cloud in the sky. I'm becoming a new person for this new world, ready for a change I never thought possible. My mind wanders less every day, and I no longer find myself someplace without remembering how I got there. But in this new world, I still get to do what I love most.

I ride for me.

I ride for those who can't.

I ride because the Wild is a part of me.

Acknowledgments

This book never would've been made into an actual book if it wasn't for certain people. Some of them had a direct hand in getting it published while others might've been there for the support of an author who sometimes needs it (always needs it).

Rachel Brooks, you are a rockstar agent and you deserve more than I can give. Thank you for being there when I needed you most and always having the right words to say.

Nicole Frail and the whole Sky Pony team, thank you for believing in this book and making it into a real thing. Also to Darren Hopes, for illustrating a such beautiful cover.

Sarah Glenn Marsh, I couldn't have asked for a better friend. I'm so lucky you live so close and always have something encouraging to say. Thank you for always being there for me.

Kay L. McCray, I can't put into words how amazing you are and I can't thank you enough for always being there when I need you most.

To my critique partners—Kevin van Whye, for always being the first reader and always having something good to say. Tricia Levenseller, for always being a text away and being the best agent sister. Dave Connis, for just being you—keep at it.

To the Insomniacs: Thank you for being the most awesome people and talking about inappropriate things at inappropriate hours.

To my family, who have always supported me no matter what. Corri, thank you for reading my books more than once when I need the help and also for watching the child when I'm on tight deadlines. Mom and Dad, for your never-ending support. And to Nina, for being that older sister everyone needs.

Joe—even though you've never, and probably will never, read my books, you're still so supportive of me and I love you for it.

Lastly, thank you to my readers, because there would be no books without you.